_et me._"

i swung around to look at him. He stood
h his back to the wide river, a tall man with
wind ruffling his coffee-brown hair.

"Let you what?" she asked.

"Read your palm." Already he was pulling her
closer, gently turning her wrist so that the back
of her hand rested against the inside of his. "I'm
a man of many talents, remember?"

It was warm outside, but inside, Tori shivered.

"Long life line," he commented. "Deep heart
line."

He was only touching her hand, running his
index finger along the lines of her palm, but her
whole body burned.

"Ah," he said, his voice low. "Just as I
suspected."

"What?"

He skimmed his thumb along the inside of her
hand, shooting a tingle clear down to her toes.

"Danger," he warned, and before she realized
his intent, he leaned down and pressed his
mouth to the sensitive flesh of her palm.

Dear Reader,

Once again, Silhouette Intimate Moments starts its month off with a bang, thanks to Beverly Barton's *The Princess's Bodyguard*, another in this author's enormously popular miniseries THE PROTECTORS. A princess used to royal suitors has to "settle" for an in-name-only marriage to her commoner bodyguard. Or maybe she isn't settling at all? Look for more Protectors in *On Her Guard*, Beverly Barton's Single Title, coming next month.

ROMANCING THE CROWN continues with *Sarah's Knight* by Mary McBride. An arrogant palace doctor finds he needs help himself when his little boy stops speaking. To the rescue: a beautiful nanny sent to work with the child—but who winds up falling for the good doctor himself. And in Candace Irvin's *Crossing the Line*, an army pilot crash-lands, and she and her surviving passenger—a handsome captain—deal simultaneously with their attraction to each other and the ongoing crash investigation. Virginia Kantra begins her TROUBLE IN EDEN miniseries with *All a Man Can Do*, in which a police chief finds himself drawn to the reporter who is the sister of a prime murder suspect. In *The Cop Next Door* by Jenna Mills, a woman back in town to unlock the secrets of her past runs smack into the stubborn town sheriff. And Melissa James makes her debut with *Her Galahad*, in which a woman who thought her first husband was dead finds herself on the run from her abusive *second* husband. And who should come to her rescue but Husband Number One—not so dead after all!

Enjoy, and be sure to come back next month for more of the excitement and passion, right here in Intimate Moments.

Leslie J. Wainger
Executive Senior Editor

Please address questions and book requests to:
Silhouette Reader Service
U.S.: 3010 Walden Ave., P.O. Box 1325, Buffalo, NY 14269
Canadian: P.O. Box 609, Fort Erie, Ont. L2A 5X3

The Cop
Next Door
JENNA MILLS

Silhouette®

INTIMATE MOMENTS™

Published by Silhouette Books

America's Publisher of Contemporary Romance

SILHOUETTE BOOKS

ISBN 0-373-27251-0

THE COP NEXT DOOR

Copyright © 2002 by Jennifer Miller

Books by Jenna Mills

Silhouette Intimate Moments

Smoke and Mirrors #1146
When Night Falls #1170
The Cop Next Door #1181

JENNA MILLS

grew up in south Louisiana, amidst romantic plantation ruins, haunting swamps and timeless legends. It's not surprising, then, that she wrote her first romance at the ripe old age of six! Three years later, this librarian's daughter turned to romantic suspense with *Jacquie and the Swamp*, a harrowing tale of a young woman on the run in the swamp and the dashing hero who helps her find her way home. Since then her stories have grown in complexity, but her affinity for adventurous women and dangerous men has remained constant. She loves writing about strong characters torn between duty and desire, conscious choice and destiny.

When not writing award-winning stories brimming with deep emotion, steamy passion and page-turning suspense, Jenna spends her time with her husband, two cats, two dogs and a menagerie of plants in their Dallas, Texas, home. Jenna loves to hear from her readers. She can be reached via e-mail at writejennamills@aol.com, or via snail mail at P.O. Box 768, Coppell, Texas 75019.

For my terrific sister, Belinda Aucoin Reeder,
role model, friend and confidante extraordinaire.
Thanks for everything—this one is all yours! *Je t'aime.*

A special thanks, as well, to Jennifer Walsh,
fairy godmother to so many dreams. May your future be
as wonderful as all the stories you helped bring to life.

Prologue

"Killed...her."

The slurred words stabbed through Victoria LaFleur like a cold knife. She quit shuffling through the file in her lap and looked at her father seated next to her on the old sofa. Agitation flashed in his glassy eyes, a distorted urgency that warned his mind was wandering again.

A chill cut through her, much like the Arctic wind whipping through the trees surrounding the hospice. Not even the heat from the furnace warmed her. Claude LaFleur looked as he always had, tall and broad, the kind of father little girls knew could slay dragons. But Tori knew looks could be deceiving. That big body of her father's concealed a heartbreaking secret, an illness that chipped away at the core of the man he'd been.

"I asked about a house, Papa. A house in Louisiana, a town called Bon Terre." Hoping to jog his memory, she handed him the faded black-and-white photo she'd found in his safety deposit box. With his health failing, she'd taken over his power of attorney, expecting routine paperwork. Instead, she found remnants of a life about which she knew nothing.

"That's you, isn't it?" In the picture, a smiling man and woman held a child in front of a rambling old house. "And Mama?" Which meant the little girl with the blond pigtails and dancing eyes had to be Tori.

Her father dropped the picture as though the paper had burned his fingers.

"Papa?"

He lifted his gaze to hers, revealing tired blue eyes awash in pain and memories. Tears. "…bad place…killed her."

"Who, Papa?" she asked, reaching for his cool hands. They were still big and strong, despite the dementia that muddled his mind. Life could be so cruel. "Who killed whom?"

"Corinne."

Tori stiffened. "Mama?" she asked. "Is this where the fire happened?"

"So beautiful…"

Her gaze cut to the tattered picture in her lap. Corinne LaFleur smiled up at her, light and energy frozen forever in that one moment in time. Losing her had devastated Tori's father. He'd never remarried, rarely dated. He had said his heart only had room for Corinne, even if an accident had stolen her from his life a quarter of a century before.

Even now the loss brought an ache to Tori's chest. She had no concrete memories of her mother, only hazy impressions. Love and comfort, security and warmth. Laughter. But that was all. Her father rarely spoke of his wife— all pictures had been destroyed in the fire that shattered their family, leaving a grief-stricken Claude to be both mother and father to his four-year-old little girl.

Now, seeing this glimpse of her parents together, Tori thought she understood why her father kept the one surviving photo locked away. From the tilted eyes to the pale hair, the wide mouth, Tori was a dead ringer for her mother.

"Stubborn," her father muttered. "Like you. Wouldn't listen."

Tori looked up and caught his gaze. She understood why he'd hidden the picture, but the other contents of the box confused her. The deed. The marriage certificate. The unfamiliar name scrawled boldly across both.

A chill seeped deep into her bones. "Who's Russell Bishop?"

"Dead and buried," he muttered. "Can't be resurrected."

"Papa, please," she implored. "Why is Russell Bishop's name with Mama's on the deed to the house? Why is his name next to hers on the marriage certificate?"

For the first time in six months her father's eyes sharpened. "Leave it alone, Victoria."

She sat back on the old floral sofa, startled by the strength of his words. She didn't want to agitate him, but she couldn't do as he asked. She couldn't leave it alone, not when every instinct screamed that she'd stumbled across something important.

What was her father keeping from her? Why had he never mentioned a home in south Louisiana? Who was Russell Bishop, and what was his relationship to Claude LaFleur? Were they one and the same? Had her father changed his name? Assumed a new identity? And most important, *why?*

Fighting a chill, Tori glanced toward the window. Outside the hospice, snow drifted through the naked branches of the trees, as white as her father's once-dark hair. She looked back and found him rocking, and her throat tightened. She wouldn't cry. Not in front of him. That's not how he'd raised her.

"Papa," she said, trying again. "Tell me about the house in Louisiana. Was that where you and Mama lived?"

He kept rocking. "Killed her. Her and Montague."

Montague? "Are you talking about the fire, Papa?"

"Couldn't stay. Couldn't let them take you from me."

"Who, Papa? Who was going to take me?"

But the moment of lucidity passed as quickly as it came. "...never go back," he said over and over. "Never go back."

Chapter 1

Six Months Later

Secrets. Echoes of the past. Remnants of lives gone by. Every house concealed them, but as Victoria LaFleur looked from the faded picture in her hand to the two-story house before her, she couldn't help but think the rambling old structure hid more than its fair share of mysteries.

Her parents' house hadn't burned down. Far from it. Shielded by an army of century-old oaks, the weathered Greek Revival still stood, beautiful even in abandonment.

Just seeing the house, with its wraparound porches and intricate ironwork, stirred something deep inside Tori. A connection. A vague sense of familiarity. This was where she'd been born. She and her parents had stood on those very steps for the picture. The only picture she had.

If she listened closely enough, she almost thought she could hear her mother's laughter dancing on the breeze.

Emotion streamed through her, forcing her to draw a steadying breath. The air was warm and thick, scented by clusters of wild wisteria that dripped from the intricate ironwork. Winter had held Nova Scotia in its frigid grip when she had left just the day before, yet here in Louisiana, spring exploded all around her.

Ignoring the No Trespassing sign, she opened the rickety iron gate and walked up the path to the wide porch. Grass sprang up from cracked concrete, while along the side of the path, pink and white azaleas bloomed vigorously.

Off in the distance, thunder rumbled.

According to the parish records, up until just a few months ago, a grandmother she'd never known had lived here. Her mother's mother. Estelle. But time had claimed her, as well. Now only the beautiful old home remained. After finding the doors and windows locked, Tori picked up a rock. Legally the house belonged to her now. She'd already had the utilities turned on. All she lacked was the key.

There could be no harm.

Candlelight flickered off the bubbles in the claw-foot bathtub, filling the small room with the scent of vanilla and roses. Had her mother bathed here? Tori wondered. Had her mother selected the quirky art-deco décor of flamingo-pink walls and cabinets with black accents? The possibility intrigued her. She knew so little of her mother, wanted to know so much more.

Enjoying the sense of connection, she pulled off her sweater and stepped out of her jeans, but paused when her fingers fumbled with the clasp of her bra. There was something odd about undressing in an unfamiliar place. Exposed. But that was silly, and she knew it. She wasn't a woman to jump at her own shadow.

"I'm here," she called out in a moment of pure inspiration. Her voice echoed through the cavernous house she'd spent the past few hours exploring. "Tell me your secrets."

Nothing greeted her but the sound of the wind rushing through the enormous oaks surrounding the house.

After piling her hair atop her head, Tori slipped into the warm water and enjoyed a welcome moment of freedom. Here she was in a forgotten house, in a town about which she knew nothing, and she was naked. What could be more liberating than that?

The warm water and subtle aroma gradually worked their magic on her tired muscles. She let her eyes drift shut, content to listen to the wind rustling through the oaks.

Her father was wrong. No evil awaited her here in this rambling old home. Only secrets. The key to a past about which her father had refused to speak. But Tori needed to know what truths hid within these old walls. She needed to know about her mother, and more, she needed to understand the documents she'd found in that safety deposit box. Why—

A scraping sound intruded upon her thoughts.

She abruptly sat up in the tub, listening closer. A branch against the window, she told herself, but then heard it again, more of a creak than a scratch.

Her heart rate accelerated, matching the wind slashing through the trees.

Bad place...never go back.

"It's just an old house," she told herself, reaching for a towel. Cool air hit the tepid water sliding down her body, bringing a shiver and making her realize how much time had passed. The candles stood less than half their initial size, afternoon having long since given way to the long shadows of twilight.

Tori thought about calling out or flipping on a light, but if someone lurked nearby, she didn't want to lead them straight to her. She slipped on her robe, then grabbed one of the iron candlesticks and stepped into the hall. If she could reach her cell phone downstairs—

The creak of a floorboard pierced her thoughts like a gunshot. She jolted from the impact, but kept moving down the staircase. There was no time to glance at the locked room at the end of the long hall. No one hid inside, she told herself. No one lurked in the shadows. Her over-active imagination had merely ascribed ominous meaning to random sounds. She'd come here expecting some grand mystery, and now—

"Hold it right there, sugar."

The steely command went through her like a jolt of live electricity. Not quite to the bottom of the stairs, she stopped dead in her tracks. Her heart kept going.

"Now turn around slowly," came the voice.

Adrenaline surged. Fight-or-flight kicked in. Knowing she couldn't outrun the intruder, she spun toward him, candlestick outstretched and ready to defend.

There was no one there.

No one right behind her, anyway.

The rough-hewn voice belonged to the man at the top of the stairs. He stood half in shadow, half in light, his booted feet shoulder width apart, his expression hard and uncompromising. He wore jeans and a black T-shirt, and in his outstretched hands he held a gun.

Bad place...never go back.

Reality proved far worse than imagination. The man's stance, the very calmness of him, indicated complete confidence, a man used to being obeyed. And why not, Tori thought raggedly. Even if he hadn't held a gun, she stood dripping wet and wearing nothing but an old terry cloth robe. If she ran, he'd be on her before she could open the door.

"Stay where you are," she said in a voice she worked hard to steady. He could be anyone, capable of doing anything. No way could she let him know the cold terror snaking through her. The vulnerability.

"I don't think you're in a position to be giving orders, *chère*."

Heart hammering, she took a cautious step backward, mirroring his pose and keeping her candle extended toward him. She hated how badly her hands shook. "Who are you? What do you want?"

"Easy now," the man said in a frighteningly calm voice. "Just put down your weapon and let me see those hands of yours."

"My weapon?"

With his gun, he gestured toward the candlestick. "Be careful. It wouldn't take much for this place to go up like a bonfire on Christmas Eve. Not that anyone would care, mind you."

The thought horrified her. "I care."

His eyes took on an ominous glitter. "Do you now?"

"Of course I do—it's *my* house." All that remained of her mother.

"This isn't anybody's house, sugar, except a couple of ghosts, if you believe that kind of thing." He finally moved, lowering one booted foot to the step below him. Then the next. "Now be a love and tell me who you are and what you're doing here. I have to warn you, though. It's a little early in the evening for a séance. Most folks wait till midnight."

She didn't know which name to give him—the one she went by, or the one she suspected appeared on her birth certificate.

Trusting instinct, she gave him neither. "A séance?"

"All those candles up there in that bathroom—"

"Don't tell me a tough guy like you is afraid of ghosts," she interrupted with a bravado she didn't feel. She couldn't keep her eyes off his gun. "What's the matter? Afraid of who I might contact?"

"No, but you should be."

Startled, Tori searched his gaze for humor, but found none. "Look," she said, mind racing, "I don't know who you are or what you want, but I know you don't belong here, and the last I heard, aromatherapy wasn't a crime—"

"Aromatherapy?" He took another step. "What do you need therapy for? Your mind or your body?"

A tight fist of panic squeezed her throat. The man was way too calm. He stood close enough now that the flickering light of her candle revealed more detail. His hair wasn't as dark as she'd first thought, but more the color of rich coffee, much like the café au lait she'd had that morning in New Orleans. A cowlick kept the bangs from his face, lending him a restless, unkempt look that might have appeared sexy, had he not held a gun in his hands. His jaw desperately needed a razor. And his eyes. Pewter, she noted, soft and steely, just like his voice.

"What are you going to do with that?" she asked, gesturing toward the pistol. "Shoot me?"

He looked at the weapon in his steady hand, then at her. "A pretty lady like you? Hurting you is just about the last thing I want to do."

She didn't like the insolence in his eyes, the awareness that flared between them, the fact that beneath her robe, she wore nothing at all.

"Then why are you pointing it at me?" she asked.

"Not as effective if I don't."

"Effective for what?"

"I can't have you running from me, and as long as I have my friend here, I'm pretty sure you won't."

The blasé answer chilled her. In his faded jeans and T-shirt the man looked harmless enough, but his iron-hard demeanor warned otherwise. If not for the gun, she would have turned and bolted the second she saw him standing at the top of the stairs.

"Quit looking at me like I'm a depraved lunatic, sugar. I'm not going to ravage you, then dump what's left out back in the bayou."

"If you're trying to put me at ease, it's not working."

"I'm not here to put you at ease."

With her gaze steady on him, she took another step

back. Her cell phone sat on a table around the corner. If she could reach it, she stood a chance.

"Come any closer," she warned, "and I'm calling the police."

The man went very still. Then he laughed. "Sugar," he drawled. "I *am* the police."

Ian enjoyed the moment of shock—the look on the woman's face was absolutely priceless. Clearly, she'd no more expected his announcement than he'd expected to find a scantily clad mystery lady frolicking inside the old Carondolet house.

The evening was shaping up to be much more intriguing than he'd anticipated when the light in the upstairs window grabbed his attention. He'd let himself in the back door, expecting to find the Melancon boy upstairs with his girl again. The kids never learned. The allure of a vacant building was too strong.

Intimately familiar with the house, Ian had taken the back staircase, figuring to sneak up on the teens before they could bolt. The surprising smell of pralines had led him to the old bathroom, where he'd found more candles burning than they had down at Sacred Lady Catholic Church. There, he'd found jeans and a sweater, matching lacy panties and a bra, and the remnants of a bubble bath.

That's when amused irritation had turned to dread.

Necking he could handle. Hell, he'd done his fair share of that during his teenage years, knew good and well what usually came next. But he didn't want to find Bo and Monique hiding naked somewhere in the house. Monique's father was one of Ian's deputies. Ian had to look the man in the eye every day. He didn't need to know what Hank's daughter looked like without clothes.

But if he had to, he figured he should scare the kids good and hard, make sure he never found them here again.

That's when he'd heard the creaking of the old floating staircase, and strode out to catch his prey.

Instead, he found a ghost.

That's what he thought at first, anyway. With all that pale hair piled atop her head and that soft white robe trailing behind her, Ian thought he was finally seeing one of the ghosts the locals insisted dwelled within the old Carondolet place.

But then he'd told her to stop, and she'd obeyed.

As far as he knew, ghosts didn't obey commands.

Nothing prepared him for the sight of her turning toward him, her striking features illuminated by the flickering light of the candle in her outstretched hands. The tilted eyes and high cheekbones. The unruly strands of pale hair that flirted with her full mouth. The scent of vanilla that rushed up to greet him, like pralines.

He didn't know who the ethereal creature was—she looked too classy to be a vagrant—but he knew she didn't belong in the old Carondolet place. No one did.

"The police?" she repeated in that distracting throaty voice. She looked at him as if he was stark, raving mad. "You expect me to believe that?"

He reached into his back pocket and pulled out a leather case, flipped it open to reveal his badge. He'd held off identifying himself as long as possible, not wanting to turn things official, unless he had to. "Ian Montague, ma'am. At your service."

"Montague?" She whispered the name like a curse.

"I'm the sheriff around these parts," he said, intrigued, "and I'd really like to know who you are and what you're doing in this house. Didn't you see the No Trespassing sign out front? I don't know where you come from, but around here, when we say 'keep out,' we mean it."

She angled her chin. "Of course I saw the sign. I just didn't see how it applied to me, since I own this house."

The repeated claim scraped a sore spot. He'd been searching for the owners for years, but no trace of the Bishops had ever been found. By all accounts, Russell and his daughter ceased to exist the night Ian's childhood crashed to an end.

"Like I told you," he said as levelly as he could. "No one owns this house. And I'm afraid trespassing is trespassing. Now, I'll ask you again." He refused to think about what she concealed under that robe, unwilling to be distracted by soft skin and dangerous curves. No way would he be taken in by a scam artist or cat burglar, no matter how sexy he found her.

"Kindly put down that candlestick and show me those pretty hands."

Temper flashed in her eyes. She spun away from him, but her feet didn't find the floor she'd obviously expected. She had one more step to go.

"Watch out—" Ian stabbed his gun into its holster and lunged for her, but couldn't reach her before she fell. She cried out and groped for the stair rail, but her foot slammed down, and her ankle twisted from beneath her. She landed hard.

Ian swore under his breath and took the remaining stairs two at a time. *"Chère?"* He was on the hard floor and by her side in less than a heartbeat. "You okay?"

Furious green eyes glared up at him. "It's a little late to convince me you're a fine Southern gentleman."

He almost laughed. Almost. Somehow, he didn't think she'd appreciate it. "I lost my shot at the gentleman part long ago," he told her instead, fighting a pang of remorse, "but I really am the sheriff."

"Then you've got a strange idea of law enforcement."

"Be that as it may—" A whiff of smoke stopped him cold. He glanced behind him, saw that her candle had landed on the throw rug near the door. Flames licked at the threadbare fabric. Pushing to his feet, he stomped out the fire before the place went up like a tinderbox.

"I guess you care, after all."

He glanced back toward the bottom of the staircase. The mystery lady no longer lay in a glorious heap, but had pulled herself into a sitting position. He wondered if she realized just how high the old robe had ridden up on her stunningly long legs. "Pardon?"

"You said no one would care if the place burned down, but you just prevented that from happening."

"My personal preferences have nothing to do with my job," he drawled. "It's that protect-and-serve thing, you know? I happen to take the oath seriously."

"Good for you." She moved to stand, but when she put weight on her right foot, her ankle buckled from beneath her, and she winced in pain.

This time Ian moved fast enough. He easily caught her before she fell and lifted her into his arms.

"Put me down," she said, struggling against him.

"Relax, or you're only going to hurt yourself more."

"I'll take my chances."

"But I won't." She was amazingly light, considering her height. He carried her into the parlor, ignoring the way she twisted in his arms, the feel of her silky, still damp skin. He looked straight ahead, refusing to glance down and see her face mere inches from his, that full, furious mouth that made a man think of tasting, not interrogating. Never had he been so physically aware of a trespasser, but then, never had he found one more naked than not.

And never had one looked like a cross between a ghost and a goddess. Her eyes, he decided. They were as green and defiant as the verdant ferns growing wild around his front porch.

The shadows playing about the old house didn't help matters.

Ian set her on one of the old sofas. A threadbare sheet covered the pink-and-red floral damask he remembered from his childhood.

"That's better," he said, going down on one knee and taking her foot in his hands. Her skin was cool, her toenails painted a soft shade of pink. Ignoring both, he worked his fingers along her high arch, then carefully inspected her ankle. "I don't think anything's broken, probably just strained."

She looked at him dubiously. "So now I suppose you're a doctor in addition to the sheriff?"

"In a small community like this, we do a lot of cross-training. It pays to know basic first aid."

"Lucky me."

He closed his fingers around her foot, covering as much exposed flesh as he could. "Your feet are cold—it's probably not good running around wet and barefoot. You're liable to catch your death."

She pulled her foot from his hands and adjusted her robe to cover her knees. "In case it's escaped your attention, *Sheriff*, I was taking a bath. If you hadn't broken in, I wouldn't be running around like this, now, would I?"

"Which brings us back to where we started." Something about this woman nagged at him, something more than her state of undress and the seductive aroma of warm vanilla. She clearly thought she belonged here, whereas he knew she did not.

"This house has been abandoned since Estelle passed on six months ago—since then I've run off local teens and vagrants alike. But never a pretty lady who obviously has enough class and sense to know better than to break into old houses. So let's start with a name? Who are you, *chère?*" He hated to think her an escapee from the mental institute west of the river. But he had to wonder. "Why do you think you own this house?"

"Are you ready to listen to me?"

"I've been ready since the moment I saw you."

Her eyes flared, for just a moment, before they narrowed spectacularly. "Spare me the gory details, Sheriff. If I answer your questions, you'll back off?"

"Now, sugar, you know I can't promise that, not until I know who you really are and what you're doing in this house."

She sighed. "Since you seem predisposed to doubt everything I say, maybe show-and-tell will work. I've found men respond better to that, anyway. My purse is on the table by the staircase. The proof you need is tucked inside.''

Ian glanced across the room and saw a sleek bag perched on the marble tabletop. He stood, but hesitated before turning his back on her. ''You're not going to try and run again, are you?''

She smiled sweetly. Too sweetly. ''You'd like that, wouldn't you? Then you could play sheriff again.'' Her eyes took on a peculiar twinkle. ''But I guess that's safer than playing doctor.''

For a moment Ian could only stare. The mystery lady had guts, he had to hand her that. A bravado he didn't often see, even if he'd poked a few holes in it. Most women he knew would be in an all-out panic in her position, hysterically trying to talk their way out of a jam. True, she hadn't really hurt anything, but trespassing was a crime, and everyone knew Sheriff Ian Montague didn't tolerate rule breakers. They knew the carefree boy who'd once haunted the swamps no longer existed. They saw the changes after his stint with the New Orleans P.D. And accordingly, they kept their distance.

''Smart lady,'' he muttered, then crossed the room and grabbed her purse. He pivoted back toward her, half expecting to find the sofa empty, that the vaguely familiar woman was only a figment of his imagination. But she sat demurely in her ivory robe, pale hair flirting with her cheekbones, watching him through suspiciously calm eyes.

She looked even more breathtaking in shadows than she had in candlelight.

''What's the matter, Sheriff? See a ghost?''

A vision was more like it. ''No such luck.'' He shook off the déjà vu and returned to the sofa. ''Here you go.''

She took the purse and hastily opened it, pulled out an official-looking document and handed it to him.

''What's this?''

"I believe it's called a deed, Sheriff. And if you look closely enough, you'll see it's for this house."

He glanced down at the old paper in his hands and went very still. His chest tightened. His insides went stone cold.

What had she said about ghosts?

"Well?" she asked.

He blinked to clear his vision, but the gold notary seal remained, the typed and signed names, the date from over a quarter of a century before. When he looked back at the woman, he found her watching him. "This is made out to Corinne and Russell Bishop."

Just saying the man's name left an acrid taste in his mouth.

"That's right." She withdrew a brown envelope from her satchel and handed it to him.

Ian held her gaze, puzzled by what he saw swirling in her striking green eyes. If he didn't know better, and he wasn't sure he did, he'd call it yearning. Maybe even vulnerability. But that didn't make sense. This woman had faced him defiantly while he held a gun on her, mocked him when he announced his position of authority, yet now, when the physical threat had clearly faded, she looked on the brink of shattering.

He lowered himself to the sofa, realizing that the way he'd been towering over her couldn't be helping matters. He was just so damn used to being a cop on the prowl, leveraging every advantage he could, particularly his size. But he could find no glory in intimidating this woman, not when she watched him with those wary cat's eyes of hers.

Not when he wasn't sure she still breathed.

Then again, he wasn't sure he did, either.

"Open it," she said.

Ian glanced at the faded envelope in his hands—he didn't know why they wanted to shake. As a homicide cop, he'd calmly processed crime scenes more horrific than most people could imagine. Nothing could shock him anymore. Nothing.

Or so he thought. But when he opened the envelope and pulled out a tattered black-and-white photograph, he knew just how wrong he was. The punch of memory, of hatred and rage and a thirst for vengeance, landed low in his gut. "Good God."

"Is that the man you know as Russell Bishop?" she asked, and her voice held its first note of apprehension.

Ian felt his fingers tighten on the paper, resisted the urge to rip it into shreds, just like the jovially smiling man in the photo had done to Ian's life. He stood there so benignly, one arm around his wife's waist, holding his little girl with the other. After ten years in law enforcement, it still turned Ian's stomach that evil could look so normal.

"Son of a bitch," he swore under his breath.

A pained, strangled noise broke from the woman's throat. "I don't think so," she choked out. "Though I never knew my father's mother, I hear she was a delightful lady."

Ian jerked his gaze from the picture to the woman seated close enough to touch. A trail of moisture slid down her cheeks. "What the hell are you talking about?" he practically growled.

She looked him dead in the eye. "I'm talking about my family, Sheriff. My name is Tori. Tori Bishop. And the man you know as Russell Bishop is the man I call Father."

He struggled to breathe. *"Tori…"*

"Short for Victoria."

Her words hit him, as debilitating as when that old barge had run aground on a sandbar last fall. He stared at the little girl in the picture, all lanky limbs and shining blond hair. His memories of her were vague and tattered, much like the photo.

"Little Vicky," he muttered, returning his gaze to Tori.

A faint smile played at her lips. "Not so little anymore, though, am I? Twenty-five years has a way of doing that to a girl."

Vague familiarity sharpened into blinding pain. He

blinked hard, but the image didn't fade. The tilted green eyes and pale-blond hair of her mother, the angular cheeks and stubborn chin of her father.

No wonder she'd withheld her name until the last possible moment. She obviously knew a Bishop was less welcome in this town than a carpetbagger.

But that hadn't stopped Ian from searching for years. God, how he'd looked. Finding her had been a blinding obsession, filling his days and nights, until he could think of little else. He hated loose ends. Needed them tied. Tightly.

Accordingly, he knew the truth. "That's not possible," he said. "You're dead."

Chapter 2

Dead. The word hit Tori hard. In a day of surprises, the little tidbit took the prize. But as she looked at Sheriff Ian Montague, at the incredulity etched into the hard lines of his face, she knew he believed what he'd said.

"I can assure you, Sheriff, I'm quite alive. Unless, of course, someone neglected to tell me something pretty important." She took his hand and brought it to her face. "See? Flesh and bone."

He swore softly. His pewter eyes were hard and seeking, but she wasn't sure he saw anything. Especially not her. His callused fingers moved against her cheekbone so tentatively it was as though he expected her to dissipate beneath his touch.

The lengthening shadows of early evening didn't help matters. They stretched across the old hardwood floor and spilled over the sheet-draped furniture, casting an eerie, dreamlike state. A stillness permeated this room time had forgotten. Only the steady ticking of the old grandfather clock that she'd wound upon arrival fractured the silence. That, and the thudding of Tori's heart.

Unease streamed through her. Fascination staggered along behind. She studied the sheriff, the way he clutched the black-and-white photo. Had the paper been glass, it would have shattered.

The abrupt shift from man in charge to man in shock unnerved her. But it also confirmed her father's changed identity. She'd suspected, but had been unable to find proof, not even from the lawyer whose name appeared on her father's documents. Carson Lemieux had asked her to come to New Orleans, but by the time she arrived, he'd been called out of town.

Now she knew. Claude LaFleur and Russell Bishop were one and the same. The need to understand twisted through her, but so did caution. The past loomed like a dark pit, and she knew better than to dive in headfirst. She had to protect her father's secret, until she understood why he'd taken such drastic measures, what he'd been hiding. Or hiding from.

Killed her, he'd said that day in the hospice. *Her and Montague.*

Montague.

Tori didn't believe in coincidences. Her father's reference to Montague had to relate to the grim-faced man who looked at her as if she was his worst nightmare come to life.

"We looked for you," he said. "But you were nowhere. No trace, no trail. It was like you vanished into thin air."

"And that's why you thought I was dead?" She tightened her robe, acutely conscious of the growing chill in the air. Montague was right. Slippers would have been nice, underwear even better.

"Cold?" he asked.

"Very."

"This house has that effect on people." He reached behind her and retrieved a faded crocheted blanket. "This might help."

She took the soft, intricately woven black-and-pink afghan and wrapped it around her. The sense of warmth was immediate.

The sheriff fingered the fabric against her wrist, where a pink daisy bloomed from a square of black. "Your mother made one just like this for my mom."

Tori looked from his hand to his eyes. "You knew her?"

He stood. "I knew them all."

Questions tripped through her. This man knew the secrets she'd come seeking.

He spun toward her. "Do you have any idea—" He stopped, visibly working to bring himself under control.

Watching him, Tori felt as she had the summer before, when she'd witnessed a horrific traffic accident. She hadn't wanted to look at the twisted aftermath, but she'd had no choice.

The good-ol'-boy sheriff was gone. The truth of her identity had stripped away all that Southern charm like a flimsy veneer. Montague's eyes were hard, his mouth a grim line. He kept clenching and unclenching his hands. He looked angry, rattled, like a man working hard to contain something dangerous before it spilled over and contaminated.

"Why are you looking at me like I've committed some terrible crime? I haven't done anything wrong."

He looked more through her, than at her. "From the time I was eight years old you've consumed my thoughts—where you were and what you were doing, if you were even alive—but somehow you stayed a four-year-old girl with pigtails and mud pies. You never grew up, even when I did."

Unease grew. He sounded as though he knew her, as though a personal connection bound them together. But he was a stranger, and his last name was *Montague*. "What are you talking about? Why did you wonder about me? Because of Mama? The fire?''

A low noise tore from his throat. ''Twenty-five years ago you and your father dropped off the face of the earth. There was a manhunt. A nationwide search. Nothing.'' He picked up the picture he'd dropped to the floor and again studied the moment captured in time. His lips twisted. ''Where have you been, damn it? Where is your father?''

''A manhunt?'' Tori whispered.

He raked a hand through his hair. ''Have you been with him all this time?''

She stood, ignoring the faint pain in her ankle. The afghan pooled at her feet. ''He's my father.''

''That's not an answer.''

''No, it's not, is it?''

Impatience flashed in his eyes. ''You have to give me more than that, damn it. You can't just waltz back into town after twenty-five years and not tell us where you've been. You can't—''

''Why not?'' The frustration in the sheriff's voice, the suspicion, pushed her to the edge. This was her life they were discussing. Her past. But instead of the answers she needed, he gave only hard, accusing looks and questions more piercing than those with which she'd started.

''Why does it matter that I lived in a small community in the northeast?'' she asked, tossing him a bone to see what came next. ''Why does it matter that my father ran a commercial fishing business and I kept the books for him?''

''Where in the northeast?''

She threw on the brakes. ''Look,'' she said, stepping away and flicking on a light switch. Shadows were giving way to darkness, creating an appalling intimacy. ''I've traveled a long way to get answers, and until I know what I'm dealing with, I'm not going to spill my life history.''

''What answers are you looking for?''

The deceptively benign question lay like a gauntlet at

her feet. She wanted to rattle off all the puzzle pieces that didn't quite fit together, but didn't want the sheriff to realize how little she knew. That gave him too much latitude, carte blanche to twist and contort.

"About my mother," she hedged. "How she died."

He stepped closer. "Why don't you just ask your father?"

"My father can't tell me anything." Grief stabbed deep. "Not anymore."

Those simmering eyes narrowed, making Montague look all cop again, as though he faced her across an interrogation table, not a dusty, shadowy old room. "Why not?"

She felt tears well, but refused to let them fall. "Trust me, there's nothing I'd like better than to sit down with my father and let him tell me everything—but he can't." Heartfelt emotion clogged her voice. She missed him terribly, but knew he'd been ready to pass. "He's with Mama now."

The thought brought Tori great comfort, but derision flashed in the sheriff's eyes. "Somehow I doubt that."

She let the snide remark slide. "Papa had Alzheimer's. He was okay for a while, but when he slipped, he gave me power of attorney. That's when I found the deed to this house in his safety deposit box."

"What else?" The question was sharp, expectant.

"My parents' marriage license," she answered, dangerously intrigued. "A few pictures." Remnants of a life she'd never known existed, despite the fact it apparently belonged to her father. And herself. "I was puzzled. Dad and I were close, but he never mentioned living in Louisiana. I figure if this is where Mama died, the memories must have been painful. But I needed to know more. I needed to find some sense of my mother." Of herself.

"So you just breezed into town without any inkling of what you were walking into?"

"You make it sound like I'm walking into a trap, rather

than the town of my birth. Of course I did research first—there was a lawyer's name among my father's things. Carson Lemieux. I called him, explained who I was and what I'd found. He asked me to get down here right away, said we had a lot to talk about.'' She'd tried to honor her father's request to leave the past alone, but as the weeks after his death stretched into months, the questions inside her had grown louder. Stronger. ''I arrived before he expected me. He's out of town, can't see me until later this week. So here I am.''

Montague's gaze flicked down the length of her body, as though again verifying she was woman and not ghost. She resisted the urge to squirm, but never had a visual inspection felt so physical. So intimate. The smolder in the sheriff's eyes made her feel as if her robe was see-through cellophane rather than thick terry cloth.

The moment stretched to the breaking point, the sounds of the old house took on exaggerated proportions. The ticking of the massive grandfather clock. Wind rushing through the trees. Crickets serenading.

When he lifted his eyes to her face, she felt as though he'd lifted a hand instead. Heat radiated from his big body, like a sunlamp turned to high. The urge to step closer, to let the warmth wash over her and through her, caught her by surprise.

The knowledge of how badly she could be burned held her back.

''You shouldn't be here,'' he said roughly. ''There's nothing for you.''

She swiped an errant strand of hair from her cheek. ''My past is here, Sheriff, part of who I am.''

He frowned. ''This isn't some juicy mystery novel, *chère,* and you're not Nancy Drew. Hasn't anyone told you sometimes it's best to leave well enough alone?''

Temper flared. All her life decisions had been made for her, as though she wasn't capable of thinking for herself. Her father—

Tori pushed away the memory before it cut any deeper. "You're right. This isn't some cozy story. It's my life, and I can't just walk away. If you won't help me, I'll find someone who will."

A soft gleam moved into the sheriff's steely eyes. "But you have no idea what answers await your questions, and I do."

"Then tell me," she said. "I won't shatter."

"Don't be so sure of that." He punctuated the curt words by turning from her and crossing the hardwood floor to the massive front windows.

Tori let him go. She needed the distance, the space. She needed to breathe without the subtle masculine aroma of sandalwood and soap. But most of all she needed a reprieve from those penetrating gray eyes.

He stood with his back to her, a tall man framed by rose brocade curtains. The sun was gone now, the moon too low on the horizon to ease the growing darkness. Century-old oaks surrounded the house, isolating them from the rest of the world. But still the sheriff stared.

Fascination pushed closer. Tori wrapped her arms around her waist and drew a deep breath. With the bright light of afternoon, the parlor had been charming. But now the sheets draped over the furniture reminded her of victims at a crime scene, she and Ian the only survivors.

Ridiculous, she admonished herself. Now was not the time for morbid imaginings.

But the silence echoed louder.

The sheriff didn't move, but not even his stillness dimmed the primal energy surrounding him. If anything, the disparity enhanced the effect. He looked so alone standing there, so apart from the world.

The urge to go to him caught her by surprise.

What could be so horrible, she wondered. Why did the mention of her father's name replace the heat in the sheriff's eyes with a bleak coldness? Her father had been a gentle man. Overly protective, yes, but after losing his wife, Tori figured it natural that he'd hung on tight to his daughter.

She couldn't fault him for that. Not entirely, anyway.

Frustration faded, replaced by a need to bridge the chasm of the past. The sheriff was wrong. She wouldn't shatter. To prove it, she crossed the room, ignoring how cold the wood floor felt beneath her feet, the swish of cool air against her bare legs.

This time it was the urge to touch that surprised her. To lay her hand against the hard muscles of Montague's back. "Tell me," she said instead. "Please."

Now he did turn toward her, slowly, and lifted a hand to cup her face. Normally she would have pulled back from the familiar gesture, but the glitter in his eyes held her motionless.

"Illusions are dangerous, *chère*. They mask reality. They make even the bitter seem sweet. Once I shatter yours, there's no going back. Do you understand what I'm saying?"

His voice was like whiskey, the words like ice. And to Tori's dismay, she realized the lamplight had done nothing to quell the tenuous intimacy. "Yes," she said, her voice little more than a murmur. "But I still want to know."

He stroked a thumb along the line of her cheekbone. "Not tonight, *chère*. The best thing you can do is go to bed, say your prayers and get some sleep. If you wake in the morning, and still want to know, I'll tell you everything. But sleep on it first. Be sure. I'd hate to dim that light in your eyes—it's too damn pretty. But I will if you make me."

The breath stalled in her throat. Sheriff Ian Montague looked casual and ruggedly male in his jeans and black T-shirt, but the glint in his eyes warned that this animal was not as tame as he wanted the world to think. He towered over her, obviously accustomed to using his size to intimidate. But her father had been a big man, too, and his over-protective nature had taught her to stand tall. And firm.

Victoria Bishop wasn't a woman to back down, much to the chagrin of the men in her life.

"Trying to scare me off, Sheriff?"

"Maybe I'm just trying to protect you. That's my job."

"I'm not going to tuck tail and run like a scared little rabbit."

A faint smile played at his mouth but nowhere else. "You don't have to run. A drive straight to the airport would be fine." His eyes met hers. "You need to trust me on this, sugar. It's for the best."

"Best for whom?"

"All of us."

She stepped back from his touch. Frustration burned deep. She hadn't come all this way to turn around and go home. She couldn't leave without the answers she'd come seeking. This was her decision, no one else's.

All her life, her father had guided and nurtured her, steered her in the directions he deemed best. Safest. That's why she'd given up her dream of leaving Nova Scotia and pursuing a career in criminal justice, because her father had begged her not to put herself at risk.

Because she loved him and knew he'd never recovered from losing her mother, she'd acquiesced and helped him run his fishing business instead. But that didn't dim the frustration, the realization that she lived like a doll on a shelf.

Never again would she let someone have that power over her. "You realize, don't you, that this big buildup is only making me more determined?"

"It should make you more cautious."

Her heart pounded harder. "I'm not going anywhere," she said, but to herself, admitted a growing unease.

The sheriff frowned. "Don't say I didn't try." He took her hand and led her to the bottom of the floating staircase.

"Put some clothes on and I'll take you to Lafitte's Landing. It's best if you stay in town."

"I'd rather stay here."

"So would vagrants and bored teenagers."

"I'll lock the doors." Realizing his hand still held hers, she slid her palm from his fingers. "Short of handcuffing me and tossing me over your shoulder, there's nothing you can do to make me leave."

Finally, the stern cop demeanor cracked, revealing a hint of the good-ol'-boy charm. "Don't tempt me, sugar," he said, and she almost laughed.

He crossed the foyer, the frayed rug muting the clomp of his boots, and pulled open the door. "I'll be back in a minute."

She curled her fingers around the top of her robe and clenched the two sides together. "That's not necessary."

"But it's going to happen all the same," he said, turning to face her. "This house is a favorite with local teens. Spending the night here is tantamount to a badge of courage. If you're going to sleep here, you need clean sheets."

Just when she thought she had a handle on the man, he proved her wrong. "So now you're a maid service, too?"

For the first time he smiled. It was a startling sight, like the sun breaking through oppressive dark clouds.

"Nope," he drawled. "I'm your next-door neighbor."

"You've got my phone number. Call if anything happens."

"Nothing will happen."

"Lock the door behind me."

"I was born twenty-nine years ago, Sheriff. Not yesterday."

Ian resisted the urge to look below her defiant gaze and see the tempting truth of her words. He'd come back with clean sheets and a blanket to find she'd changed into a pair of well-worn jeans and a bulky sweater. Fuzzy blue slippers concealed the pale-pink polish on her toes. All that blond hair fell loose now, flirting with her cheekbones and streaming below her shoulders. She no longer looked like a siren or a vision, but the casual look held equal power to punch.

Never had he been so relieved to have a pretty lady put *on* clothes.

Ian winced, telling himself his reaction to Victoria Bishop was simply that of a healthy male, not a lech. Or a traitor.

"Good night, Sheriff," she said, and moved to close the door.

He stuck out his arm. "Just one more thing."

She lifted a brow. "You said that five minutes ago."

"Be careful with those candles. This place is a tinder-box."

Something dangerously close to a smile broke on her lips. "Anyone ever mention you take the whole protect-and-serve thing a little too seriously?"

Her words sobered him like a bucket of ice water. "Not many," he snapped. Only one, actually. But now she was dead. "I won't have anyone hurt on my watch, *chère.*"

"How gallant."

Realizing he was stalling, he let his arm drop. What the hell was he doing lingering over Russell Bishop's daughter, anyway? If he had one ounce of sense, he'd drag her to his squad car and take her to the New Orleans airport this very moment, watch until she boarded a plane and he knew she was gone.

"I'll be around first thing in the morning," he told her.

"Lucky me," she said, then closed the door between them.

Ian waited a heartbeat, long enough to hear the dead bolt click into place and the chain jingle. He listened for footsteps, but figured fuzzy slippers wouldn't make much sound.

Then the night went dark.

He looked at the extinguished porch light and almost

laughed. Miss Victoria Bishop wasn't one to mince words, or actions. He doubted the word *subtle* resided in her vocabulary, though it was the only word he could think of to describe her appeal. Hers wasn't an in-your-face beauty like so many of the women in south Louisiana, but rather, a gradual intoxication of the senses, the kind you weren't aware of until you craved your next fix so badly you shook.

Craved? The dangerous analogy destroyed the allure.

He had a town to protect and inherently knew Tori's presence here would destroy years worth of healing.

He turned and headed toward his house, tromping between the knobby roots of the massive oaks separating his property from hers. Spanish moss dangled from the branches, like memories twisting from the gallows of sins past.

Across the yard he heard the sound of a dog barking. "Hold on, boy. Papa's coming."

The worthless hound bayed even louder.

Ian grinned. Gaston had that way about him; he couldn't retrieve worth a damn, but he could brighten the darkest of Ian's moods, with little more than a pitiful howl or a pathetic thump of his tail.

Abruptly Ian turned back toward the old Carondolet place, where light glowed from the upstairs window. The guest room. The room where Russell Bishop's daughter would slide between sheets he'd brought her. His sheets.

She came into view, a sinuous shadow framed by the large window. She was looking off toward his house, but through the trees and the darkness, he knew she couldn't see him.

But he could see her.

And he knew what the pale light of morning would bring. What her decision would be. It had been there in the stubborn tilt of her chin, the defiant green glint of her eyes.

Ian didn't fear much. In his years as a New Orleans

homicide cop he'd seen and done things he would never talk about with decent folk. All in a day's work, he'd told himself. For the better good.

But Victoria...Victoria Bishop had no idea what demons awaited her here. She had no idea her world, her ideals, were about to go up in smoke. His, too, if she dug too deep.

By damn, he didn't relish the thought of what tomorrow held. He didn't want that woman in town one second longer than necessary. But he didn't want to utter the brutal words that would crush her rose-colored glasses either. The past belonged in the past, not dragged up and desecrated.

Just how the hell did you tell a woman the father she adored was a cold-blooded murderer?

The bed stole her breath. Solid, yet exquisite, it easily dated back to the mid-1800s. French, she guessed. Noble. Four intricately carved posts stretched up toward the ceiling, standing sentinel.

In that bed Tori knew she would feel safe.

Had she felt that way before, she wondered? Had she slept in this bed as a little girl? It wouldn't have been her parents'. The room was too small, the comforter too frilly.

Shaking off the questions, Tori stripped the old linens and replaced them with the ones Montague had brought. Funny, she would have taken him for a black silk man, not these taupe sheets of soft Egyptian cotton.

They smelled like him. That was her first thought when she turned out the lights and slipped between the cool linens. She shifted restlessly, but the distracting combination of soap and sandalwood lingered. It was as though Montague lay in bed with her. Uneasy, she turned to her side, only to confront an equally unsettling thought. The sheets touching every inch of her body had embraced his, as well.

The realization was surprisingly erotic.

She didn't know how long she lay there in the darkness,

but at some point she drifted off. When she opened her eyes again, sunlight whispered through the gauzy curtains.

Knowing the public library wouldn't open for a few more hours, she dressed and wandered down to the parlor. The sheet-draped furniture gave the room an otherworldly look and made Tori feel like an intruder.

What lay beneath the covers? What secrets? What treasures?

She went to work and, bit by bit, the grand room took shape. First the camel-back sofa, then a coffee table, an old sideboard, a few wing chairs. The grandfather clock presided over her excavation, rhythmically clanging as she worked. Shards of dust went flying, illuminated by the early-morning sunlight streaming through the window.

Her heart slowed when she found the piano. She'd always wanted to play, but her father had never agreed to lessons. Had her mother played? Is that why he'd never allowed the tinkling of piano keys in his home? Because memories would have been too strong?

Tori couldn't imagine a love that deep and abiding, that fierce. She'd dated, but no one had ever rocked the foundation of her world. She didn't want anyone to, either. Wouldn't allow it. An all-consuming love like that gobbled up the core of who and what you were, leaving you nothing more than an invalid.

Frowning, she shook off the unsettling thought and folded the yellow sheet. The emptiness of the house was getting to her. If the library was closed, she'd go to the coffee shop or find another way to occupy her time.

In the foyer the singed throw rug returned her thoughts to the night before. Thank God the sheriff—

She bit back the thought. She didn't want to feel gratitude toward Ian Montague. Yes, he'd stomped out the fire, but his heavy-handed tactics had also caused it.

Tori pulled open the front door and stepped onto the shady porch, eager to find out what secrets Bon Terre had in store for her. Instead she went absolutely still. Deadly still. All but her heart. It started to pound. Hard.

She didn't know which chilled her worse. The rusty hunting knife stabbed into the door. The blood. Or the note.

GO HOME BITCH.

Chapter 3

She wouldn't scream. She would *not* scream. She absolutely refused to yield to the horror sloshing through her like corrosive acid.

But deep inside she trembled.

Blood dripped from the yellowed scrap of newspaper, the offensive words scrawled in a heavy dark marker. And the knife. Dear God, the knife was huge. Its rusted tip speared into the wood, making the door look like the carcass of a hunting trophy.

Bad place...never go back.

Her throat burned, and her stomach turned. She hadn't expected to be greeted with open arms, but this—

"Waiting for me, sugar?"

Tori stiffened. Last night the seductive drawl had intrigued her, but this morning it pushed her to the edge. Who the hell did he think he was?

"Got your bags all packed?" he asked.

She didn't stop to think. He didn't deserve it. She turned and lunged for him. "You coldhearted son of a—"

"Whoa, there," Montague said. Already on the wide porch, he easily caught her wrists in his big hands. "I didn't exactly expect a kiss hello, but—"

"You've got some kind of nerve," she snarled, struggling to pull free of his grip.

He wouldn't let her go. "Still carrying a grudge from last night?" he asked as though this was all a big joke. "I thought we got past that."

She fought the way his big hands manacled her wrists, but the sheriff's strength far surpassed hers. "No one gets hurt on your watch, but threatening and terrorizing are quite fine, is that it? Or do you just save all the fun for yourself?"

"What are you talking—" His words died abruptly, and in the space of a heartbeat, the good-ol'-boy veneer hardened into a mask of cold fury. He shifted her to his side and pulled the gun from his holster, letting out a string of curses so inventive, Tori wasn't sure she heard him right.

"Is this supposed to scare me?" she asked, twisting against his hold on her. "Trying to make me realize you were right last night and send me running for the interstate?"

He looked from the defiled front door to her. His gaze was narrow. "Where did this come from?"

Fury galvanized her. Disappointment followed in its wake. What a fool she'd been to think, for even one second, that this man was anything more than a predator. The feel of his body against hers, all that heat and hard muscle beneath his loose, olive button-down and faded jeans, reinforced just how dangerous he could be.

"If you ever get tired of fooling the folks of this town, maybe you should give Hollywood a try. You're quite good."

"What the hell are you talking about?"

"My little housewarming gift. Thanks all the same, but it really wasn't necessary."

His pewter eyes took on a dangerous glitter. "You think I did this?"

"Who else knows I'm here?"

He had her crowded against the side of the old house before she even realized he'd moved. "Stick around here long enough, *chère,* and you'll realize I don't play games. If I want something, you won't have to wonder."

Her breath caught. She didn't know whether it was the simmer in his eyes or the barely concealed anger in his voice, the strength of a body that could protect as easily as it could threaten, but something deep inside responded to his ferocity.

She swallowed hard. "If you didn't do this, who did?"

Gun in hand, he turned and surveyed the densely treed front yard. The old oaks sprawled across the lawn, beautiful but secretive, Spanish moss dripping and swaying from the thick branches. But other than two squirrels playing chase, nothing moved.

"Did you hear anything?" he asked. "See anything?"

"Just you."

He spun toward her. "Damn it, Tori—" He stopped midflow and let out a harsh breath, visibly working to bring himself under control. The transformation fascinated her. It was like watching the rough, violent waters of the Atlantic Ocean going suddenly calm. Like glass.

"I'm sorry," he shocked her by saying. "You have every right to be upset, and absolutely no reason to trust me. You have no way of knowing what my word means. But I do. I also know the truth, and until you realize you can't conquer the world single-handedly, that's going to have to be good enough for both of us." He shoved his gun into his shoulder holster. "I intend to find out what happened here," he said, his gaze dipping down over her ivory sweater and tan slacks. "Are you okay?"

She hugged her arms around her waist. "It'll take more than a junior-high stunt to scare me off, Sheriff."

"The note, have you touched it?"

"No."

"Good. We'll dust for prints, see if we can get a match. Who else did you talk to? Who else knew you were coming here?"

The abrupt shift from hostility to what sounded like logic stripped the edge off her anger and left her facing a chilling question.

If he hadn't stabbed the note into the door, who had? "No one."

"Anyone in town?" he persisted.

"No. I came straight to the house."

"What about the lawyer's office in New Orleans?"

"I was there, but I didn't tell them my intent."

He shoved the hair back from his face. "Someone must have seen you, then. One look and there could be no doubt."

He sounded all cop now, looked that way, too. A man didn't need a badge when he had Montague's hard body and even harder eyes. He filled out the olive shirt and jeans well enough to be a poster boy for strength and confidence. His chest alone was enough to intimidate a man, distract a woman.

Only moments before, she'd interpreted the way he pressed her against the side of the house as a threat, but now a little voice deep inside pointed out that the way he had his body between her and the outside world could just as easily be construed as protection.

"No doubt about what?" she asked.

He lifted a hand to her face and slipped a strand of flyaway hair behind her ear, making her wish she'd pulled it into a ponytail. "All that blond hair and those pretty green eyes...you're a dead ringer for your mother."

Tori cringed at his word choice, though she'd thought the same thing upon discovering the photo in her father's safety deposit box. "You think someone drove by and saw me, and without knowing a thing about why I'm here, decided to put a bloody note on my door and run me off?"

The notion sounded ridiculous, but Montague's unyielding eyes revealed his answer before he spoke. "Yes."

Her throat tightened. "But why? I'm not here to hurt anyone."

"Have you decided?"

"About what?"

"Whether you're staying or going."

Tori glanced beyond his shoulder to the lush front yard. She knew what he wanted to hear. She knew what her father had wanted. But after less than twenty-four hours in Bon Terre, she couldn't leave, not without knowing the truth of why her father fled and hid her heritage from her.

She looked back at the sheriff. "I'm not leaving."

A grim smile played at the corners of his mouth. "Now, there's a surprise." His eyes met hers. They were warmer now and lingered a heartbeat longer than comfortable. "I'll call one of my deputies to process the scene. We'll send the note down to the lab in N'awlins. Find out if the blood is animal or human."

"Human?" The thought hadn't occurred to her.

"Hold your imagination, *chère*. Just because all those vampire books are set here in Louisiana, doesn't mean your pretty neck is in jeopardy."

God help her, she almost laughed. She didn't know how he did that, for a fraction of a second make her forget the circumstances that brought them together, and see only the ridiculous.

Going along with him, she lifted a hand to her collarbone and lightly rubbed, ignoring the way his gaze tracked her movement. "Do you take anything seriously?"

"Mais oui." The easy drawl should have warned her, but the slow smile caught her off guard. In the blink of an eye, the cop vanished, the unaffected charmer returned.

A defense mechanism? she wondered. A coping device? She knew cops often defaulted to humor, dark humor, to deal with the horrors they saw day in and day out. But what could be so horrible in a sleepy bayou town like Bon Terre?

He lifted his hand toward her face, but rather than touching her, he braced his arm against the side of the house and leaned closer. "I take a great many things seriously. My job. Protecting the good people of this town. And a few other, more pleasurable, quests. Shall I go into more detail?"

Maybe it was his voice, the glint in his eyes or the way his hair fell on either side of that distracting cowlick, but Tori sucked in a sharp breath, shocked by the image instantly flooding her mind. Heat. Deliberation. A slow but thorough seduction. Lingering. Inch by inch.

Her body betrayed her, clenching in all the wrong places. "Thanks," she said, ducking under his arm and crossing the wide porch, "but I think I'll head down to the library instead."

He caught her wrist. "You won't find the answer there."

She turned and served up an overly sweet smile. "But I will find what I need. Microfiche. And if you won't tell me the big secret, I'll find out on my own."

"I'm only looking out for your best interests, Victoria Bishop."

The use of her given name, a name that appeared on her birth certificate yet meant nothing to her, jarred her. "I can take care of myself."

His expression sobered. "That's what worries me."

"Oh, dear Lord in Heaven. It's true."

Tori spun toward the strained voice, finding a tall woman with long, graying dark hair standing on the top step of the old porch. The early-morning breeze played with the hem of her floral dress in soft pastels. She had a hand to her throat.

The pale woman looked like she faced a ghost.

Montague hurried toward her. "Mom, what are you doing here?"

Mom? Surprised, Tori watched the sheriff take the woman's fine-boned hands in his own. The resemblance was stunning, not just the height, but the pewter eyes and full mouth.

"Are you all right?" he asked.

His mother didn't even look at him, just stared across the porch, her gaze on Tori. "It's like seeing a ghost," she murmured.

Tori stiffened. She'd read the woman's expression correctly, but she didn't much like that the ghost in question appeared to be her.

"I'm Victoria Bishop," she said, crossing the porch and extending her hand.

Montague's mother freed herself from her son's grip and took Tori's outstretched hand in both of hers. Her flesh was cold, the gesture warm. "I'm Laurel. Laurel Montague." A soft, acutely sad smile graced her features. "Little Vicky. I held you when you were just a babe."

Oddly moved, Tori smiled. "It's nice to meet you."

Laurel's eyes misted over. She released Tori's hand and gently touched her hair. "You look so like *votre mère, mon ange.*"

"Thank you," Tori managed. She knew enough French to recognize Laurel's words as *my angel.* The endearment sat better than being called a ghost, but both referred to a person no longer living.

Montague put his arm around his mother's shoulders and tried to steer her away from Tori. "Mom, now isn't a good time—"

"It's a wonderful time," she corrected. She released her grip on Tori's hands and pulled her into an abrupt embrace. "It's a miracle, *non?* Here you are, right as rain."

Tori hugged the thin woman back and felt her composure unraveling like a spool of frayed thread. Animosity she could handle, but this feminine display of affection touched a place deep inside her, an aching emptiness, the little girl who grew up longing for a mother's touch. Her love.

"I never stopped worrying about you," Laurel murmured, "wondering what happened to you. Where you were. If he'd hurt you."

"If who hurt me?" Tori asked, pulling back.

Laurel sent her son a nervous glance.

Something hot flickered in his eyes. "She doesn't know."

A shocked little "oh," slipped from Laurel's mouth. She released Tori and backed away. "Oh, no."

Tori glanced from the mother's shocked expression to the son's somber gaze. She didn't like the secrecy, the talking around her as if she was a child incapable of dealing with adult circumstances.

"If you're talking about my father," she said more sharply than she'd intended, "he would never hurt me."

Laurel's retreat was visible, though she didn't move a muscle. "There's so much you don't understand. You—"

"Mom." The sheriff moved between the two women, his back to Tori. "I'm taking Tori down to the library— I'm going to tell her everything."

With sadness in her eyes, the older woman glanced around her son to Tori. "I'm sorry, *mon ange*. So sorry. You're an innocent in all this."

Tori didn't know what to say.

Fortunately, she didn't have to. "I'll be right back," Montague told her. "Don't go anywhere, don't touch anything."

She lifted her chin. "I don't need a baby-sitter, Sheriff."

He barked out something unintelligible. "We can debate that later, but for now I need to get the boys out here to process the scene." His gaze cut to the bloodied note on the door, then back to her. "It's not a good idea for you to go into town alone. Five minutes. That's all I need. Please. Let me make the calls."

It was the *please* that got her. Or perhaps it was the

shock. All Tori knew was she didn't want to go into town alone. Numbly she nodded. "All right. Five minutes."

"I'll be right back," he said, then led his mother down the wide steps and across the heavily wooded lawn.

Through the dense oaks, Tori made out the outline of a grand old house she figured to be his. Thick white columns supporting upper and lower wraparound porches evoked an image of frayed grandeur, not bachelorhood.

The sheriff was a walking paradox—seductive and teasing one minute, all business the next. Men like him were dangerous. Like chameleons, they changed their colors with the wind, being who they needed to be at a particular moment to come out on top. Making decisions for people. Controlling circumstances. The needs of others never entered the equation.

The sooner she could learn Bon Terre's secret and leave, the better off she'd be. She'd already had one man protecting her from her shadow. She didn't need another.

"I want that note taken to the lab in New Orleans," Ian barked into his kitchen phone. "If there's so much as a fraction of a fingerprint there, I want it. The blood, too. I want it typed."

His own blood boiled. He'd spent the early hours of the morning in an old rocking chair on the front porch, staring off toward the bayou. Except for the crickets and occasional toad, Ian hadn't heard a peep, not a twig snapping or a step creaking. Neither had Gaston. The dog couldn't hunt, but Ian had held out hope he'd at least cut it as a watchdog. But, no. With those allegedly supersonic canine ears, the dog had slept at Ian's feet, while just next door, through the cluster of ancient oaks, someone had crept through the shadows and attacked the old Carondolet place.

Again.

There'd been no screams this time.

But there'd been a knife. And blood.

And a woman sleeping upstairs, completely unprotected and vulnerable.

And Ian hadn't noticed anything wrong. Not a damn thing. He'd just sat there morosely staring into the darkness, a warm, forgotten beer cradled in his hands.

What the hell kind of sheriff was he?

What kind of man?

What kind of son?

No one gets hurt on your watch, but threatening and terrorizing are quite fine, is that it?

She couldn't have cut deeper with the knife speared into her door.

He could still see her standing there, trembling but defiant. Trying to be brave, when she had to be scared to death. And he was pretty sure she hadn't noticed the worst of it—the paper the perp had used to scrawl his warning. But Ian had. Newsprint. From twenty-five years before. If Tori looked close enough, beyond the blood and the threatening words, she'd learn the ugly truth before Ian had a chance to tell her.

He didn't know why that possibility disturbed him so.

But he was pretty sure she hadn't noticed. She'd been too shaken. He couldn't see her getting any closer to the knife and defiled paper than she had to.

He finished barking orders to his deputy, then hung up the phone. He needed to head next door before Miss Tori Bishop did something rash, like go downtown without him.

"Why haven't you told her already?"

The voice jarred him. For a moment he'd forgotten his mother had come home with him. He turned toward her and came face-to-face with the past. The sight of her holding a dish towel and standing in the sunny kitchen of his youth unlocked a door, and like an overcrowded closet, memories came crashing down—her making a roux on Fridays, French toast on Saturdays, pralines on Sundays. The time she and Ian had decided to surprise his father by painting the house themselves. His mother's easy smile and infectious laughter.

Before.

Before screams ripped the night and Ian learned first-hand how ugly life could be. Before his childhood shattered into fragments of horror and betrayal. Before his mother ran into the night and refused to step foot in the home she'd both created and loved.

The loss still had the power to cut him to the quick.

On a silent oath, he crossed the bright kitchen and took the dish towel from her hands. "I'm thirty-three years old, Mom. I can clean up after myself."

She smiled. "Then why don't you?"

The closet to the past still hung open, and another memory blindsided him, hitting Ian so hard he braced a hand against the Formica counter. For a crushing moment he was an eight-year-old boy, grinning sheepishly at his mother after she'd discovered a trail of mud leading across her freshly mopped floor, from the back door to the kitchen. The innocence of that long-ago time, when he'd thought being scolded by his ma or paddled by his da was as bad as it got, almost stole his breath.

Laurel touched his face in concern. "Ian?"

He shook off the remembrance, shoving the memories back where they belonged, down deep, where he didn't have to face them on a daily basis. So deep they couldn't even seep into his dreams.

"Are you okay?" his mom asked.

He gave her his best Ian-the-Unaffected smile. "I was about to ask you the same thing."

"I'm not the one who just went sheet-white."

Ian turned and reached for a clean coffee mug, then filled it to the brim. He took a long, hard swallow of the dark roast coffee his mother called river mud and waited for the warm liquid to work its magic.

"Seeing the Bishop girl has got to have been a shock for you," he commented.

"A shock?" Laurel shook her head, sending one strand of still-dark hair straying against her cheekbone. "More like a scare. That girl shouldn't be here. It's not safe."

Ian glanced past the windowsill herb box and beyond the sprawling oaks, to where Victoria Bishop and the old Carondolet place waited in the distance.

"She won't be here long. After I tell her the truth, I'm betting she'll be gone before nightfall. With any luck, she'll sell me that old firetrap while she's at it, and I can have it condemned once and for all."

"I'm concerned about *her,* Ian. Not the house." The words were sharp, her voice compassionate. She picked up a plastic New Orleans Saints cup, filled it with water, then leaned across Ian to water the withered herbs she'd brought him a few weeks before. "Just because the girl loves her father doesn't make her guilty by association. But some people won't see it that way. Hurting Bishop's daughter would make an awful lot of people happy."

Ian dumped the rest of his coffee in the sink and took his mother's hands. As always they were cold, but unlike too many years before, now they were strong. Her grip firm and reassuring.

"You are one amazing woman," he told her.

A smile lit her eyes. "You just now getting around to realizing that, *mon chou?*"

Love and admiration mingled. It had taken years, but his mother had emerged from the darkest of hells intact and determined to face the future. He had to make sure Victoria Bishop's arrival didn't suck her back down.

"You're defending her. You, of all people. You have as much reason to want her gone as anyone else."

She glanced back toward the window. "Hard to believe that elegant young woman is the rough-and-tumble girl from all those years ago. She grew up well, didn't she?"

He tried not to remember the sight of her last night, on the staircase with that blond hair piled onto her head and those mysterious eyes of hers glinting at him. Those defiant cheekbones. That provocative mouth. The robe wrapped around her praline-scented, freshly bathed body. Her bare feet with the pink toenail polish.

"She's an innocent," his mother said. She looked back toward him, catching his gaze in that pointed manner that always meant business. "I loved her like my own. I don't want to see her hurt."

Ian frowned. "There's nothing I can do about that, Mom. The writing's on the wall. Not even a sandblaster could change the truth."

Or the past.

Ian steered his cruiser down Riverside. To his left, Bayou Grand, a tributary of the Mississippi, snaked its way toward the Gulf of Mexico. To his right the sights of Bon Terre ambled along, the old buildings that many a town spent a fortune to recreate—the bookstore and the card shop, the florist, the barber, even the fancy coffee shop in the renovated dime store.

Tori sat by his side. Silent. Unmoving. Hair twisted behind her head, she had her face angled away from him, as though watching the sights go by. But Ian had been a student of human behavior too long to accept the obvious that easily. He saw the tension in her angular jaw, the way she held her shoulders high, her back straight. Her hands in her lap, clasped and pale. Resolve glinted in her eyes.

No, Miss Victoria Bishop wasn't just watching the sights go by. As much as he hated the analogy, she was coiled as tight as a pretty rattler, ready and waiting.

And for a moment a blade of compassion cut through Ian's determination. Despite the blood in her veins and the danger she posed, she didn't deserve what lay in store for her. No one did, but especially not the courageous woman seated next to him. There was a stabbing vulnerability about her, a yearning for something he knew didn't exist. He would have admired her fearless determination, if it hadn't chilled him to the core. In his line of work, bravery and tenacity served a man—or woman—well. In civilians the traits got people killed.

"Well, here we are," he said, parking the cruiser in front of the century-old library.

She didn't move, didn't speak.

"Chère?" He reached over and laid a hand on her wrist. "Change your mind?"

She flinched at his touch, then glanced down to where his palm rested against her forearm. The scars on the back of his hand contrasted sharply with her cool, flawless skin.

A beat of silence passed before she looked up and caught his gaze. "You wouldn't believe how hard my heart is pounding right now."

Yes, he would. "That's understandable."

A tentative smile played at her lips. "I didn't expect to feel so much."

Neither had he. "We don't have to go through with it," he said, ridiculously propelled to comfort. "We can always go back."

"No." The light in her eyes sparked brightly. "This is something I need to do." She opened the door and slid from the car.

Ian followed, lifting a hand to the gun in the holster around his shoulder. The gesture was automatic, but completely unnecessary.

He didn't need a bullet to end life as Tori Bishop knew it.

Chapter 4

The sun shone brightly from a vivid azure sky, but a chill hovered in the air. It was one of those deceptive days that looked all spring, but still felt like winter. Up and down the street, the town seemed to go completely still. For a minute, there, Ian would have sworn he'd stepped into a painting. People stopped walking. Heads turned. Eyes narrowed.

They knew. Already. News traveled fast in a small town.

"They're staring at us," Tori said when he reached her side.

He took her hand and led her across the sidewalk. "They're just curious." The words tasted phony even to him.

"They know who I am."

"Kind of hard not to."

"One of them could have done it," she said. "One of them could have put the note on the door."

"Maybe." He opened the library door and let her enter

before him. Following, he paused, his eyes adjusting to the low lighting after the bright sunshine.

The musty old library was just about empty. Once a week the ladies auxiliary gathered to discuss their next project, in this case, next week's Spring Festival. Either today wasn't the day, or they'd migrated to the coffee shop. Now that the Java Café had an espresso machine, the town flocked there like it was Mecca.

He glanced back at Tori. At first she appeared perfectly composed, but the fine lines around her eyes and the tightness of her mouth gave away her anxiety. And when he took her hand, her cool flesh confirmed his suspicions.

"This way," he said, leading her across the matted green carpet between towering shelves of books. "The microfiche is back here."

She didn't say anything, just kept walking.

"You okay?" he asked. Worse, he realized he cared. Destroying wasn't his style, stomping his foot down on a pretty magnolia blossom and crushing it against the punishing concrete.

Tori flashed him a tight smile. "I'm not so fragile that I'll shatter."

He wasn't so sure about that. He reached for the doorknob, saw the woman marching over too late.

"It really is her," Kay Roubilet snarled. She stopped and crossed herself. "You've got a lot of nerve showing your face in this town, girl."

Tori stiffened. "Pardon?"

Ian stepped between them. "Leave her alone, Kay."

"Sheriff or not," the tall, matronly woman seethed, "you have no right to tell me what to do, Ian Michael Montague. This girl's father single-handedly—"

"Go on inside, Tori," Ian said abruptly. He didn't want her to hear this from Kay. "I'll be right there.

She looked from him to the tight-lipped woman glaring at them both. "I want to know what she was going to say."

"And you will, but from me. Not her."

"You're not my protector," she bit out.

"You need to trust me on this," he said. Then, because it seemed to work before, he added, "Please."

Her eyes flashed fire, but by some miracle she acquiesced. "Fine." She turned the knob and went inside.

Ian closed the door behind her.

"You're just like your father," Kay accused in that sugary, condemning voice of hers. "Can't see beyond a pretty face."

He glanced toward the young librarian at the checkout desk. "Do me a favor, Lily, and call Autrey, tell him to come get his wife before I have to take her in for disturbing the peace."

Kay's eyes glittered. "Are you threatening me, Ian Michael? Why, I'm going to call your mama—"

"You go right ahead. But in the meantime, you leave police business to me."

"That girl is not welcome in this town, *Sheriff*, not unless she can lead us to her father."

"Her father is dead."

The older woman paled. She seemed to sway for just a moment before recovering her composure. "Then you best get rid of her, before someone decides to visit the sins of the father on the daughter."

That's exactly what Ian planned to do. "I'm going to pretend you didn't say that, Kay, but if anything happens to Victoria Bishop while she's here, there won't be any pretending when I come looking for you. Are we clear?"

"It's not me you need to be worried about." With an indignant lift of her chin, she marched between the overflowing shelves of books.

He took a moment to bring his temper under control, but Kay's words left an acrid taste. She'd been hurt badly by Russell Bishop. And though the sins of the father had nothing to do with the daughter, he knew many wouldn't realize that. Wouldn't care. The thirst for vengeance ran too deep.

Bon Terre would not welcome back little Vicky Bishop. If she was lucky, the worst they would do was run her off.

If she weren't lucky— The thought didn't bear considering. After today the lady with the determined glint in her eyes would be gone, and that would be that.

It struck him as ironic that he, of all people, had to be the one to both protect and destroy her.

He opened the door, and though she'd only been in the room a few minutes, she'd accomplished much. For starters, the smell of pralines already mingled with that of dust. He would have grinned, if he hadn't seen her leaning over the table and sifting through microfiche. She looked eager. Almost excited.

Inevitability stabbed through him. "Tori."

She glanced up, the question in her eyes before she gave it voice. "Mind telling me what that was all about?"

"That's why we're here, sugar." With a nonchalance he didn't feel, he strolled to her side and took over for her, quickly locating the right microfiche. "I don't suppose I can convince you to change your mind?"

"After this morning? No."

"It was worth a try." As a New Orleans homicide detective, he'd learned to separate the man from the case. The emotion from the facts. It was the only way he could stand over the beaten body of a child or the bloodied body of a woman and still function.

"Like I told you," he said matter-of-factly. There was no time for feeling now. No time for anything but the truth. "The past isn't pretty. A lot of people got hurt. Kay was one of them."

"Who else?"

He ignored the strand of blond hair scraggling against Tori's mouth. Even more, he ignored the desire to slide it behind her ear. Touching her was a bad idea. "Just about everyone."

Frustration flashed in those amazing green eyes. "What?" she asked. "What does everyone think my father did?"

Ian cringed. He heard the desperation in her voice, the need to know. He knew she thought she was tough. He even admired how well she'd handled the nasty scene that morning. But that was child's play, while this was as adult as it got. For a moment, though, Ian had the ridiculous notion to pull her into his arms and just hold her. Make it all go away. Protect her from the inevitable.

But the past couldn't be changed, and this was one woman who would never run from an oncoming train.

She was Russell Bishop's daughter.

Ian looked away from her eyes and finished loading the microfiche. "On the night of November 16," he began, "twenty-five years ago, the sheriff and one of his deputies were found slain in the deputy's house." *By a young boy.* "The murder weapon was recovered three days later, full of your father's prints."

Shock flooded Tori's eyes, followed closely by horrified suspicion. "But that doesn't mean—"

"No, it doesn't," Ian acknowledged. Earlier she'd commented on how hard her heart pounded. Now it was his heart pounding, his blood roaring. He forwarded through the old newspaper articles, until he found the one from the day after the murders.

Then he looked at her, straight-on. He might as well have held a gun in his hands. "Your father disappeared the night of the murders. So did you. And so did a fortune in diamonds. No one has seen or heard from either of you since."

Tori paled. All that fire and brilliance, suddenly dim. "What about my mother?" she whispered. Her voice was hoarse. "How does she fit into all of this? Is that when the fire happened?"

Ian pulled back the trigger, and fired. "No," he said. "She was the deputy."

* * *

Tori went very still. "What did you say?"

She'd misunderstood him. That was all. This would all make sense in a moment.

Montague's expression hardened. The grim lines around his pewter eyes deepened. "Your mother was the deputy found dead with the sheriff."

The words slammed into her, well-timed fists. "And you think my father killed her? Is that what you're trying to say?"

"Her and the sheriff. The evidence is overwhelming."

The room tilted. Or maybe it was the world. "No," she rasped. Her airways tightened. She couldn't breathe. Couldn't think. *"No."*

Montague crossed the room and reached for her. "Tori—"

"No," she said again, batting away his hand. His concern. To steady herself she braced her palm against the table and focused on facts. "There's a mistake. My mother died in a fire."

"Is that what your father told you?"

Instead of the scorn that typically hardened Montague's voice when he spoke of her father, Tori heard caution. She opened her mouth to answer but found herself gulping in air instead. She just barely managed a nod.

Cold. Dear God, she was so cold.

"You need to sit down." He'd pulled out a chair and put his hands on her shoulders before his movement consciously registered.

"No," she said again.

He eased her down onto the old wooden seat. "Lean forward and take a few deep breaths."

She wanted to protest, to tell him she could take care of herself, but found herself following his instructions.

"That's a love," he murmured, running his hands along her upper back. "Good girl."

A cacophony of protests vaulted through her, sharp, jagged, vehement, but none of them punctured the soothing feel of his hands along her back, his hypnotically Southern voice, the oxygen he encouraged her to draw into her lungs.

"Just give it a minute, *chère*. Shock is a scary thing."

Shock.

She was the deputy.

The deputy, the deputy, the deputy.

The horror surged back, and Tori abruptly looked up. "My father did not kill my mother."

Montague went down on one knee, bringing himself eye level with her. "You're white as a sheet," he said, skimming his index finger along her cheekbone. "Cold, too. Just give yourself a minute."

She batted his hand away and stood. Or tried to. Instead she swayed.

He pushed to his feet and quickly had a hand on each shoulder, steadying her. "Look at me."

She stared straight ahead, just barely registering the width of his chest. The olive shirt seemed to go on forever—

"My eyes," he clarified, then placed a finger under her chin and tilted her face upward. "Concentrate on my eyes."

She didn't want to do that. Eyes were dangerous. Eyes were intimate. Eyes didn't lie.

And what she saw in his eyes stole her breath.

Strength. Derision. And an unshakable belief in the horrible accusations he'd made.

"Breathe, damn it. You have to breathe."

She obeyed, gulping in another breath of air. All the while, his hand continued to cup her face, and she continued to look at him. Focus. Concentrate. Just as he'd commanded. The hard, unforgiving lines of his face, the thick hair the color of pecans. That damn cowlick. She looked for the cop, for the good ol' boy, but found neither. Just a man. A tall, strong, protective man, ready to pit himself against the world.

Or, in this case, everything she believed to be true.

"That's right," he murmured, his index finger sliding up her cheek to just below her eyes. "Easy does it."

A man, she thought again. A man who thrived on being in the driver's seat.

Abruptly she pulled away. "No, easy doesn't do it," she bit out, withdrawing from his too gentle touch. Fog fading, the punishing glare of his words returned. Cut deep.

"There's been a mistake," she insisted. Her thoughts jumbled and twisted, blurred. Memories bled through. "My father loved my mother with all his heart. He mourned her, never got over losing her."

"Crimes of passion usually involve deep emotion," Montague countered, his voice curiously hoarse. "Russell Bishop wouldn't be the first killer to love his victim."

"Don't call him that!"

"You said you wanted the truth."

"And you wanted to tell me," she recalled in a near-blinding wave of incredulity. "Why?" she wanted to know. "Why did you want to tell me? Did you want to see my reaction? To see if I'd believe your every word? If I'd turn to you for consolation?"

He stood still as a statue, his hard gaze unreadable. The tension emanating from his body indicated he wanted to pounce, but it was as though he had some invisible strait-jacket on, and wouldn't let himself move a muscle.

The restraint fascinated her. Even as it terrified.

"If that's what you'd like to believe," he said, "be my guest."

"Don't tell me what I can and can't believe," she almost growled. As much as she loved her father, he'd done that all her life, and look where it got her. If he'd just been honest with her. If he'd told her about the past, she'd be able to refute these horrible allegations. Instead she faced an arsenal of lies with no ammunition except the love and memories in her heart.

But it was those memories that gave her strength. She knew her father, knew him to be a good man. Which left only one possibility. The sheriff was lying to her, using poison darts to force her to leave town, like she'd refused to do last night. It was the only explanation that made sense.

"I've heard about cops like you," she said, softly, deliberately. "Cops who get their kicks by holding people's lives in the palm of their hand, then closing their fingers as tightly as they can. Cops who enjoy strolling up to a quiet house in the middle of the night and telling the occupants that daddy won't be coming home ever again. Is that how you get your kicks, Sheriff?"

Something hot flicked in Montague's eyes, but didn't move his body. "You're forgetting a few details, *chère*. You're forgetting that I wanted you to turn around and go back to your fishing village. You're forgetting that I warned you about unearthing secrets."

She wanted to lash out at him, to pound her fists against his chest and force him to take back the horrible accusations. But one look at his stony face, and she knew nothing she could say or do would change his beliefs. Touch him.

"You wanted to protect me from your own lies," she amended. "How gallant."

"Believe what you will about me, but this is not a conversation I'd choose to have."

His voice was hard and indifferent, cold, and for a fractured second, Tori found herself longing for the easy drawl of the good ol' boy. But that was just an act. With his shield of banter in place, Ian Montague hid his shadows from the world.

She watched his fingers curl into a tight fist and felt herself take a step back.

"I didn't sleep last night," he said in a dangerously quiet voice. "I sat on my back porch, watching the night push closer, trying to will you to leave but knowing with cold certainty what the morning would bring.''

"My little housewarming present?'' she asked pointedly.

His eyes went wild. He looked straight at her, but Tori got the distinct impression he saw beyond the four walls of the small room in which they stood. To what, she didn't know. The past?

Silence gathered, thick, punishing, like the thrumming of her heart. With each second the low hum of the overhead light became louder, until Tori wanted to slam her hand down on the switch and cast them into darkness, anything to quiet that constant droning.

But she didn't move. Didn't speak.

"Trust me, Tori, I'm not enjoying this any more than you are. This isn't what I wanted. That's why I warned you to leave. I don't want to hurt you.''

She fought the lure of his voice, his eyes. He had to be at least six-two, but the small room made him look taller, broader, like an animal in a cage several sizes too small. "But you're going to, anyway, is that it?''

"The writing on the wall can't be changed.''

"Why? Why can't it be changed?''

"Because you didn't listen to me and leave well enough alone. With your father gone, I didn't see any point in dragging out the past for a dog-and-pony show. What happened that long-ago night doesn't really matter anymore.''

"It matters to me!'' she protested, crossing the room and putting the length of the small table between them. Emotion ripped at her. "You may not care, but it matters a great deal to me that everyone in this town thinks my father killed my mother and the former sheriff.''

Montague went very still. "I care.''

Somehow, she doubted that. "Why? Why would you care about a crime committed a quarter of a century before? So you can play hero and secure justice once and for all?''

"Not heroics, Tori. My father. I care about my father."

The light-green walls closed in on her. Her airways constricted. "Your father?"

"My father. He was the sheriff. The man your father killed in cold blood."

Tori wasn't sure how she stayed standing. Just when she thought she had a handle on Montague, he hurled a curve ball. This one wicked. Dangerous. Hitting low. Hard. Finally, finally, she understood the glint she'd caught in his eyes. The hardness. The struggle.

Her own breathing turned jagged. Choppy. She felt as if someone held a thick wet cloth over her face, and each breath became more difficult than the last. More vital. But the someone was only Montague, and the thick cloth was just the past.

"That's why you look at me so strangely, isn't it?" Sickness churned through her. "Why you want me gone. When you look at me, you see the daughter of the man you think killed your father."

Ian heard the horror in her voice, but couldn't deny the truth of her words. He looked at the visibly shaken woman standing across the room from him, with the cluttered table between them as if it could somehow protect her from him, from the past, the truth, and felt a surprising blade of compassion.

A blade he immediately destroyed.

"You have your mother's eyes, but, yes, I see Russell Bishop looking out from them."

"That's why you want me gone," she whispered.

He hated how pale she was, even as he admired the resilient light in her eyes. "Losing my father nearly destroyed my mother. For a long time…for a long time the doctors didn't know if she'd pull out of it. But she's back now, and I'll be damned before I let her be hurt again. The best thing you can do for everyone is sever your ties to this town, relinquish rights to that old house and go back to where you came from.''

Her hands curled into tight fists. ''Relinquish rights to the house? Why would I do that?''

''So I can tear it down.''

She winced, and for a moment he thought she meant to hurl an angry retort. But then she went very still, and Ian could almost see the very second recognition hit.

''My God,'' she whispered. ''That's where they died.''

The long-ago night reared back to life and cut through the thick veneer he'd perfected over the years, and once again Ian was an eight-year-old boy running across the tangled path from his house to the old Carondolet place. Tripping. Praying. Shouting for his father.

''I found them there,'' he confirmed. Still saw them, too, often, when he tried to find sleep.

Bishop's daughter just looked at him, as though he spoke a forgotten ancient language, and she couldn't comprehend what he was telling her.

''Why?'' she asked. ''What possible reason could my father have had for killing them? What motive?''

He'd asked those same questions. They'd consumed him, followed him around the baseball diamond while he was growing up, into the back seats of cars with girls, eventually driving him to Tulane and a degree in criminal justice. He'd learned the importance of turning over every stone, digging deep, deeper still, even when everyone else was satisfied.

Ian was never satisfied.

''Some folks say they were having an affair—your mother and my father. Some folks believe that's why Russell snapped. That he found his wife with her lover and shot them in cold blood, then ran off with his daughter.''

''And you?'' Dread and hope twisted through the question. ''What do you think?''

Ian didn't think. He knew. ''My father was a dedicated

cop who spent more time on the job than off, but he loved my mother. No way was he unfaithful to her.''

''Then why? What else is there?''

''They were working on an investigation together, your mother and my father. I saw them together down by the bayou a time or two, arguing. From what I could gather, your mother was keeping information from Dad, and he didn't like it. He said secrets got people killed. She called him that night. Dad and I were eating ice cream. Your mom said she had something to show him, something important, and he raced out the door.''

Ian had never seen his father alive again.

To this day, he couldn't eat ice cream.

Tori put a hand to the table, but the tremble in her fingers didn't stop the stream of questions. ''What had she found? What were they investigating?''

Ian hesitated. He'd warned her. He'd told her she didn't belong in Bon Terre. He'd made it clear nothing awaited her but disillusionment. But she'd stayed, anyway.

And now here he stood, firing bullet after bullet.

She took each of them valiantly, wincing on impact, but remaining standing. And demanding more.

Ian didn't like it. No matter who she was, he'd never been a man to take pleasure in hurting others.

''What?'' she asked again. ''Tell me. I have a right to know.''

''Not what, Tori, but who.''

''Who, then?''

For so many years Ian had dreamed of securing justice. Of punishing Russell Bishop. But now that the opportunity lay at his feet, now that he had the man's daughter in the palm of his hand, a strange reluctance nagged at him. He found he didn't want to close his fist and crush.

But he did so, anyway. ''Your father, Tori. Your mother was investigating your father.''

Chapter 5

"No."

She spoke only the one word, but it summed up everything.

"From the day your mother came back to Bon Terre," Ian went on, "pregnant and with a husband in tow, the town watched Russell Bishop like an insect under a microscope. They never thought he was good enough for the town golden girl. They didn't understand what she saw in the rough-looking man she'd hooked up with during her brief stint with the New Orleans P.D."

"I never knew Mama was a cop," Tori murmured in a whisper-fine voice.

Ian wondered what other lies her father had plied her with.

"Bon Terre's first female deputy," he told her. "Folks didn't understand why pretty Corinne wanted to do police work, but from what I hear she always had a taste for adventure."

"And my father? What did he do?"

"He tried to fit in." Lied. Cheated. "Sold insurance for a while, then took a job down at the auction house with Guy Melancon. Put on a suit and tie every morning, while your pretty mama put on her badge. Folks were just starting to accept him when your parents separated."

Tori put her other hand against the table. "Separated?"

Ian noticed how rigid her fingers were, how pale. Her courage impressed him more than he cared to admit. Her composure. She was reeling, yet she struggled to keep dignity draped around her like a coat of armor.

"No one knew why, but your dad just up and moved out of the house one day."

Those catlike eyes of hers flared. "That's not possible."

"Your mama didn't think so, either. She thought he must have gotten into some kind of trouble. That he'd moved out to protect his wife and daughter from something dangerous. She just didn't know what."

"To *protect* her?"

She made it sound like a crime. "Two months later she and my father were dead, you and your father were gone, and close to a million and a half dollars in uncut diamonds vanished."

The blood drained from Tori's face. "Diamonds?"

Instinct almost sent Ian across the room. For a second, there, he wanted to reach out to her. To fold that lithe body of hers into his arms and hold her, give her an anchor in the storm. Give her security. Assure her everything would be okay.

But he couldn't do that.

She was Russell Bishop's daughter.

And everything would not be okay.

"That's what your mama found that night, what she wanted to show my dad. But they were killed first, and the diamonds vanished."

"But…where did the diamonds come from?"

"The antiques. Your father and the owner of the auction house, Guy Melancon, used the antiques to smuggle in jewels from Europe. They auctioned them off, escaping taxes. Shortly after your father disappeared, the feds closed in on Melancon, but he swallowed the barrel of a gun before they could take him in.''

''My God.''

Ian looked at her standing across the room, and for a disorienting moment, saw neither Russell Bishop nor his wife, Corinne. He saw a dangerous mirage, a woman in a soft cream sweater and matching tailored slacks, silky blond hair and smooth ivory skin. She reminded him of a delicate flower, except for the fire in her eyes. Strength and determination glowed there, and just a hint of trust.

A trust he had to crush.

Something deep inside him shifted. She looked so damn alone. So...betrayed. By whom, he had to wonder. By him? Or the father she obviously loved?

''The diamonds were never found, and the auction house burned to the ground, reducing Bon Terre's economy and livelihood to ashes with it. Many people in this town lost everything.''

''That doesn't mean my father was involved.''

He admired her loyalty, even as he sought to destroy it. ''Your mother stumbled across the scheme, found the diamonds. I have no idea exactly what she planned to do, whether she planned to turn your father in or try to help clean his hands, but your father took that choice from her. He found her and my father with the diamonds, realized his goose was cooked, took you and the diamonds and ran. Melancon was left holding an empty bag, the feds closing in from one side, the New Orleans crime syndicate from the other.''

Tori struggled to take in all that Montague was saying, but couldn't, not when the foundation of her world had shifted so violently. She groped for balance, but felt the way she had fifteen years before, when she'd lost her footing on an outcropping and slid ten feet to the frothing

Atlantic. She'd grabbed at the rock, but her hands had slid and scratched, cutting her palms.

This time when she landed, everything inside her went very still. Even her heart. She wasn't sure it beat. Too well she remembered her father's reaction when she asked him about Bon Terre and the old Carondolet house.

…killed her. Her and Montague.

She started to shake. "This isn't possible."

"I'm afraid it's a lot more than possible. It's fact, and it's truth. Your father is still a wanted man."

She looked across the table, toward Montague. "He's beyond the bounds of the law now."

He watched her peculiarly, as though he could see the turmoil inside. "Be that as it may, that's not going to change the way the people of Bon Terre feel. Particularly Kay Roubilet."

An image of the woman came back to Tori, of a face carved with lines of rage. Kay Roubilet wore her hate like a badge of honor. "Why Kay?"

"She's Guy Melancon's daughter. She lost everything when her dad took his life."

Tori squeezed her eyes shut, but in the darkness she saw her father standing in the dimly lit catholic church, lighting a candle every Sunday in honor of his wife. Down on his knees. Praying. Crying.

He could not have killed her.

"My father…we grew up as close to poor as you can be. He was a fisherman. He coached soccer! He didn't have a malicious bone in his body."

Montague sorted through the microfiche. "That fits the profile. Crimes of passion don't typically repeat themselves."

"But the money…he didn't have any."

"He wouldn't be the first criminal to start over," he said blandly. "To shut the door on the past and assume a new identity, a new life. To think that if they change, they could erase the sins of the past."

Violence had never played a role in Tori's life, but the urge to hit tore through her, to pound her fists against cool, calm, collected Ian Montague and his accusations, the table, the microfiche machine, to make the lies go away and restore her father's good name. Restore life as she'd known it.

A life that had never really existed.

Who was Victoria Bishop, after all?

She'd grown up Victoria LaFleur.

Because her father had lied to her. "I don't…I can't…"

Montague finally moved. With strides full of purpose, he rounded the table and sent Tori's heart hammering, his long legs eliminating the distance she'd put between them.

Now she just stood frozen, watching him approach her. Instinct told her to move out of the way of a speeding train, but her heart tripped and her legs wouldn't cooperate.

He stepped closer, stopping inches from her body and putting his hands on her shoulders. "I know it's a lot to absorb."

The stab of longing surprised her. The last thing she needed was for Montague to come closer, to slide his arms around her back and pull her against his chest. To hold her. Tell her everything would be okay. Make it so.

That was just shock, she knew. The need to connect with another human, when everything she'd ever believed had been stripped away in the space of a few minutes.

Ignoring the misplaced need, she focused on the heat of his hands against her shoulders and looked up at him. "He loved her," she said quietly. She couldn't get past that one fact. "Losing her destroyed him."

Montague's mouth became a hard, uncompromising line. "I don't doubt that for a second. However, that doesn't mean he isn't responsible."

Answers drifted closer to the questions tearing her apart. On the surface his allegations explained so much—why her father had changed their identities when Tori was too young to realize it, why he'd never told her how her mother really died, or about the small bayou town in south Louisiana. Why he'd become agitated when she asked him about the safety deposit box.

Tori had grown up like many little girls, thinking her father could climb every mountain tossed his way. But now, doubts undermined confidence. If he'd lied about their names, if he'd lied about their past and how her mother died, what else had he lied about?

She'd never questioned her father's love for her mother. But now she had to wonder. When had he really lost his wife? When she died? Or had it happened before then, when he moved out of the house? Had he heard the rumors about her and the sheriff? Had he known she was investigating him?

No. *Lies,* Tori told herself. Stories. Rumors.

The sensation of falling intensified, no longer from a rocky outcropping, but through the cold darkness of time and space. A free fall. Long. Hard. Endless.

"Tori?"

She blinked up at Montague and found his gaze concentrated on her. An intensity glittered in the pewter of his narrowed eyes, a low current that reached deep within her.

She pulled away from him and rounded the table.

"Where are you going?" he asked.

Away. Away from the man who looked at her and saw a killer. Who wanted to run her out of town.

"I need the words, Ian." To see the allegations in unbiased black and white, not through the filter of a little boy who'd lost his papa and his childhood to a heinous act of violence.

"I've already told you everything. There's no point in torturing yourself."

She sat at the table behind the microfiche machine and looked at what he'd loaded. "You've told me your point of view. The son of one of the murder victims. I need to see more, newspaper articles, police reports."

"They all say the same thing."

"Fine. Then I'll read the same thing."

She heard him swear softly but didn't look back, didn't speak. Just focused on what needed to be done. The words on the screen. The pictures. They jumped out at her, headlines and quotes and evidence. Bodies found. Shot to death. A fortune in diamonds, missing. Little girl gone. Statewide manhunt.

Tori sucked in a breath and blinked several times, but the newspaper stories blurred. Jumbled.

"Hey."

She felt the whisper of Montague's breath on her neck more than she actually heard the word. Numb, she glanced to her side, where he'd gone down on one knee.

With surprising gentleness considering his grim expression, he lifted a hand to her face and wiped the moisture from beneath her eyes. "You've seen enough."

In his voice she found a lifeline she didn't trust enough to grab. "Either you're my friend, Sheriff, or you're my foe. You can't be both."

He let his hand linger against her face for a moment, then eased a strand of hair back from her cheek before making his decision and severing contact. "Let's get out of here. I'll take you home and help you get all packed. You can make New Orleans by nightfall."

Something oddly close to disappointment drifted through her. She reached for the heated emotion of earlier, but found only a painful residue, a resolve to find the truth, no matter what.

"Thanks, but I'm not ready to accept my father as a murderer that easily. I need to see the police reports, and I have a meeting with Carson Lemieux in New Orleans tomorrow. He said he has a lot to tell me. Maybe he can shed some light on what really happened twenty-five years ago."

Montague didn't look so sure. "It's not smart to get your hopes up."

"It's even less smart to believe only the worst."

"At least that way you don't get hurt."

She turned off the machine and rose from the chair. "But you don't enjoy life much, either, do you?"

Montague stood. "Touché."

"Wait here."

Tori stood on the wide front porch and watched the sheriff round the side of the old house. His movements held purpose; the gun in his hand indicated caution.

The combination sent a thrill pulsing through her.

The reality sobered her good and quick.

Despite the strength he so easily conveyed, despite the simmer in his eyes that made her breath catch, Ian Montague was not a man to be admired. He thought her father a murderer.

In the distance, thunder rumbled. A cool breeze sent hanging baskets of bushy ferns swaying wildly. An afternoon storm, she figured, glancing south and seeing the dark clouds gather. Somehow, that fact didn't surprise her.

"Everything's secure," Montague announced, coming around the far side of the house. He still held his gun, still wore that steely expression in his gaze, but the lines around his face didn't look quite so hard. "Doors are all locked, windows secured. The glass you broke out last night has been replaced."

"You don't waste any time, do you?"

He eased the gun into his shoulder holster. "I linger when it's called for, *chère,* just not when it comes to police business."

A gust of heat swirled through her, reminding her why she had to keep this man at arm's distance. His easy charm was dangerous. If she swallowed the bait, he could lure her in for more lies. "You should go now. Everything's fine here, and the storm's about to break."

"*C'est vrai,*" he said, laser eyes locking onto hers. "That it is. But getting wet has never bothered me."

"How about getting struck by lightning?" After the revelations at the library, that's exactly how she felt.

"Can't say as that's happened yet, but I haven't ruled out the possibility. A man never knows when and where the next strike will be."

She slid the key into the lock and turned. He was doing it again, she realized, reeling her in with well-crafted words and smoldering eyes. Where in God's name was the man from the library? The boy who'd found his father's body? The sheriff who wanted her out of town?

Veneers, she reminded herself. The man had more layers than many of the refinished antiques inside.

"Not feeling so adventurous anymore?" he asked quietly.

She turned and found him watching her with a speculative gleam in his eyes, like a panther watching an elk drink from a stream. "I've had enough adventure for today," she said, rising to the challenge, "but don't let that stop you. If you want to tempt fate, be my guest."

The breeze ruffled the hair against his cowlick. "That's okay. Temptation isn't a demon that strikes when I'm alone."

She opened the door. "Too bad."

"Wait here," he said, starting past her. "I'll check inside."

"No." The word came out sharper than she'd intended, but she'd already spent too much time with the good sheriff. Now she just wanted to be alone. "If the exterior's in good shape, I'm sure everything's fine inside."

He turned back toward her. "Is that really what you think?"

She met his gaze, not surprised to find the simmer gone. In the space of a heartbeat, he'd taken a sharp turn back toward the past. He knew the answer to his question as well as she did. He was living proof of the fact that too often a perfect exterior concealed damage within.

"I think it's time for you to go, Sheriff."

He didn't move, didn't speak. Just held her gaze with an unnerving intensity. It was the cop this time, carefully assessing her. Again. And just as before, her airways tightened and her breathing turned shallow.

The moment stretched taut. Too well, Tori could see Montague using the technique on a suspect, staring a confession out of them. Being behind bars seemed preferable to being the object of his penetrating gaze.

Then a flash of lightning split the sky and shattered the spell. Thunder rolled along behind it. Then came the rain, big fat drops falling hard.

"Not just gutsy, but smart, too." His smoky gaze dipped down over her sweater, then slowly rose to her face. "Don't forget to lock up. Wouldn't want the boogeyman to bite."

"Don't worry about me, Sheriff. I can take care of myself."

"Like I said this morning, that's what worries me." But rather than forcing the issue, he turned and strode down the wide steps of the porch.

Tori moved to the railing, watching his long legs carry him across the weed-tangled path between the houses. The wind whipped at his brown hair and splatters of rain fell around him and against him, but he seemed oblivious to the elements.

The blade of fascination nicked harder, exposing a dangerous attraction.

She stood there for a long while, enjoying the storm. She loved the rain, found she missed her home by the ocean. When a storm gathered, she'd often found herself standing on a rocky outcropping over the Atlantic, lifting her face to the wind and enjoying the stinging spray of crashing waves.

On more than one occasion, her father had bolted to her side, insisting she come home with him. That she not take chances. Over the years, despite her love for him, she'd come to resent the leash he'd tried to keep on her.

The memory kindled an anger she tried to suppress, and along with it came a punishing blow of guilt. How could she feel both grief and anger at the same time?

Because he'd lied to her, a voice pointed out deep inside. He'd kept secrets. And in doing so, he'd not prepared her for what she now faced. The journey that had started out nostalgic, a grand mystery to be solved, had taken a sinister turn.

And Ian Montague resided at the heart of the darkness.

Illusions are dangerous, chère. *They mask reality. Once I shatter yours, there's no going back.*

The wind picked up, blowing sheets of rain onto the old porch and splattering Tori. Suddenly shivering, she headed inside, locked the door behind her and flipped on the lights. She started upstairs, but then paused and simply drank in her surroundings. Her parents' house. The home of her birth.

Where her mother died.

The enormity of the past twenty-four hours closed in on her, and with a strangled sob she dashed upstairs. At the end of the hall the locked room beckoned, and again she shivered. Before, she'd wondered what lay in the room beyond. Before, she'd imagined all sorts of intriguing secrets.

Now she knew. And she hated.

Sooner or later she'd have to confront that room, just as she would confront the horrible accusations against her father.

But not now. Not yet. Not when she felt so damn cold. Not when all she could think about was stripping off her damp sweater and slacks and pulling on thick sweats. Maybe she'd build a fire downstairs, she thought as she entered the room with the gorgeous antique bed. Maybe—

She stopped dead in her tracks.

It was impossible to enter the small room and not immediately notice the big bed with the intricately carved posts jutting up toward the ceiling. Each time she opened the door, her breath caught. As it did now. She stared at the carefully made bed, the thin comforter pulled up tight beneath the flimsy feather pillows. And her heart surged into overdrive.

That morning she'd stretched languorously, enjoying the moment until the scent of sandalwood and soap had reminded her where she was. In whose sheets she slept. Uncomfortable with the odd intimacy, she'd rolled from bed and hurriedly dressed.

She hadn't taken time to straighten the comforter.

She swung around now, looking for her suitcases, but finding no trace of the battered brown bags she'd found in the basement of her father's house.

Alarm crashed up against caution. Someone had been in the house. Someone had made up the bed she'd slept in. Someone had taken her belongings. Someone could still be inside.

Thoughts jumbled. She ran to the bathroom, found the same thing. Her brush, her makeup, her shampoo, everything, all gone. She ran from room to room, found nothing. Down the hall. Down the stairs. Her heart racing faster than her feet.

The parlor was empty, but for the sheets, once again draped over the furniture. The dining room offered nothing different. In the kitchen she found much the same—everything in order. The dishes she'd used for breakfast no longer sat in the sink. With a sick feeling in her stomach, she opened the cabinet and found the small plate and mug sitting on a shelf.

"Oh, God." First the note instructing her to leave and now this. All traces of her presence erased.

The chill deepened, the horrible feeling that the walls had eyes. That they were watching her. Waiting. Jeering.

"No," she whispered, looking out the kitchen window to where the storm raged. "No." And that's when she saw them. Her suitcases.

Sitting in the rain.

Chapter 6

Tori ran outside and grabbed her bags, dragged them back to the porch. Out of the rain's stinging spray, she shoved damp hair back from her eyes and opened the suitcases, found all her belongings nestled inside, neatly folded.

The sense of violation was swift and brutal.

Someone had touched them all—her jeans and sweaters, her pajamas, a bra. Her panties. Someone had run their hands over them. Arranged them in an almost artistic manner.

Her first thought was Montague.

Fury muscled its way past the horror and sent her back to her feet. She ran down the steps and toward his house, not giving a damn about the wind and the rain and the mud. But then lightning split the storm-darkened sky, and Tori realized her mistake. Montague had been with her all day.

"Oh, God," she whispered. Call him, some voice deep inside insisted. He was the sheriff. He would know what to do. He would—

He would look at her with those searing eyes of his. He would tell her he'd warned her. That she wasn't wanted here. Then he'd tell her to leave.

Russell Bishop's daughter wasn't going anywhere.

And she wasn't going to run to Sheriff Ian Montague, either. Instead she turned and trudged through the mud and puddles back toward her parents' house, where the back door hung open. The rain still hadn't let up. Nor had the wind. But a cold certainty marched through her.

She would not be bullied into believing her father a murderer. She would not be bullied into leaving town. And she would not be bullied into leaning on the broad shoulders of the cop next door, not with his simmering eyes and twisted accusations about her father. Not even in an official capacity.

Inside, she found the purse she'd dropped on the floor, fished out her cell phone, and jabbed 911. Montague would find out eventually, but from one of his deputies. Not her.

Rain slashed across the narrow two-lane highway, drowning out the jangly Zydeco tune blaring from the radio. The windshield wipers slashed back and forth, but they couldn't keep up with the downpour. Lightning flashed and thunder rumbled, and still Ian drove.

In the passenger's seat of the Jeep, his big yellow dog, Gaston, sat with his nose pressed to the window. He wanted his master to roll it down so he could hang his head out, but Ian didn't want to deal with 110 pounds of wet dog.

So Gaston just sat there, pouting.

Damn. Ian clenched the wheel tighter. Victoria Bishop didn't belong in Bon Terre. He didn't want her here, either. Didn't want to go to sleep every night with the knowledge that Russell Bishop's daughter lay between his sheets in a bed just next door. Didn't want to lie awake, unable to forget the note someone had speared into her door, wondering if they'd strike again. Didn't want to jar himself awake, heart pounding at the memory of what had happened in the house where she now slept.

And wondering if it could happen again.

Too easily she could wind up paying for the sins of her father. And Ian couldn't let that happen. By virtue of the law he'd sworn to uphold, he couldn't stand by and do nothing when a threat had already been made.

Ian took a curve in the road faster than he should have and felt the Jeep slide into a hydroplane. He skillfully regained control, but kept up the speed. Gradually, the thick sheets of rain thinned, and Ian turned toward home, deciding he wanted to run, not drive.

"Hang on, boy," he told Gaston. "We'll be home in a sec. Promise not to get muddy, and you can run with me."

The lab's droopy ears perked up. Ian had said the magic word. He flicked the windshield wipers down a notch, his body already craving the release of endorphins soon to follow.

The sight of the squad car parked in the street, its lights flashing garishly, changed everything.

Ian threw on the brakes and slammed the Jeep into park, reaching out an arm to keep Gaston from flying against the dashboard. He flung open the door and tried not to run. But God it was hard not to, when his heart thundered louder than the storm. His boots sloshed down hard, sending puddles of rainwater splattering. The stairs to the porch he took two at a time. At the door, he knocked. Loudly.

But no one answered.

Dear God. Tori.

His pulse kicked up another notch. He put his hand to the knob and turned. Found the door open.

Ian charged inside, slammed into a wall of déjà vu. He'd run to this house before. Run inside, not knowing what he'd find. Then he hadn't possessed a weapon. Then he'd only had a childhood.

Now he had neither.

But he had his hands and his body, and with them he could not only defend, he could protect.

Voices drew him across the foyer and through the dining room, toward the kitchen.

"So let me get this straight," Deputy Hank Fontenot was saying. Tall and slightly balding, Fontenot had been with the department for almost thirty years. He was a passable deputy, but he'd never wanted the responsibility of being sheriff. "You got home and found your bed all made and the dishes washed and put away?"

"That's right." Tori's voice. Strong. Angry. Defiant.

Alive.

He saw her then, through the doorway separating the dining room from the kitchen. And for a moment he just stared. She stood at an angle to him, chin high, soft white sweater soaking wet and molded to her chest. Her arms were wrapped tightly around her waist. Her wet blond hair looked darker than it had before. Sleeker. Her eyes were huge.

The urge to cross to her, to fold her in his arms and stop the trembling, caught Ian by surprise. Beneath all that tough, she looked shockingly vulnerable. She was scared, he could tell, even though she fought like hell to hide that fact from the world. From him.

Reality left a bitter taste in his mouth. She didn't want his help. She hadn't turned to him, hadn't called him. He lived next door, but she'd called the department instead.

Fontenot looked up from his notepad. "Well, hell, honey, whoever did this, we need to catch them. I could use them over at my place. Ever since the wife left me—"

"Knock it off, 'Tenot." Ian strode into the kitchen, perversely pleased by the way Tori's eyes flared at the sound of his voice. "What's the matter with you? Can't you see this woman is shivering?"

"Sheriff," the deputy drawled. "They didn't need to call you. Everything's under control here."

Like hell. He turned to Tori. "Go put some dry clothes on, *chère*. You'll catch your death—" His words died when he saw the suitcases sitting by the back door. "Decided to take my advice, after all?" he asked more coldly than he'd intended.

A brittle smile played at her mouth. "Don't get your hopes up, Sheriff."

"Then what's going on here?" he wanted to know.

"Ask your deputy." That said, she picked up the dripping suitcases and swept past him, heading for the stairs. The exit would have been elegantly scathing, had she not left a trail of rainwater in her wake.

Ian watched her go. Only when he neither saw nor heard her, did he turn toward Fontenot.

"Why you sticking up for Bishop's daughter, Sheriff? I'd think you, more than anybody, would want her gone."

The boy who'd run into this house twenty-five years before did. The man who stood there now wasn't so sure. "What I want doesn't amount to a damn. We have a job to do, and we do it, whether we like it or not. Now tell me what's going on."

Fontenot did. When he finished, Ian swore under his breath. Something cold twisted through him. He should have gone inside with her, damn it, whether she'd wanted him to or not. Someone was playing games with her. Nasty games. Mind games. He hated thinking about Tori walking into that room alone and finding the bed made, her suitcases gone. Not knowing if someone still lurked in the shadows.

"She could be making it up, Sheriff, like her nana did. Remember how Corinne's mama called us from time to time, said someone had been inside the house, but there was never any proof? Never anything missing, just slightly rearranged. Crazy as a loon, that woman was. Never the same after Bishop killed her daughter."

Ian remembered. At the time, he'd written off Estelle's

claims as a lonely woman's ramblings. Now he had to wonder.

"I'll take it from here," he told Fontenot. "Have a report on my desk first thing in the morning."

The deputy frowned. "I know she's a pretty thing, Ian, but that don't change who she is. Where's she been all this time, anyway? Where's that lowlife she calls Daddy?"

"She didn't pull the trigger, Hank. Russell did."

The older man grunted. "Don't matter. Out of respect for your dear sweet mama, you should send Bishop's girl on her pretty little way. She's not welcome around here."

"Careful, Hank. You're starting to sound an awful lot like the note we found on her door this morning."

"Your dad was a good man, Sheriff. One of the few men I've ever called friend. I won't apologize for not welcoming his killer's daughter with open arms." Hank flipped his notebook closed and grabbed his keys from the table. "I'll have that report on your desk."

Ian watched his deputy stalk out the back door. Through the window he saw him cross the porch.

Damn.

Someone wanted Russell Bishop's daughter gone. Badly. So far they hadn't made a move against her person, but he found little consolation in that flimsy fact.

Mind games, he thought again, turning to inspect the rambling kitchen. If he couldn't convince her to leave, he'd have to get better locks for her. Maybe a security system. And by God he needed to make it clear she was to call him, and him alone.

He wouldn't have another death on his watch.

Several minutes passed before Tori returned to the kitchen. He heard her before he saw her, soft footfalls across the hardwood floor. Turning from where he stood at the chipped sink, he found her standing in the doorway, dressed in a soft pair of moss-green knit pants and a huge sweatshirt with Discover Canada emblazoned across the front. Thick cream socks covered her feet. Her hair was still damp, but she'd run a comb through the tangled strands.

Soft, Ian thought. She looked soft. Almost cuddly. All but her eyes. Disillusionment glinted there. A shard of loneliness. And for the first time, he saw a hint of the little girl who'd been lied to her entire life. Victoria Bishop lost her mother twenty-five years ago, but today, she'd lost her father. Her ideals. Those illusions he'd warned her about.

For only the second time in his life, Ian hated being so damn right. The first time had resulted in the death of an innocent woman. *Meghan.*

The grim memory twisted him up inside. He knew he should say something to Tori, but he'd be damned if he could think of the right words. What he wanted had nothing to do with the verbal art of communication and everything to do with the physical. Watching her stand there assessing him with those huge, betrayed eyes, part of him wanted to pull her into his arms and hold her, promise her everything would be okay. *Make* everything okay. But the rest of him—the sane, rational part—never wanted to see her again. Only twenty-four hours into their relationship, and she'd scattered his beliefs like leaves in a harsh fall wind.

Cop, he reminded himself. She needed the sheriff, not the man who looked at her and saw a woman who twisted him up inside.

Objective, he added. Be objective. Focus on the facts. The routine.

Indifferent, he admonished. A cop would ignore the vulnerability in those bottomless green eyes of hers. A cop would ignore the fact her father was a cold-blooded murderer.

The sheriff's responsibility to a visitor who'd been threatened had to supersede the son's hostility toward the suspect's daughter. Both had to override the man's reaction to a woman too stubborn to admit her own vulnerability.

Yeah, and while he was at it, he might as well yank the sun out of the sky and turn it into a yo-yo.

"Is this some sort of contest?" she asked.

"Pardon?"

"My dad and I used to call it the quiet game. See who could go the longest without saying anything. Or laughing."

He just stared at her. In addition to changing out of drenched clothes and running a comb through her hair, she'd gathered all those jagged emotions and shoved them out of view. Where? he wondered. Where did Victoria Bishop hide what she didn't want the world to see?

"You should get out of those clothes," she said.

"What?"

"Your clothes. They're dripping all over my floor."

Ian glanced down and saw that she spoke the truth. His shirt and jeans were plastered to his body. A puddle formed at his feet. "That's what happens when you run through the rain." The shock of driving up to see the garishly flashing lights of Hank's car reared back to life. "Why didn't you call *me,* damn it?"

She shrugged. "I called 911. That's what you're supposed to do in case of an emergency."

"Not when a cop lives next door."

"Is that coffee I smell?" she asked.

Frustration tightened through him. Maybe he deserved her dismissal, but he damn well didn't like it.

"I thought it might help you warm up," he growled, feeling like an idiot. If he were smart, he would have just turned and walked away. Never stopped in the first place. Let Hank Fontenot handle her.

"Thanks." She crossed the large kitchen and picked up the old drip pot from the stove, took a mug down from the cabinet and poured a cup of coffee. After taking a deep sip, she turned to him. "Go ahead and say it."

A myriad of possibilities slid forward—you're amazing, you're beautiful, you're dangerous as hell—but he didn't think she wanted to hear any of them. And even if she did, love for his father would never let him voice them. "Say what?"

"I told you so."

That got his attention. "Oh?"

"I know you want to say it—I can see it in your eyes. You warned me to leave. You told me I wasn't welcome."

Ian moved to her side and fixed a mug for himself, careful not to touch her as he did so. "Just looking out for your best interests, *chère*. Contrary to what you think, I don't want to see you hurt."

"But that won't change the writing on the wall, right? Isn't that what you said earlier?"

He didn't appreciate having his words thrown back at him. "Staying here is just asking for trouble. We'd all be better off if you just sold me this old house, went back to where you came from, forgot about Bon Terre altogether."

She put down her mug. "How long have you lived here?"

"I was born here," he said, then took a deep sip of coffee. *Bitter* coffee.

"So you probably know most everyone?" she asked.

"Some better than others."

"Grandparents?"

That made him smile. "Of course."

"Aunts, uncles, cousins?"

Once, Montague family reunions had been legendary. *Before.* "Your point, *chère?*"

She took his mug from him and put it on the counter beside hers. "I grew up with no one, Sheriff. No one but my father, a father I now realize I never really knew." She glanced around the kitchen, at the ceramic flower wind chimes hanging in the window, the old tin canisters still sitting on the counter, the table where various names were carved into the old wood. The cracked countertops and peeling linoleum, the frayed gauzy curtains. Then she smiled. "This house…this house is part of me."

"You haven't lived here since you were four years old."

"But my family did."

The soft, resilient light glinting in her eyes surprised him. After this afternoon he hadn't expected to see it again. "Look, Tori—"

"I understand you want this house gone," she rolled right on. "It's an albatross. A reminder. But for me..." She gazed at him, and damn near knocked the breath from his lungs. "This house is like family for me. A long-lost relative. I can't say goodbye, not when I've just barely said hello."

Ian swore softly. "You're talking like the house is alive."

Her smile turned ethereal. "For me it is."

Late that night Tori turned away from the locked door at the end of the upstairs hall. Quiet blanketed the house, but for the rhythmic ticking of the stately grandfather clock. It seemed to echo, a constant reminder of time slipping by.

Tomorrow, she told herself. After her trip to New Orleans, she would find a way to gain access to the mysterious room. But for now, she wandered the house, avoiding the big bed where she'd slept the night before. Where someone else had straightened the sheets. Montague's sheets. Tomorrow she'd buy a new set. A set that didn't carry the scent of the man she didn't want to think of, especially when she lay alone in bed.

She'd never seen eyes as fierce as his that afternoon. As raw. Standing there in the kitchen, his wet clothes plastered against hard muscle, he'd looked as though he'd walked in on a murder scene rather than the aftermath of psychological warfare.

She refused to let the memory unnerve her.

Curiosity drew her from antique-packed room to antique-packed room, until she found the armoire in one of the bedrooms, the box inside. The pictures. She sat cross-legged on a handmade rug and spread the photos on the wood floor. Her family. Embraced by tarnished silver frames, image after image smiled up at her.

That's what she noticed. The smiles. Bright, genuine, full of happiness and laughter.

Her throat tightened. She picked up one of the frames and ran her finger along the images of her mother and father, frozen forever on that bright sunny day in what looked like Easter finery. They looked so…happy. Normal. In love. No traces of anything sinister or untoward lurked in their gazes. No warning of the bloodshed that lay ahead.

Tears welled. "Oh, Papa," she whispered into the quiet house. "Why didn't you tell me? Why didn't you realize secrets only make everything worse? How can I help you now?"

No answers came. There were none.

Time passed. Tori inspected each photo, the early years of her childhood dancing around her, love and happiness, warmth, security. A time when darkness came only at night and tomorrow held nothing but promise.

The cold jarred her awake. She opened her eyes against the wash of bright light and found that she lay on the hardwood floor of the bedroom, an old photo clutched in her hand and pressed to her heart. She'd fallen asleep amidst images of a time long gone. And now the sun shone like a spotlight, glaring intrusively through the window.

Momentarily disoriented, Tori quickly recovered, bathing and dressing, readying herself for her meeting with Carson Lemieux in New Orleans. Answers lay just hours ahead. Maybe then she could wake from this nightmare once and for all.

Slinging her purse over her shoulder, she opened the door and stepped into the cool air outside.

"Morning, sugar."

He sat in an old rocking chair, his long legs stretched before him and crossed at the ankles. He looked relaxed and confident, completely at ease. He wore olive pants with a tan button-down shirt, open at the throat, revealing a medal of some sort, one she hadn't noticed before. His hair was neatly combed and falling on either side of that damned sexy cowlick, drawing her attention to those gun-metal eyes.

An unwanted sensation curled low in her belly. She refused to call it heat. Or excitement. Especially not relief. "What are you doing here?"

"Waiting for you."

He made it sound like the most natural thing in the world. "Sorry, Sheriff, but I don't have time for another round of listening to all the reasons I shouldn't be here. I've got to be in New Orleans by ten."

He stood. "I know, sugar. That's why I'm here. I'm going with you."

Alarm shot through her. "That's not necessary."

"Maybe not, but it's going to happen, all the same." He strolled toward her. "You're a visitor to Bon Terre. As sheriff, it's my job to make sure you leave here as safe and pretty as you arrived."

She turned to lock the door, needing to do something other than look at him. The longing was ridiculous. Misplaced. Wholly misguided. But for a second, there, she found herself wanting to believe him. Dangerous.

"After everything you told me in the library, how do you expect me to believe you can really put my best interests first?"

"Today's a new day, *chère*."

She glanced beyond the intricate ironwork to the front yard, the brightness of the green grass, the clear blue sky overhead. No remnants of yesterday's storm remained.

"You can't quit being Saul Montague's son," she said, looking back toward the sheriff, "any more than I can quit being Russell La—Bishop's daughter."

"Nor would I ever try." Entreaty glinted in his eyes.

"But today that little boy is tucked away. Today I'm just a cop."

She noticed the harness around his shoulder, the gun resting snugly in its holster. He may have looked all cop, but his words, his voice, his eyes, held nothing but Southern charm.

"Does this usually work?" she asked, mildly amused.

"All the time." Grinning, he extended his hand. "What do you say? A truce. Twelve hours. What can it hurt?"

A whole hell of a lot, the voice of caution pointed out. "Sounds more like a dare."

The simmer in his eyes deepened. "You're not afraid, are you?"

Her heart thrummed low and hard, but she didn't hesitate. "Not on your life," she said, and placed her palm to his.

Victoria LaFleur never walked away from a dare.

"I can't believe he wasn't there."

"He's a lawyer—since when did they start keeping promises?"

Tori finished off her second beignet, savoring the last sugary bite. A cacophony of tourists and locals crowded the open-air café, while on the adjacent sidewalk, a bearded man played "Somewhere over the Rainbow" on the sax. At a nearby table two older men carried on an animated conversation in what had to be Cajun.

The accents reminded her of home. *Papa.*

"It doesn't make sense," she said, pushing aside a blade of sadness. "When I called, Mr. Lemieux sounded eager to talk to me. Asked me to come down. Said he had a lot to tell me."

Montague took a sip of café au lait, his big, olive-skinned hand making the mug looked smaller, whiter. "Try not to worry about it."

Impossible. They'd waited at the lawyer's Canal Street

office for two hours. His assistant kept assuring them Lemieux would be in any minute, but he'd never shown.

"Do you think he forgot?"

"It's possible." Montague set the mug next to his empty plate—he'd eaten four of the French doughnuts. Now, his gaze lingered on her mouth, the low sizzle in his eyes making Tori feel as if she'd just become a menu item. And he was still hungry.

"What?" she asked, more than a little uncomfortable.

His hair fell around the cowlick on his forehead, making him look dangerously benign, wholly irreverent. "Just admiring the view."

She resisted the urge to squirm. "Don't."

"How can I not? With that powdered sugar on your face, you look like you should be on the menu."

Flustered, Tori grabbed her napkin, but Montague was leaning across the table and rubbing his thumb against the corner of her mouth before she could do anything.

"Pink becomes you," he drawled, licking the sugar from his fingers.

She sighed. "I should have known it was too good to last." Up until that moment he'd been a gracious host. She'd actually found herself glad he'd insisted upon coming along, particularly when trying to parallel park a few blocks from Jackson Square.

"Come on." He stood and reached for her hand. "Let's get out of here."

She started to protest, but realized doing so would be futile. When the man had his mind made up, not even a papal proclamation could change it. She barely had time to run the white napkin across her mouth before he dragged her from the crowded café. His strides were long, his grip firm. She could barely keep up with him. "Where are we going?"

"I want to show you something." He led her across a tree-shaded breezeway and past a bronze plaque, with words in both French and English. To her right and across the street, a beautiful old cathedral stood at the back of the vibrant park area, but Montague steered her left and up several rows of steps. The sun had burned off the early-morning chill, leaving a comfortable warmth in its place. The humidity was high, but a gentle breeze kept it from being too stifling.

"Here you go."

The sense of awe was immediate. Wide, grand, dotted with an array of barges and steamboats packed with tourists, the river stole her breath. Its muddy water ambled along lazily, inevitably, as if it hadn't a care, a hurry, in the world.

"It's...beautiful."

"They don't call it the Mighty Mississippi for nothing." Montague started walking again, tugging her hand and leading her across railroad tracks and down the cracked steps of the levee. He didn't stop until he reached the rocky area at river's edge. "I never get tired of seeing her."

Tori didn't think she would, either. There was something pure and elemental about being so close to the water. Cleansing. They were in a busy city, but down here it was as though they'd entered another world. Another time.

Montague gazed off to the right, where the massive river made a tugboat look like no more than a toy. "When I was a kid," he told her, "the river seemed magic. It's always been here, you know? Long before we came."

And it would be there long after they left, too, ever-lasting, like the love she'd thought her parents shared.

Oddly moved by the undercurrent to Montague's voice, Tori looked at him standing beside her on the rocky riverbank. Sunlight glinted against pecan-brown hair in need of a trim and curling slightly at his nape, shimmered in his pewter eyes. His gaze wasn't as hard as usual, or as condemning. It was almost reverent as he watched a barge steaming by. Somehow he looked as though he belonged.

Longing speared through Tori. She didn't know where she belonged. Not anymore. When she'd arrived in Bon

Terre, the sensation of homecoming had been sharp. Almost profound. But in the wake of all that had transpired since then, she knew she didn't belong here, no matter how badly she wished otherwise.

Downriver the tugboat blared its horn. The wind whispered harder, louder, but Montague seemed oblivious to his surroundings. To her.

Not so for Tori. Her chest tightened as she studied the hard lines around his eyes and a mouth that was as sensuous as it was scornful, the very stillness of his body. What would it feel like to rest her head against his chest, to feel those arms close around her and hold her tight? How long had it been? How long since someone had held her? Since she'd let someone?

Would Montague's wrinkled shirt smell like his sheets, that intriguing combination of soap and sandalwood? Would the chest hairs beneath the vee of his shirt feel as wiry as they looked? And his arms, would they provide the comfort they promised?

No, she answered abruptly. No, no, no.

This man was not a shelter in the storm.

If anything, Montague was the storm itself—swirling and ever changing, unpredictable, dangerous. She'd been uneasy around him from the first moment she saw him standing at the top of the stairs with a gun trained on her, but now she realized the danger stemmed from a different direction than she'd first thought. The man wouldn't hurt her in a physical sense, but on an emotional level he'd already started to unravel her like a spool of thread. Not just her need to stand on her own two feet and make her own decisions, but his distorted version of the past had planted seeds of doubt where certainty once thrived.

Caution, she reminded herself. Caution was key. If Sheriff Ian Montague slipped further under her skin, too easily she could wind up as debilitated as her father had been.

"The Acadians called it the river of life," he commented. "Fitting, *non?*"

Tori looked out over the water and smiled. "I know. Dad told me the stories all the time—they were my favorite." That had been their special time, when her father sat on the edge of her bed and closed his eyes, let his voice grow heavy with a French accent and stories spill from his heart. "Little did I know I'd be replicating their journey."

"Replicating?" Montague turned toward her, his voice as sharp as his gaze. "You're from Nova Scotia?"

Realizing her mistake, Tori held her face expressionless. "I spent some time there," she said, hedging.

For a moment he said nothing, just studied her with those all-knowing, all-seeing eyes of his. Then a change came over his face, like a curtain going down on a play, and his expression lightened. "Did he tell you about the crawdads?"

Tori could only stare—she couldn't believe he was letting her off the hook. *A truce. Twelve hours. What can it hurt?*

"Crawdads?" she asked.

"Mais oui." His voice was softer now, thicker. And his eyes, all deep-set and narrow, they almost seemed to shimmer. "Everybody knows about de Acadians, how dey were exiled from Nova Scotia and forced to seek refuge. To start over. But not many folks know about de crawdads."

Tori tried not to grin, but felt her lips twitch. Big, bad Ian Montague in storyteller mode was a sight to behold, and against better judgment, something deep inside her stirred. "What happened to them?"

He picked up a flat rock, then lazily flung it out over the river, where it skipped twice before sinking beneath the muddy water. "De Acadians were a happy people. Warm and loving, lively. When dey were exiled, the lobsters of de Atlantic were heartbroken. So heartbroken, in fact, dat dey followed 'em."

She cocked a brow. "Followed them?"

"Mais oui. Dey found der way to de Miss'sipi and

trekked all de way down to Louziana. But de journey was a hard one, yah? Long. Arduous. By de time dose mighty lobsters found deir Acadians, the muddy river had turned dem brown, and they'd shrunk. De Acadians didn't recognize dem as their beloved lobsters. Called 'em crawdads instead.''

She couldn't help it. She laughed.

And Montague smiled. It was a startling sight, all the more stunning for its rarity. His whole face seemed to lighten, his lips curling up and revealing startlingly white teeth. Eyes entirely too concentrated on her, he lifted a hand to her cheek and eased a strand of flyaway hair back from her face.

"I like it when you do that," he murmured, his hand lingering.

Tori couldn't look away. The air around them seemed to thicken. They stood in a wide-open expanse, a warm breeze caressing them, yet the spell of his words, his eyes, wove around them like a net. Her heart took on a low staccato rhythm, and her breathing deepened. She felt herself reaching toward him. For him.

Montague stepped closer. So close she felt the heat of his body. The raw energy. Saw his head lowering toward hers.

"We should head on back," she said abruptly, glancing toward the bustle of the city. "I was hoping to walk through Jackson Square before leaving."

A wicked light glinted in his eyes. "The day is still young, sugar. No need to rush."

She tried to pull away from him, found she couldn't. "I need to run through a hardware store, too."

Needed away from *him*. Fast. Before she did something irrevocable, like surrendered to the draw that pulled at her like the dangerous eddies in the river.

He skimmed a thumb down to her lower lip. "What are you so scared of, *chère?* Me? Or yourself?"

Chapter 7

She stood on the bank of a river in humidity thick enough to cut with a knife, but Tori's mouth went dry. The challenge in Montague's voice touched her as intimately as his hand against her cheek. On her mouth. But she couldn't rise to it—survival instincts ran too deep.

The man was like the river beyond, its deceptive laziness making it all the more luring. Dangerous.

"I appreciate the truce," she said with a breeziness that pleased her, "but let's not get carried away." She pulled away. "I was hoping to have my palm read before we leave."

His eyes took on a peculiar gleam, but he didn't move. "Your palm read?"

"I've wanted to for as long as I can remember." But whenever she mentioned it at a festival, her father had become agitated, telling her it was a waste of time. Witchcraft.

"Don't tell me you believe that garbage?"

"What can it hurt?" She turned to head up the steps of

the levee, but Montague caught her wrist before she got far.

"Let me."

She swung around to look at him, felt an increasingly powerful rush go through her. He stood with his back to the wide river, a tall man with the wind ruffling his thick brown hair. The tan shirt and olive pants made him look like he belonged in an outdoorsman catalog.

"Let you what?" she asked.

"Read your palm." Already, he was pulling her closer, gently turning her wrist so that the back of her hand rested against the inside of his. "I'm a man of many talents, remember?"

Apprehension gathered. "I think you're taking this cross-training thing a little far."

"A man never knows when certain talents will come in handy."

It was warm outside, but inside Tori shivered. Standing there with her hand in his, her palm up and open to the breeze, to his eyes, she felt surprisingly vulnerable. The urge to curl her fingers into a protective fist was strong.

Ridiculous. What could the man see after all? Just flesh and a bunch of wrinkles.

Montague drew her closer and lifted her hand toward his face. His gaze turned serious, intent. He skimmed his index finger, callused and blunt tipped, along her flesh, murmuring "ah," or "hmm," as he did so.

Amazing that hands so hard and battle-scarred could touch with such tenderness. If she closed her eyes, she would think he stroked her flesh with a feather.

"Long lifeline," he commented. "Deep heart line."

On cue, her chest tightened, her pulse deepening. The longing was acute. She hadn't realized how intimate his perusal would feel. How exposed. Like making love in broad daylight. He was only touching her hand, running his index finger along the lines of her palm, but her whole body burned.

"Ah," he said again, his voice low. "Just as I suspected."

Instinct demanded she pull away, but she found herself leaning closer. Breathing choppier. The world around her, the river and the tourists, faded. "What?"

He skimmed his thumb along the inside of her hand, shooting a tingle clear down to her toes.

"Danger," he warned, and before she realized his intent, leaned down and pressed his mouth to the sensitive flesh of her palm. She felt the moist warmth of his breath first, then the press of his lips against her skin.

A ribbon of heat unfurled up her arm and pooled low in her belly. Eddying. Unraveling. The feel of his mouth against her palm unleashed a dangerous longing to feel his mouth elsewhere. His lips. Moving gently. Confidently. Seductively.

Then he looked up and straight into her unprepared eyes. His smile was lethal. "Needed to get a little closer to your fate line," he explained.

God help her, everything inside her went warm and liquid, as if he'd just kissed her thoroughly, mouth to mouth, rather than merely on her hand. Disoriented, she fought the need to brace herself, knowing that if she touched his body, all bets were off.

"And just what did it tell you?" She barely recognized the breathless voice as her own.

He grazed his index finger where his mouth had been, then pressed it to her lips. "What do you think it told me?"

The ache in her chest deepened. The longing. "That you've forgotten who we are."

The words scraped on the way out.

She tried to pull her hand free, but the sheriff had other ideas. His hold tightened, making it very clear that Ian Montague wasn't a man to let go easily. Not until he wanted to. *Unless* he wanted to.

"I haven't forgotten anything," he said hoarsely. "Maybe I'm just tempting fate."

The bold proclamation jolted her. Caution crashed in from all directions. "I'm the daughter of the man you think killed your father," she reminded him. And herself.

He frowned. "Non, *chère,* the real problem is you're a woman who refuses to listen to people looking out for her best interests. That's a good way to get hurt."

"What makes you think you know what's best for me?"

"What makes you think I don't?"

Everything! The racing of her heart, the blurring of her thoughts. The crumbling of her defenses.

Abruptly she yanked her hand from his. "You're out of your mind," she snapped, then turned and hurried up the steps.

His parting words echoed on the breeze. "Next time, *chère,* you won't pull away."

"Wait here."

Standing next to a caricature artist, Tori lifted a hand in mock salute. "Aye, aye, cap-i-tain."

Ian shot her a hard look, then turned and made his way through the mass of tourists and street performers crowding Jackson Square. He had a call to make, but didn't want her to hear. Didn't want her to worry. Didn't want her to know. She would only become more defiant then. Put herself in greater danger.

Glancing over his shoulder, he saw her standing in front of the intricate iron fencing around the park in the center of the square, watching him. She lifted a hand and waved.

Mocking him, damn it. She was mocking him.

His body tightened in irritation. Not at her, but himself. Tempting fate, his ass. He knew better than to tempt the grand dame. No matter how in control he felt, she always found a way to remind him otherwise.

Tori. God, he should never have taken her to the river. Should never have subjected himself to seeing her standing there against the soft blue sky. The breeze played with her pale hair, sunshine sparkled in her vivid green eyes. He should never have touched her, never have given in to desire and put his mouth anywhere on her body. Just kissing her palm, the rest of his body had surged to life, hardening in a heartbeat.

A string of frustrated curse words tore from his mouth, earning the shocked gasp of a cluster of elderly tourists.

Ian didn't care. He didn't want to make memories with Tori. Didn't want to hear that damned sexy voice of hers shake as she defended her father. Didn't want to cut her slack. Didn't want to feel compassion for a woman who reminded him of the biggest mistake of his life.

Didn't want anything to do with Russell Bishop's daughter.

And yet, the pull was there. The draw. The connection. When she smiled, when she leveled him with those mysterious, tilted eyes of hers. She intrigued him. And she was right. Too easily she made him forget who she was and the magnitude of bloodshed and betrayal that stood between them.

A safe distance away he turned back and found her laughing at something the caricature artist had drawn. Probably a tourist in Elvis or Dolly Parton drag. Frowning, Ian pulled his cell phone from his belt and jabbed out his former partner's number. During his days on the streets of New Orleans, he and Aaron Fourcade had boasted the highest solve rate in the city.

"Damn, son," Fourcade drawled a few seconds later. "Your hunches always did creep me out."

Ian tensed. "What the hell are you talking about?"

"The lawyer. How the hell did you know we'd find his place trashed?"

Ian squeezed his eyes shut. He'd wanted to be wrong, for a change. Wanted to be paranoid. "What happened?"

With the detached voice of a cop, Fourcade recounted the scene at the lawyer's French Quarter town house. The furniture strewn and drawers opened. The missing electronics and jewelry. Blood on the bedroom floor. But no body.

A robbery, like hell. Ian didn't believe in coincidences any more than he believed in happily ever after. There was always a catalyst. A lead domino. Cause and effect.

Tori.

He barked out a final request to Fourcade, then ended the call and turned back toward the square. He would have to tell her. But not now. Not here. He needed to get her away from the busy city with its anonymous crowds and back to Bon Terre, where he could keep an eye on her. Keep her safe. *Keep her alive.*

Like he hadn't done with Meghan.

A group of senior citizens congregated directly between where Ian stood and where he'd left Tori. They laughed and pointed and snapped pictures and completely blocked his view.

The jolt of panic was ridiculous. He took off, telling himself not to run, but acutely aware his legs weren't obeying. He pushed through the horde and emerged on the other side, only to find the caricature artist sitting alone.

"Where is she?" he demanded, but the young man just looked at him and shrugged.

Ian pulled back and scanned the crowded piazza. The bright sun glaring off the pavement nearly blinded him. She had to be somewhere, damn it. She couldn't just disappear.

But of course she could. She and her father had for twenty-five years. His own father and Meghan had, forever.

Blood roared through his veins. His heart pounded. He tore through the crowd like bare hands ripping frayed fabric. A middle-aged man barked something about manners, and a young woman with dreadlocks gaped, but Ian didn't slow down. Didn't care. He could think of nothing but Tori.

"Hey, mister. Betcha twenty dollars I knows where y'got those shoes."

Ian glanced hotly at the grinning young man, then pulled out his wallet and flashed his badge. "I got them on my feet, slick."

The street performer's eyes widened, and he scurried away to scam some unsuspecting tourist.

A cluster of artists sat at the base of the steps leading to the cathedral. Nearby two acrobats performed adjacent to a trio of mimes. On the corner five old men sang the blues.

No Tori.

Adrenaline surged, the instincts of a cop kicked in. He knew this city, knew the seduction, the danger. She did not.

He took off toward the river, pushing his way through meandering groups of children and adults, lovers and vagrants. The carnival-like square revolved around him, a cacophony of sound and color and sensation. Restaurants, vendors, gift shops.

No Tori.

The sun beat harder, the sweet smell of beignets sickening. She was fine, he told himself, trying not to run. Not to panic. Not to call Fourcade. She was close by. No one had followed them to the city—he'd made sure of that. She was a smart woman. She'd just wandered into a shop. She wouldn't have gone far.

He was on his third round of the square when he saw her, and his heart squeezed. Hard. Fury came next.

She sat beneath a colorful parasol at the far side of the plaza. The warm breeze played with the strands of her pale hair, while the bright sun kissed her gorgeous skin, making her smile more breathtaking. She sat leaning forward, her right arm outstretched before her, like a junkie awaiting a fix.

Ian swore hotly and took off. His long strides quickly

ate up the pavement. "I told you to stay put," he barked as he approached her.

She glanced up and shot him a wry grin. "I figured being the big bad sheriff and all, you'd find me."

"Damn it, do you have any idea—"

"You don't own me, Montague." Her voice was firm, her eyes glittering. "You can't tell me what to do."

"The hell I can't," he growled. His heart was still pounding. Reeling. He knew what happened to unsuspecting tourists. He'd seen the aftermath, the sickening images that would stay with a man forever. "You don't know this city. You don't know the risks. Wander into the wrong back alley—"

"I wasn't born yesterday," she said, cutting him off, then glanced at the colorfully dressed woman seated in front of her. "Excuse the good sheriff, madame. He's a tad overprotective."

An odd light glinted in the palm reader's eyes, but rather than the reproach Ian expected, her expression looked more like apprehension. "He has good reason to be," she said.

That seemed to startle Tori. The amusement faded from her gaze. "Wh-what?"

"I don't need to see his palm to see that he takes life seriously. That he would lay his life on the line for those he cares about."

"That's it," Ian barked, reaching for Tori's wrist. "This is hogwash."

She shot him a heated glance, holding her hand in place with surprising resolve. "Be that as it may, Sheriff, it's my hogwash." She returned her attention to the woman who watched them carefully, no doubt looking for cues to play off of.

"Ignore him, please," Tori said, "and continue."

Madame Rousseau met Ian's gaze for a heartbeat before returning her attention to Tori's palm. "There's danger in your hand, girl. This man obviously knows that."

Tori paled. "Danger?"

Ian tensed. "Damn it, Tori—"

"What kind of danger?"

The older woman leaned down, running her thumb along the center of Tori's palm. "You've lived with it your whole life," she said. "Even when you were just a wee thing. I see hardship early on, but perhaps that's why I also see courage and resilience, a thirst for life. Determination."

"Wow."

The intrigue in Tori's voice shot through Ian like a cold knife. Apprehension bled through. "That could apply to anyone, Tori. I've yet to meet a man or woman who escaped childhood unscathed."

"Yours is a long journey," the psychic said, as though Ian hadn't spoken. "Physical and emotional."

Tori leaned closer. "That's right."

Madame Rousseau ran her finger along a line from the base of Tori's palm up toward her middle finger. "I see independence, but only recently. This is why you left your home."

Tori went very still. "Yes." Her voice was a whisper.

"What else do you see?" Ian drawled. He didn't like how pale Tori had gone. Didn't like how dark her eyes had become. "What she had for breakfast? How many children she'll have?"

The psychic smiled serenely. "What are you really asking, Sheriff? If our girl here will fall in love while on her journey?"

Ian stiffened. "I suppose a vivid imagination comes in handy for a profession like yours."

"Stop it," Tori said, and the pleading in her voice grabbed him somewhere deep inside.

"Go on," she told the psychic.

Madame Rousseau traced her thumb along a vertical line in the middle of Tori's hand. "You've not known love yet, girl, not the kind of love that binds a man and woman together for a lifetime.'' She hesitated for a brilliantly dramatic moment. ''But you will. Ah, yes. You will.''

Tori released a shuddering breath. ''Love like that doesn't exist.''

For once Ian agreed with her.

The old psychic smiled. ''Yes, it does, child, though often it gets off to a rocky start. Such will be yours. You have difficulty separating intellect and emotion, but once you find a man who fulfills you on both levels, your union will overcome even the greatest obstacles.''

Tori glanced away from the woman and toward the big white cathedral, blinking rapidly.

The moisture glistening in her eyes punched Ian in the gut.

''That's enough,'' he said.

She was silent a moment, breathing deeply. ''I'll stop,'' she surprised him by saying. ''If you let her read yours.''

Ian stepped back. ''No way.''

She looked up at him, her composure rapidly returning. ''Why not? Scared of what she might see? Of what I might find out about *you?*''

The gauntlet landed hard at his feet. It glistened. Taunted. ''Storytelling doesn't scare me.''

Tori stood. ''Then prove it.''

Ian thought about taking her hand and leading her back to the Jeep, but knew he'd never hear the end of it. She'd harass him forever. ''What's in it for me?'' he asked.

She tilted her head, smiled innocently. ''Pardon?''

''You want me to have my palm read—I'm asking you why I should. If I do this for you, what will you do for me?''

Those luminous green eyes of hers came to life. ''That's easy. I won't be able to call you a coward.''

God help him, he almost laughed. He didn't know how the hell she defused him like that. Across town, blood stained Carson Lemieux's Garden District town house. Across the river, someone in Bon Terre wanted Tori gone.

But here Ian was, letting the daughter of the man who'd killed his father goad him into having his palm read.

"Five minutes," he grumbled, taking Tori's place in the hot seat.

She put her hands on his shoulder and leaned over him. "Give her your hand."

Ignoring the faint aroma of pralines and roses, the feel of her soft body entirely too close, Ian extended his arm.

Madame Rousseau took his hand, running her fingers along the back of his before exposing his palm. "Yours has not been an easy life," she murmured as she did so.

Ian barked out a laugh. "Gee, what was the giveaway? The scars?"

Somber black eyes met his. "Your scars are not of the flesh, *mon chou.* Not all of them, anyway. Not the deepest."

His gut clenched. "So now you're into psychology, too?"

The older woman shot Tori a placid glance. "This one's a handful, girl."

Tori laughed, but Ian growled. "Spare me the psychic humor." He couldn't believe he was freaking having his palm read. A man was missing. A man linked to the smiling woman standing beside him. A man linked to the past.

"You've got fabulous hands," Madame Rousseau said, running her fingers along the inside of his square palm. He remembered doing just the same thing to Tori, the feel of her soft skin, the rapid fluttering of a pulse point. And for a fleeting moment he wondered what her elegant hands would feel like holding his. Touching. Stroking.

"You're a man of deep passion and conviction," the psychic said. "You take life seriously. Responsibility defines you, but you're not as hard as you want people to think. You feel things deeply and profoundly."

Ian felt Tori stiffen. She still leaned against his shoulder, enabling him to feel her chest expand with each breath she drew. They were slower now. Deeper.

"Go on," he said ambivalently.

"See these chains here along your lifeline?" the psychic asked, tracing what looked like fragmented lines along his palm. "Your life hasn't been easy. Like the lady, your childhood was marked by tragedy and sudden loss."

Ian went very still, all but his heart. It staggered. Reeled. *She couldn't know.*

"Not just your childhood, either," Madame Rousseau said in a trancelike voice. While she spoke, she skimmed her finger to the vertical line between the base of his palm and his middle finger. "You've loved before," she murmured. "Briefly. Intensely. And then you lost. Abruptly. And you blame yourself."

Ian jerked his hand from hers and stood. "That's enough."

Tori looked up at him, alarm sharp in her eyes. "Ian—"

"It's okay, child," the psychic said, touching Tori's arm. "This man has survived a lot. There's no need to torture him."

"How much do we owe you?" Ian growled. It was too damn hot in the square. The humidity too damn thick. How the hell was a man supposed to breathe?

He settled with the psychic and turned to leave.

"There's one more thing," Madame Rousseau said.

Instinct told Ian to keep walking, but something in the older woman's voice stopped him cold. An odd note of warning. A fierce gentleness. He turned toward her, saw her watching him through impressively grave eyes.

"You've tried to shut yourself off from the world, *mon chou,*" she said gently, somberly, "but fate has much in store for you. Your sense of responsibility will serve you well, but if you keep denying your strong emotions, you'll have yet another tragic ending."

Ian swore hotly. "Your tactics may work on tourists, *Madame Rousseau,* but they don't work on me." He took Tori's hand and guided her through the swelling crowd, toward the riverside parking lot and away from words that chilled him to the core.

She couldn't know about Meghan. She couldn't.

They drove in silence. Uneasy, suffocating silence. Thick and ominous, like the dark clouds gathering down south, over the Gulf of Mexico. Tension hovered and stretched, settling around them and between them, keeping them apart even as it drew them together. Making it difficult to breathe.

Ian steered the Jeep off the two-lane highway and eased to a stop at the traffic light. He stared straight ahead; sunglasses shielded his eyes. His mouth was a hard line, his big body still. All but his hands. He held them at the bottom of the steering wheel, where he rubbed his left thumb against the inside of his right palm.

The palm Madame Rousseau had read.

Tori fought a chill deep inside. She'd gone to the palm reader in jest, out of fun and in the name of adventure. To rile Ian. But she'd done more than rile him. She'd shut him down. He'd barely spoken to her since they left the French Quarter. He'd practically dragged her through the swelling, merry crowd and to the car, where he'd merely barked, "Get in."

The light changed to green and Ian gunned the Jeep, sending them jerking forward. Still, he neither spoke nor glanced at Tori. It was as though he drove alone.

She touched a hand to her stomach and thought about the other vendor she'd visited. He'd be furious, she knew. To herself, she admitted that had been part of the thrill. The satisfaction. To prove that Montague couldn't dictate to her.

But now regret pushed in. Seeing such a passionate man completely expressionless unnerved her. That's not what she wanted. Despite the magnitude of lies and betrayal that stood between them, she found she missed the simmer in those smoky eyes of his, the way he prodded her. Challenged her. The way he sent her pulse racing with no more than a look.

And his touch…

Good God. Earlier, on the levee, the feel of his fingers skimming along the sensitive flesh of her palm had been almost excruciating. And his mouth… It was hard and grim now, but earlier, when he'd put his lips to the inside of her palm, there'd been only gentleness. And promise.

Madame Rousseau's words had changed everything— shattered, actually—like the dark storm clouds blotting out the rays of the sun. What had she said, Tori wondered. What had disturbed Ian so deeply? What had fortified the wall between them and erased the seductive man who'd stood alongside the Mississippi, the wind ruffling his hair, talking to her with easy intimacy in his voice? Who'd kissed her palm.

And touched something far deeper.

The sense of loss was powerful. In place of Ian, the good ol' boy, stood a man who looked much as the sheriff had that first night, when she'd revealed her identity. Ian the Unaffected.

Your scars are not of the flesh, mon chou. *Not all of them. Not the deepest.*

Tori looked from his big hands to the sunglasses hiding his eyes, the rigidity of his body, and wondered what he was thinking. What he was remembering.

"Madame Rousseau upset you," she ventured.

"Don't be ridiculous."

The finality in his voice didn't deter her. "You've barely said two words since we left New Orleans."

"Maybe it's the company," he said without looking at her. "Maybe I don't have anything to say to a woman who refuses to listen."

The tone, more than the words, robbed her of breath. She hadn't realized he could hurt her so. "Ouch," she said as casually as she could, then looked out the window toward the cypress trees whizzing by. She didn't want him to see her face. Her eyes. She didn't want him to see the pain she hadn't expected.

Ian swore under his breath, and the Jeep swerved onto the bumpy shoulder. Gravel spewed into the air as the vehicle jerked to a stop. Tori swallowed hard and focused on a cluster of trees, jutting up toward the increasingly ominous sky. Her throat was surprisingly tight. Scratchy.

The car engine idled and thunder rumbled, but neither of them spoke. Silence gathered. Stretched.

"Look at me," Ian said a moment later, and his voice was hoarse, rough hewn.

Tori blinked rapidly. Her heart staggered and stumbled. She didn't know why she felt so raw and exposed. So vulnerable.

She felt him move before the actual touch of his finger beneath her chin. He turned her toward him, held her face so that she had no choice but to look at him. At the dark glasses hiding his eyes.

"I'm sorry," he startled her by saying. "That was uncalled for."

She ignored the ache, forced a smile. "You don't need to tiptoe around me, Ian. I know I'm not your first choice of who you'd like to spend the day with."

"So now *you're* psychic, too?"

A fat raindrop splattered against the windshield. "A woman doesn't need to be psychic to read you, Ian. It's in your eyes. Your touch."

The rest of his hand joined the finger beneath her chin, sliding to curve around the back of her neck. "And what about my kiss? Was it there, too?"

Sensation closed in on her. Memory. A flash of heat. The yearning, the reaching. The feel of moist warmth against her palm. The irrational desire to lift her mouth to his, to—

It happened before she realized his intent. Before she

could stop him. Before she could breathe. His mouth lowered to hers, his lips skimming. Searching. Gently. Tentatively. A match in search of tinder.

"Yes," she whispered. "Yes."

Chapter 8

Ian changed the direction of the kiss, but not the intensity. He didn't go deep, just skimmed, the way his finger had danced along her palm, lazily. Inquisitively. She could feel tension beneath his touch, could feel the restraint, and it sent her heart pounding even harder.

Then he pulled back, not far, just enough so she could see his face. "You scared me today."

Tori felt the emotion bleed from her heart and into her eyes. She tried to label what she'd felt in his kiss—a test, a taunt, a challenge, a way of distracting her, throwing her off the hunt—but came up blank. She searched his face, lingering for a moment on the brown hair falling recklessly to either side of his cowlick, then to his shielded eyes. She wanted to see them, damn it. Only then would she know.

"Take off your sunglasses."

"What?"

"You're not a man to hide, Ian. Don't start now." Not after the odd intimacy they'd forged through the day.

Surprisingly, he obeyed. One hand still pressed to her neck, he used the other to remove the dark aviator glasses.

Tori's breath caught. Ian's pewter eyes gleamed as raw as she felt, volatile and turbulent, almost violent, like the waters off her coastal home when a hurricane churned nearby.

"Tell me, Ian. Tell me why you look like you want to rip someone apart with your bare hands."

His gaze dipped to her mouth. "Is that what you think I want to do?"

She curled her fingers around his wrist and pulled his hand from her neck, only to have it settle against her thigh. "Yes."

The moment of emotion vanished as quickly as it came, retreating under a veneer of nothingness. "Leave it alone, Tori. I've just got a lot on my mind."

Disappointment careened through her. She wanted the intimacy, not this cold facade. "That phone call you had to make?" she asked.

"Among other things."

The palm reader's final words came back to her. *Your sense of responsibility will serve you well, but if you keep denying your strong emotions, you'll have yet another tragic ending.*

"Who was she?" Tori asked, knowing she shouldn't but unable to hold back the question.

Ian pulled back, physically, and every other way imaginable. All but his hand. The fingers splayed against her thigh tensed. Tightened. "Who was who?"

Tori couldn't believe how fiercely her heart beat. How deeply the answer to her questions mattered. "Who did you love, Ian? Who did you lose?"

The rain was falling now, hard, strong. Big fat drops had given way to a steady downpour, pounding the Jeep and eliminating visibility. "You know the answer to that," Ian said. "My father."

Tori refused to let him off the hook. Because of the hand

he held against her leg, the way he kept moving it against the cotton of her slacks. "Who else?"

He frowned. "Come on, Tori. You didn't really believe that crazy old woman, did you? She's there to prey on gullible, unsuspecting tourists, not a smart lady like you."

"Then why do you keep rubbing your palm?"

He looked down at his big, battered hand pressed against her leg, then abruptly returned it to the steering wheel.

The withdrawal stung. "I may have grown up sheltered," she said, "but I know that if you don't exorcise your demons, they'll consume you."

Her father had taught her that—he'd been living proof of how a physical life could continue, long after the spiritual ended.

"My demons are my business, sugar." Ian checked the rearview mirror, jerked the Jeep into drive and gunned back onto the rain-slicked highway.

Tori just sat there, stunned, aching. *Sugar.* The word played over and over in her mind, all the times Ian had used it.

Hold it right there, sugar.

Waiting for me, sugar?

That's okay, sugar. Temptation isn't a demon that strikes when I'm alone.

The word sounded like an endearment, but it was one of distance, used by Ian when he wanted to appear in charge and removed, distant, unaffected. When he wanted to throw up a veneer. A defense mechanism.

Illusions are dangerous, chère.

Her chest tightened as she thought back on the other endearment he used, the one that rolled off his tongue thick and sensuously, like a gentle caress. The one that made her heart strum and something deep inside shift. Yearn. The one that weakened the barriers between them as effectively as sugar fortified them.

I won't have anyone hurt on my watch, chère.

Non, chère, *the real problem is you're a woman who refuses to listen to people looking out for her best interests. Next time,* chère, *you won't pull away.*

Dear God, she thought. Dear God. The man was more than just an enigma, he was the walking wounded, torn between two worlds, two desires, a past that would never let go and a future that would never take hold.

Just as she was.

"Here we are," he said as the Jeep slowed in front of the old house.

Tori glanced up the heavily treed front yard and felt something deep inside her stir at the sight of the grand old home. Weathered now, but beautiful once. She wondered if it could ever be restored to its original splendor.

"I suppose you want to check out the house," she said, reaching for the door handle.

"Trying to keep me around, sugar?"

The cavalier question burned. He spoke easily, as though he hadn't just tacked up veneers to shut her out. "In your dreams," she drawled.

In the hollow of his cheek, a small muscle thumped. "Is that what you want? Me dreaming of you?"

Her heart surged. His words were seductive, the tone was not. She didn't appreciate being played with. "Dream whatever makes you happy," she said curtly, then opened the door and climbed into the rain. "We both know they don't come true."

Ian reached the porch before she did. In silence she let him inside, but chose to wait outside. She didn't feel like going into the darkness with him.

Across the porch the old rocking chair moved to and fro. Hanging baskets of bushy ferns swayed. Close to five minutes passed before Ian emerged from the house. His soaked and clinging shirt emphasized the firm lines of his chest, just as the damp hair he'd shoved back from his face emphasized the hard pewter of his eyes. "Everything's fine," he said, stepping onto the porch. "Lock the door behind me."

She looked at him standing there, but rather than seeing the passionate man she'd spent the day with, saw only Ian the Unaffected. It was as though the intimate moments down by the river had never happened.

"Oh, come on," she said unwisely. Frustration drove her. "Where's your sense of adventure? I was thinking about leaving the door wide open."

A low growl broke from his throat. He started toward her but then stopped, visibly caging the demons he refused to admit. His hot gaze revealed the struggle within.

"You were right," he said in a curiously hoarse voice. "About before. I forgot who we are."

Then he turned and stepped into the rain.

Tori refused to watch him walk away. She went inside and closed the door, only then letting her shoulders slump. Her chest was tight, her emotions surprisingly raw. Leaning against the hard wood, she breathed deeply, absently watching rainwater drip from her drenched clothes and soak into the rug with its fire-singed edges. Then she gathered her composure and turned the lock, fastened the chain.

Upstairs she bathed and changed, trying not to think of the cop next door. She was safer thinking of him only in that regard—the increasingly strong draw she felt toward him could only lead to trouble. When he looked at her, he saw the daughter of a murderer. He wanted to direct her activities and make decisions for her, just as her father had done her whole life.

But Ian Montague didn't have the blanket of love to motivate his actions.

No matter how strong the draw, she couldn't let him barge into her life and take over. She couldn't abandon her quest and leave Bon Terre just because he said it was best. She couldn't stop digging into the past just because he wanted her to.

And she would not, under any circumstances, believe

her father a murderer just because Ian Montague believed that to be the case. It was her life, her father, her past.

No one would dictate her decisions but her.

The storm raged well into the night. Tori lay atop the covers of the big four-poster bed and stared out the window, watching slashes of lightning illuminate the darkness. She blinked when light came spilling under the closed bedroom door, but when she sat up and looked closer, she found only darkness. But still, her heart pounded and her throat tightened.

Ian, she thought, but didn't call.

She could take care of herself. *Had to.*

Thunder rumbled and the wind shrieked through the oaks, at times sounding oddly human, like laughter and cries and screams. *Ian,* she thought again, this time sharper than before, but then listened closer and realized she was only imagining things.

Still, she rolled from the high bed and hurried for the door. But instead of opening it, she secured the back of an old chair beneath the glass knob. Just in case.

Grabbing an iron candlestick, she climbed back onto the mattress, this time slipping between Montague's sheets. The increasingly familiar scent of sandalwood and soap settled around her and through her, almost like a drug, easing her into a fitful sleep.

It was as close to the cop next door as she could allow herself to become.

Morning came quickly. Tori awoke with the sun and opened the gauzy curtains to discover a brilliant, storm-washed day. The sky looked as if it had been painted with an artist's palette of vivid blues and whites, clear and crisp and sharp. Opening the window, she breathed in the cool air, smiling at the heavy scent of jasmine and honeysuckle.

It sure beat sandalwood and soap.

During the long hours of the night, she'd lain between Ian's sheets, playing over all that had transpired since traveling south. She'd been hopeful about her meeting with Carson Lemieux. She would call again today, see if the lawyer had surfaced.

But she couldn't depend on him, she knew. If she wanted answers, the truth, she had to take matters into her own hands.

In the bathroom she glared at the old claw-foot tub. It had been charming at first, but now she found herself longing for the hard, warm spray of a shower. There wasn't a single one in the house.

She wondered about next door. Surely one had been installed there. She had a hard time imagining a man like Ian Montague soaking in a cramped tub, though the thought of his big body draped in a tub two sizes too small and covered in bubbles, his arms and legs hanging over the rim, made her grin.

Which in turn made her frown.

Banishing the image, she secured her hair in a French braid and dabbed on a touch of makeup, then eased into her favorite pair of jeans, soft and faded and worn at the knees, and a cotton, cream-colored jersey. She was downstairs fighting with the drip pot when the doorbell rang.

Ian. Again. Already. After the way they'd parted the night before, she hadn't thought to see him today, but she should have known better. He may have been rattled after their trip to New Orleans, but the good sheriff had a ready supply of veneers.

Today, just as the storm had chased away the darkness leaving only a clear blue sky, Ian would act as if nothing had happened. A clean slate. A blank canvas. It would be as though he hadn't taken her down to the riverbank and entertained her with stories, the palm reader hadn't rattled him, he hadn't slid a hand around Tori's neck as he put his mouth to hers. And lingered.

He would pretend they hadn't touched on a subterranean level that sent them vaulting in opposite directions.

"If you're looking for coffee," she said, as she opened

the door, "I'm afraid you're in the wrong—" Tori stopped abruptly. Ian didn't stand on her frayed welcome mat. "Ms. Roubilet."

"You're still here," the matronly woman said. Her graying ebony hair was pulled tightly back from her face, making her eyes look severe. "I'd hoped that you would take my advice and be on your way by now."

"I'm sorry, but I can't do that." Tori wanted to slam the door in the woman's face, but instead stepped onto the shady porch. "I have as much right to be here as anyone else."

"Memories are long here, girl. There was never a trial, never any justice. Why would you want to be somewhere where the thirst for revenge lingers? Where you're nothing but a surrogate target?"

Tori stiffened. Her gaze instantly darted between the sprawling oaks toward Ian's house. "Are you threatening me?"

"I speak for the town," the older woman said with a hard smile. "There was a meeting. It's been decided—" The sound of a car screeching to a halt stopped her vengeful flow of words. Kay swung toward the street, where a man raced from the driver's side of a silver town car and ran across the lawn. "Kay!"

She stiffened. "Stay out of this, Autrey!"

"I told you not to come here," the silver-haired man said as he strode up the steps.

"You can't tell me what to do," Kay shot back.

He reached her side and put an arm around her shoulders. "Honey, please. Listen to me," he said in a gentle voice. A concerned voice. "This isn't the answer."

The matronly woman refused to back down. "What is, then?"

Tori watched in fascination as the elegant man slid a strand of graying hair behind Kay's ear. "Go wait in the car, honey. I'll be there in a minute."

The hostile woman of moments before seemed to dissolve on the spot. Her hard eyes turned fragile, broken and filled with tears. "You've been itching for an excuse to come see her, haven't you? To see if she looks like Corinne."

He brushed a kiss on her forehead. "Now you're talking nonsense."

She looked up at him with those shattered eyes, suddenly appearing as fragile as the Spanish moss swaying in the morning breeze. "Make her go away, Trey. Just make her go away."

"I will," he murmured, running the back of his fingers along the side of her face. "Just give me a second."

Kay looked at him for a long moment, then turned and walked stiffly toward the big white Cadillac parked in the street. She didn't say a word to Tori, not goodbye, not go to hell.

The man waited until Kay slid into her car before looking away from her. "She's right, you know. Bon Terre is no place for Russell Bishop's daughter."

His tone was gentle, the words harsh. The continuous badgering was wearing thin. "Too bad," Tori said, again glancing toward Ian's house. She kept waiting for him to come tearing through the trees, barking one command or another.

She didn't know why his failure to do so bothered her more than her early-morning visitors.

"I'm here and I'm not leaving," she said, her gaze skimming over the empty rocking chair, where Ian had sprawled the day before. "I have to tell you, though, this town really knows how to lay it on thick."

Surprisingly, the man laughed. "Whoa there, get your hackles down. I'm not the enemy here."

"Could have fooled me."

A wide smile split his face, revealing dimples deep in his weathered cheeks. *"Mon dieu,"* he drawled, hooking his thumbs on pinstriped suspenders. "You've got your mama's spunk."

Tori looked at him a little closer, keying in on blue eyes that held unmistakable intelligence. And compassion. "You knew her?"

He offered his hand. "I've been meaning to get by here and say hello, apologize for what happened at the library. The name is Autrey. Autrey Roubilet. I publish the weekly newspaper. Kay is my wife." He closed his fingers around Tori's and gave a gentle squeeze. "Don't look so wary, sweetheart. I'm not here to run you off, though I hear my Kay has already tried. Memories are long here, *ma petite*. Your father hurt a lot of people."

Tori pulled her hand from his. "My father is an innocent man."

"Then why did he run away?" he asked in that placating tone. "Why did he take you and vanish without a trace, not even sticking around long enough to bury your sweet mama? She deserved better than that."

The questions scraped. The obvious answers scraped even harder. "Maybe he was scared," Tori said. More than anything, she wished she could pick up the phone and just call him, demand answers. Make him make her understand. "Maybe he was being framed, and he realized he might not be able to win. Maybe he was just trying to protect me."

It was all she could come up with.

"Protect himself is more like it," Autrey countered. "Look, sweetheart, your dad and I were friends. We fished together on Saturdays. Played a hand or two over at Buddy's on Tuesday nights. No one wanted to believe in his innocence more than I did, but he made that impossible. Surely you see that."

She did, that was the problem. Her father had built lie upon lie, making it almost impossible to defend his innocence. "What I see is a town that can't let go of the past."

"*Touché.*" Autrey glanced back at the car, where Kay had lifted her head from the steering wheel and now watched them intently. "I better head on into town," he said, returning his attention to Tori. "The Spring Festival planning meeting starts at ten. It's in just a few days, you know. If there's anything I can do...anything at all, you let me know."

"If I think of anything, I'll do that."

"Very well, then." He turned to leave but glanced back before dismounting the steps. "I'm sorry," he said, bracing a hand against the intricate ironwork, dripping with sweet smelling clusters of light-blue wisteria. "I'm sorry about before and about Kay, but most especially, I'm sorry about your ma. She was a good lady."

Tori's throat tightened. "Thank you."

It wasn't exactly kindness, but it sure beat a bloodied note stabbed into the door and her luggage sitting in the rain.

"Now why would a pretty little thing like you want a gun?"

"Same reason as most folks, I suspect."

"You going hunting?" the pawnshop owner asked. The sign on his cluttered desk, back behind the counter, read Lenny Leonard.

Tori tried not to groan. "No," she said, politely but firmly. "I'm interested in protection."

The second the words left her mouth, she realized how they could be construed. Cringing, she braced herself for a lewd comeback. Or worse, consequences. She didn't need Ian Montague learning that she'd requested "protection."

But the big bear of a man just scratched his head. His nearly black hair was obscenely thick for a man who had to be pushing sixty. His eyes were dark and a bit far apart, his nose wide, giving him a look dangerously close to that of a caveman.

"Protection?" he repeated, glancing up to the camera mounted in the corner of the crowded shop. "What's the matter?" he asked, returning his gaze to her. "You wor-

ried someone in Bon Terre is going to take the sins of the
father out on the daughter?''

She stiffened. Lenny had seemed so harmless, the words
caught her off guard. But he was right. Tori wanted to
believe the threats were just cruel pranks, but her father
had taught her to take nothing for granted.

And when she closed her eyes, she still saw the blood-
stained note stabbed into the front door.

''A girl can never be too careful.'' In all likelihood she
would never need the gun, but if she did, she wanted to
be prepared.

''The sheriff's just next door,'' Lenny said. He actually
sounded confused. ''You don't really think someone will
try and hurt you with him that close, now do you?''

The question sent an odd rush humming through her.
She wished having a cop next door made her feel safe, but
the cop in question was Ian Montague, warrior extraordinaire and son of one of her father's alleged murder victims.
His presence left her feeling anything but safe.

''The sheriff has his own life,'' Tori said in dismissal.
''He's not my bodyguard.''

Lenny's droopy-eyed gaze dipped to Tori's chest, which
was just barely visible above the high counter. ''His loss.''

Her patience slipped. She'd hoped to dash in and out of
the pawnshop as unobtrusively as possible. Now she realized she should have gone to New Orleans to buy a gun.
She would have had to drive several hours, but at least she
would have enjoyed anonymity. And for Tori anonymity
equated with safety.

''About the gun,'' she said. ''I'm looking for something
small but reliable, like a Ladysmith or Lady Derringer.''

Lenny wandered past a grouping of guitars and a set of
drums over to a display case on the other side of the cluttered store.

''Don't got any of those, but I do have this nifty little
Colt Mustang .380.'' He unlocked the glass panel, picked
up the stainless steel pistol and handed it to her. ''My wife

Lindy prefers this darling, says it's the perfect size for her hand."

Tori took the gun and curled her fingers around the cool grip, trying not to think about the similarity between the weapon and Ian's eyes. They were both hard and unyielding, capable of destroying.

"I'll take it," she said, deciding she liked the way it felt. Solid, but not too big.

"Don't you want to know how much it costs first? She's a bit pricey, that one."

"Doesn't matter." She needed a gun she felt comfortable with, not one that didn't cost much.

"You don't say?" Lenny took the gun and returned to the main counter, where he pointed to another display case. "Think I can interest you in some of this jewelry, then? I've got this one-of-a-kind gold nugget bracelet over here. Or maybe this pretty little opal ring?"

Laughter bubbled up, but Tori bit it back. She didn't know if Lenny was serious, didn't want to offend him. "Just the gun."

He sighed. "All righty then. I just need your driver's license."

Tori went very still. "My driver's license?"

"Gotta run you through NICS."

"NICS?"

"The National Instant Check System, doll. It's the law, you know. I gotta make sure you don't have a criminal record before I can let you walk out of here with this gun."

"Oh." She held her purse close to her body as her mind raced. Even though she'd lived in Nova Scotia, she was a United States citizen and she had a valid Massachusetts driver's license. But it had been issued to Victoria LaFleur, not Bishop.

Realizing she had no choice, she fished out her wallet, withdrew the small plastic card and took a deep breath.

Lenny took it and started tapping into his computer, but

then looked up. "This here says LaFleur—I thought you were Bishop's girl."

Play it cool, she told herself. Be unaffected. Like Ian. "Does your wife still go by her father's last name?"

Lenny's gaze instantly dropped to her left hand. "Course not, I just didn't see a ring on your finger."

She smiled sadly, spoke softly. "Whether or not I wear a ring has no correlation to whether I've been married." She paused to let the implication sink in. "Can we get on with this, please?"

He frowned. "Sure thing. This will just take a few minutes," he said as he entered more information into the computer. "You know, they promised thirty seconds when the system first rolled, but it's more like three to five minutes."

"That's fine." She glanced around the overcrowded store, fighting claustrophobia. She'd been in here too long. Anyone could have seen her.

True to Lenny's prediction, close to five minutes crawled by before the system granted approval. She paid in cash and stood impatiently while he fiddled with the cash drawer.

Buying a firearm was shockingly easy.

At the front of the shop, the door burst open, triggering an obnoxious electronic parrot to say, "Welcome, mate."

Tori took a wad of bills from Lenny and shoved them into her wallet.

"Hold it right there," came a dangerously soft voice from several feet behind her.

Stiffening, Tori swung around and felt her heart explode into a cruel staccato rhythm. Late-morning sun glared in through the front windows, casting two men in silhouette and making them look more threatening than the guns in their outstretched hands.

Chapter 9

A dizzying charge went through Tori, an increasingly familiar rush. She looked at Ian standing there, all tall and rough around the edges, jaw unshaven, hair falling around his cowlick, and felt the breath back up in her throat.

"Well, it's about time you got here, Sheriff," Lenny said, rounding the counter. "I was just about to have to let her go."

Tori gaped at him. "You called the sheriff?"

"He activated the silent alarm," Ian said, shoving his gun into its holster. Deputy Fontenot continued to hold his. "Thought there was a burglary in progress."

She rounded on the shop owner. "How dare you—"

"I thought the sheriff should know Russell Bishop's daughter is buying a gun," Lenny explained, pointing to the Colt Mustang on the counter. Then he looked at Ian. "She plans to use it, too, Monty. On someone in Bon Terre. She told me so."

Tori couldn't believe she'd actually thought this Cro-

Magnon harmless. He'd just been stringing her along. So much for Southern hospitality.

"That is not what I said," she corrected. "I said I'm buying this for protection."

Ian strode to her side and took the sleek pistol from the counter, turned it over in his hands. "Nice."

She reached for it. "If you don't mind, I'll be heading out now."

He took her wrist. "I mind."

"We can't let her have that," Deputy Fontenot said, ambling over. "She'll pose a danger to everyone in this town."

"I have as much right to buy this gun as anyone else," Tori said, fighting the emotion tearing through her. Everything inside her felt jagged, violated. Just as she'd suspected, Ian was back to his cold, unaffected self. A stranger would never suspect the intimacies they'd shared the day before. The laughter. The kiss.

No way would she let him know how deeply the hard glint to his eyes hurt. "It's not against the law. There's no waiting period in Louisiana, and my record is clean."

"But your father's as dirty as they come," Fontenot drawled.

Tori glared at him. "He's not buying the gun. I am."

"Sugar, why don't you start over and tell me why you think you need a gun." Ian's grip loosened, his thumb skimming the inside of her wrist. "Did something happen last night? Something I don't know about?"

Sugar. Never had Tori imagined such a sweet-sounding word could feel so bitter. "No."

"Then don't tell me you took that palm reader's predictions of doom and gloom seriously?"

The teasing in his voice pushed her to the edge. She didn't know if he was insulting her or playing big bad sheriff in front of his deputy and the pawnshop owner, but she didn't care, either. Disappointed and angry, she pulled away from him and shoved a loose strand of hair from her face.

"I'll tell you what I took seriously," she said, realizing her twelve-hour truce with Ian had long since expired. "The bloodied note speared to my door and the fact someone put their hands all over my clothes."

Ian frowned. "I've already told you to let me take care of that. I'm a cop and I'm next door—"

"We're not talking a cup of sugar, Sheriff. We're talking about my life. And we both know you won't always be there." The words stuck on the way out. Hurt. "What happens then? What happens if I let myself depend on you, but then you're not there?"

He moved closer. Spoke softer. "I'll be there."

The other men in the store were forgotten. "You can't know that," she said, glaring up at him. The whiskers on his jaw made him look rougher. More dangerous. "You can't promise me that."

"Damn it, Tori," he growled, reaching for her.

She slapped his hand away and stepped back. "All my life my father promised to take care of me. To protect me. But he can't do that now, can he? In all of his quests to do what was best for me, all he did was lead me like a lamb to slaughter. I can't let that happen again."

The pewter of Ian's eyes darkened. "Guns aren't the answer," he said roughly. "Do you know how often firearms are used against their owner?"

Yes, she did. "It's just a precaution."

He shoved a hand through his hair, leaving the pecan-colored strands to fall against his cowlick. Yesterday, she'd found the gesture sexy. Today, she found only volatility.

"Fine," he snapped, reaching for her. This time he took her hand, not her wrist, and clasped their palms together. "Have it your way."

"What are you doing?" she asked as he dragged her toward the front of the musty pawnshop. "Arresting me?"

He pulled open the door and ushered her out into the bright sunshine. "Don't tempt me."

Ian shucked out of his long-sleeved olive shirt with the unaffected confidence of a man at ease with his body. He tossed the wrinkled cotton to the ground, then looked across the clearing, where a cypress tree full of watching crows jutted up toward a pale-blue sky. When he lifted a hand to shade his eyes, the muscles in his back flexed against a well-worn khaki T-shirt. Down lower, faded jeans curved over his distracting rear and hugged his long legs.

"Ready?" he asked, turning toward Tori. His eyes were hard.

She told herself to ignore the silver chain hanging around his neck, not to wonder what dangled beneath the T-shirt. Seeing him standing there, all tall and grim-faced and ready to teach a lesson, drove home just how dangerous Ian Montague really was. Because as much as she wanted to destroy the arrogance in his gaze, she wanted to replace it with the sizzle that made her pulse race.

And that would only lead to disaster.

Even were it not for the past, Ian Montague would still be the kind of man who believed he had to protect everyone in his path. That he had to think for them. Act for them. Live for them. Even die for them.

Tori couldn't live that way. Didn't consider a life like that "living."

Ian stepped closer. "What's the matter? Tough Tori didn't change her mind, now did she?"

She tucked a wisp of hair behind her ear, acutely aware of the sun beating down on her. "Just say the word," she said in a strong, firm voice. "I'm all yours."

His gaze dipped down over her cotton knit jersey, further down to her faded jeans, then returned to her face. "Somehow, I doubt that."

The heat curling through her was ridiculous. "Let's get on with it, then."

He headed over to a table and picked up her new purchase. She watched him load the Colt Mustang, noticing how the T-shirt made his arms look bigger. Harder. Incredibly well-honed.

Anticipation whirred closer, like the warm breeze blowing through the cypress trees at the back of the shooting range. She knew better than taunting a wild animal, but a long-suppressed need drove her. The need to stand on her own two feet. To fight her own battles. Savor her own victories. Her father had denied her that for as long as she could remember.

She wouldn't let Ian Montague do the same.

And while she could have just told him the truth, she'd always found showing to be much more interesting. Memorable.

Ian finished preparing the gun and picked up a pair of goggles. "Just one more question, sugar."

"Shoot," she invited, but when his eyes narrowed and his gaze hardened, she decided against grinning. "No pun intended."

He didn't see the humor. "Guns are serious. This isn't a time for joking." He paused, his gaze searing into her. "I've seen you. Beneath all that bravado, you're a gentle woman. I know that. But before I show you how to use this baby, I need you to think about whether you're ready to *kill* someone, if you think they're threatening your life."

Her heart pounded harder. "I'd rather just stop them."

He shoved unruly brown hair back from his face. "That's not what guns are about, Tori. Someone who wants to hurt you isn't going to just change their mind and walk away, merely because you wave a gun in their direction."

She watched his mouth as he talked, how hard it looked, how uncompromising, and wondered how he could have kissed her so softly just the day before. So sensually. She didn't want to label the odd hollowness as loss. But it was.

"If you pull the gun, you need to be ready to shoot. And not just once, either. You need to be ready to shoot over and over, until you've taken your target down. You need to expect screaming. Blood. The sight, the smell, the feel."

She cringed. "You're trying to scare me—"

"You're damn straight I am. Violent attacks are never clean and seldom go down the way you expect. They change your life forever."

"Being unprepared to protect myself would change my life pretty dramatically, too."

He held her gaze a beat longer than comfortable. "So it would." He handed her the goggles and ear protection. "Let's get to work, then. You need to practice. Watching television and movies won't cut it."

Dangerously intrigued by his soldier-of-fortune attitude, she slid the eyewear into place.

"First, let's get you in position." He nudged his boot between her feet. "Spread your legs for me, sugar."

Tori stiffened. The command, the tone, they sizzled and crackled. "I think you're enjoying this a little too much," she said dryly.

He cut her a hard smile. "This was all your idea. Not mine."

Glaring at him, she moved her feet shoulder width apart, careful not to lock her knees.

Ian moved to stand beside her. "Now, before I give you the gun, I want you to practice with just your hands. Focus on the target. Concentrate. Raise your hands and pretend you're holding a weapon."

She did as he said, lifting her arms and holding them before her, hands linked and forefingers extended like the sights of a gun. She pointed them toward one of the human forms outlined on a big white board.

"Good," he said. "Now, when you actually fire, there'll be a recoil. You need to be ready for that."

"I'm ready."

The gun came next, offered up to her like some ignominious prize. "Hold it in both hands," he instructed.

She curled her fingers around the handle and turned toward him. "Okay, ace, what next?"

He took her wrist and eased it toward the target. "Keep your finger off the trigger, and never point the gun at anyone unless you plan to shoot them."

"Don't tempt me," she drawled.

"No warning shots. A bullet shot in the air has to come down somewhere."

"Got it."

"Bullets fired into the ground can ricochet or fragment. Walls are too thin."

"Got it," she said again. "No warning shots. Shoot only to kill."

"Curl your right hand around the grip, like this," he said, lifting his hands to hers to demonstrate.

Tori looked at their joined hands, his so big and tanned and scarred, hers so fine-boned and pale, and felt an odd rush go through her.

You've got fabulous hands, Madame Rousseau had said.

And he did. Strong. Gentle. Determined. She loved the way they felt wrapped around hers.

"Use your left hand to cup the butt," he added.

The grin appeared on its own. "Are you going to demonstrate that, too?"

He shot her a heated look that said he wasn't amused. "Lift your hands toward the target, try to bend your left elbow just a tad." As he spoke, he moved behind her. Standing entirely too close, he mirrored her pose, feet apart, arms outstretched, his body bracketing hers, making Tori acutely aware of the primal male animal standing behind her.

He leaned closer. "Concentrate."

She swallowed hard. She *was* concentrating. Concentrating on ignoring the assault of sandalwood and soap that made her think of soft cotton sheets and hard man. The feel of whiskers against her cheek that made her long to run her fingertips along his jaw. The solid male animal behind her that tempted her to just lean back, let him catch her if she fell.

"This is like a scene out of a bad movie," she observed.

He didn't laugh. "If you don't know how to use our friend here, it could get a lot worse. Now, I'm going to let go of you and step back, and I want you to try and hit the target. Don't worry about precision right now, just get a feel for how you and the gun can work together."

"I'm ready," she said, and was. She knew what she had to do, even if it destroyed the rare moment of togetherness.

"Good girl. Now show me what you got."

She took a deep breath, but it didn't slow the hammering of her heart. The sun beat down, hard. Adrenaline crashed and surged inside her, almost violent. Anticipation tingled. Even the birds seemed to quiet.

For a moment she almost felt regret.

Banishing the useless emotion, she repositioned her feet slightly and lifted her arms. She ignored the fact that Ian stood behind her, and concentrated on the outline of the human form, put her finger to the trigger and pulled. The gun recoiled slightly, but she readily handled the kickback, kept her arms outstretched and kept firing.

She didn't stop until she'd emptied the clip.

The smell of burned gunpowder hung heavily in the air. The silence was almost deafening. The beat of the sun, blistering.

Tori stood there, arms outstretched, empty gun in hand, and tried to catch her breath. She could feel Ian staring at her. Feel the heat. The accusation.

She let her arms fall.

Ian curled his fingers around her upper arm and turned

her to face him. Fury darkened his eyes. "What the hell—"

Her heart stuttered. "What's the matter, Sheriff?" she asked, pulling off the goggles. "Did I do something wrong?"

He released her abruptly and tore across the clearing, toward the remains of the target.

Apprehension tittered through her. This was what she'd wanted, she reminded herself. If she played with fire, she had to face the consequences, even if that meant getting burned.

Setting the gun on the table, she hurried to join him. He just stood there, staring.

"Did I kill it?" she asked casually.

Slowly he turned toward her, revealing the coldest eyes she'd ever seen. "You lied to me."

Her mirth, her satisfaction at one-upping him, started to fade. "About what?"

"You shot the hell out of the target—no way was this your first time."

"I never said it was. You just assumed."

"Damn it, Tori—"

"Damn it, what?" Temper spiked. "I was minding my own business. You're the one who barged in and took over. You're the one who said you had to teach me a thing or two. I wanted to see if you could."

A muscle in the hollow of his cheek twitched. "You should have told me."

"Told you what?" The truth bubbled up, spilled out. "That my father taught me to shoot before he taught me to ride a bike? That he made me practice until I had blisters on my hand? Until I could hit the target blindfolded? Over and over, until I cried? Is that what you wanted to hear?"

He closed his eyes, opened them a moment later. "If it's the truth, yes."

She didn't understand what she heard in his voice, the

restraint, the anger, maybe even sorrow, but she knew better than to yield to it.

"Your mistake, Sheriff, is exactly what you said yesterday. You think you know what's best for me. How many times do I have to tell you I don't need you leaning over my shoulder, playing tough guy? I need respect and consideration, not a knight in shining armor."

He came alive, stepping closer and taking her upper arms in his hands. "You think this is funny, don't you?" He brought her close, so close there was no mistaking the fury blazing in his eyes. It burned clear through to her heart. "Here I am twisted up inside about the thought of you having a gun you don't know how to use, a gun someone could turn on *you*, could *kill* you with, and you just strung me along, like some damned joke."

The words sounded torn out of him, and in turn, they tore into her. "That's not what I meant," she said softly, realizing she'd just made a grave mistake.

She'd only meant to teach him a lesson. To show him that she could stand on her own two feet. That she could take care of herself. That she didn't need him. *Couldn't* need him.

Why, then, did the outcome she'd deliberately engineered leave her cold inside? Aching. Longing for something she knew better than to want.

Those eyes, she knew. Ian's eyes—narrow and deep set, the dark pewter glittering like stars in the night sky, scorching through her defenses to touch her on a level she'd never been touched. All she had to do was see them, see him, and her insides turned hot and molten. Wanting.

But now his gaze was hard. Angry. Betrayed. He looked as if she'd slapped him in the face, then when he'd turned the other cheek, slapped him again. Which she had.

He released her and started across the clearing. "Come on."

"What…where are we going?" She tried to keep up with him.

He never even slowed down. "This lesson is over."

* * *

Tori looked out the upstairs window toward Ian's house, not surprised to find no light shining through the trees. Shortly after he'd driven her home, she'd heard his Jeep tear down the street.

Even now, hours later, the chill remained. She'd never seen eyes that cold.

Regret pushed at her. She'd been trying to teach him a lesson, while he'd been trying to help. Granted, he'd gone about it in a frustratingly macho manner, but the tone of his voice and the ferocity glittering in his eyes had told her the truth. Despite the walls he kept between them, despite the fact he hadn't called her *chère* since the French Quarter, he didn't want to see her hurt. But like her father, he demonstrated his concern in a manner dangerously close to a straitjacket.

Frowning, Tori turned and picked up the gun. She doubted she would need the sleek little Colt Mustang, but if she had it, she might as well keep the weapon handy. Down the long hall she stopped in front of the locked door—tonight was the night. She'd swung by the hardware store before going to the pawnshop and bought a few tools. Tonight she would greet the room shut off from the rest of the world.

The task wasn't as easy as she'd hoped. Opening the series of bolts and locks installed by her grandmother required specialized tools, time and patience. No wonder the teenagers hadn't found their way inside, she thought with an ironic smile. Even if they'd had the right equipment, she couldn't see them dedicating themselves to the task, not when the house offered so many other avenues for mischief.

After more than thirty minutes of jimmying, the locks gave way. Cautiously, with a deep breath, she straightened and turned the glass knob, let herself into the room and flipped on the light.

And came face-to-face with her mother.

Tori's heart staggered, and her breathing hitched. Her hands started to shake. In stepping over the threshold, she'd done more than enter a room, she'd stepped into a whole other world. Her parents' world. Perfectly preserved, the room looked as though they would come sashaying through the door any minute. The big bed with the soft pillows. The tea-washed comforter with big pink roses. The towering armoire and matching chest of drawers, the silver comb and hairbrush waiting on a mirrored tray. Even a bottle of perfume.

Shock held her immobile, followed by a stab of grief so intense she almost doubled over. The room had a texture to it, a feeling. Memories lived there. Hopes. Dreams.

All destroyed by a well-aimed bullet.

Coldness came next. A chill from within and without. Why had someone locked away the room? Why had her grandmother left it intact?

Confused, Tori crossed to the dresser and picked up her mother's brush. The sight of a few blond hairs still trapped among the bristles brought tears to her eyes. "Oh, Mama," she whispered, pressing the brush to her heart. With her free hand she picked up a perfume bottle and drew it to her face, where she could only smile at the subtle aroma of roses.

The memory hit hard and fast. *Roses.* Her mother had loved roses. Grown them. Arranged them. Worn them as a fragrance. The scent unearthed smiles and laughter, hugs—fierce hugs that brought a little girl to her mother's bosom, where the scent of roses comforted her.

Now the aroma, the memory, shattered.

…bad place…killed her.

"No, Papa. No." Tears welled and spilled over, fell unabashedly. Tori let them.

Replacing the brush and perfume bottle, Tori picked up a long silver chain, at the end of which dangled a locket. Her fingers trembled as she worked at the clasp, her heart pounding. Her emotions reeling. When at last she pried open the oval, her throat closed up on her.

They were all there. Her mother. Her father. Herself.

And they all looked so heartbreakingly happy.

"What happened?" Tori looked into the tarnished mirror, as though she expected to find someone there. To find answers.

Only her reflection stared back at her, eyes like dark pools of green against unnaturally pale skin, tangled blond hair, wrinkled cotton pajamas with pink and red roses scattered about. A gift from her father...

Emotion ripped in, bittersweet memories and shattered dreams, fragmented hopes. She carried the locket to the big bed, which she climbed atop of, then pulled her knees to her chest. And wept.

She must have fallen asleep—one minute she was picking yellow roses with her mother, in the next she was lying very still, straining to hear the noise that destroyed the idyll. She couldn't move. Could barely breathe. Her limbs were leaden.

But she heard nothing, just wind tearing through the trees.

Shivering, Tori sat up and squinted, but the darkness revealed little more than shadows, shapes more than details. Odd, she didn't remember turning off the lights. And then she heard it again, a noise downstairs, like a door closing.

Her heart took off on a mad sprint, like her first night in the house, when Ian had let himself in the kitchen door.

That was it, she realized. Ian was back, playing more of his macho games. Testing her, probably. Ready to see if she'd listened to him that afternoon.

Relief flashed through her, followed quickly by irritation. She didn't like being played with. Slipping from the bed, she padded across the hardwood floor and reached for the doorknob.

And remembered she hadn't closed the door.

Games, she told herself. That was all. Her fingers curled around the glass and she turned, but the door didn't open. She jerked it harder, but the solid wood door wouldn't budge. Locked, she realized. From the outside.

A shaft of light cut in from under the heavy door. Bright. Intrusive. Then came the voices. The laughter. The screams.

Panic speared through her. Terror. Her lungs quit working. Someone was in the house, and it wasn't Ian.

If anything happens, call me.

She ran to the side of the bed and grabbed the phone, but found no dial tone. *Ian,* she thought maniacally. Dear God, Ian. She was trapped. She was alone.

And someone was coming up the stairs.

The crickets were out in full force, humming with relentless disregard for the lateness of the hour. On his front porch, Ian sat in an old rocking chair, legs stretched out and propped on the railing. He held a bottle of beer in his hands, but hadn't brought it to his mouth in over an hour. A snoring Gaston lay at his side, oblivious to the unease crawling through his master.

Tori.

After New Orleans he'd told himself to stay away from her. To treat her like any other visitor to Bon Terre. To pretend she hadn't invaded entirely too many of his thoughts. To forget the drugging sensation of his mouth against hers.

But then the silent alarm had sounded at Lenny's, and Ian had charged in to find Tori standing there. With a gun.

Now he looked toward the darkened house next door. She'd be sleeping, he knew. In the big poster bed. All that glorious blond hair fanned out across a pillow.

The simple thought had him hard in a heartbeat.

What kind of lech was he? What kind of fool?

He could still see her standing in the clearing, in her soft ivory jersey and faded jeans. Her braid had allowed an unobstructed view of her face, those shockingly green eyes, swirling with secrets Ian couldn't seem to unearth. She'd reminded him of a doe looking up from a babbling spring—he'd never known a human could look wild and untouchable, yet vulnerable at the same time.

The gun in her hand had sickened him.

Her little surprise had shredded his illusions.

Told you what? That my father taught me to shoot before he taught me to ride a bike? That he made me practice until I had blisters on my hand? Until I could hit the target blindfolded? Over and over, until I cried?

What had her father done to her? What had her life become after that brutal night so long ago? What scars did she carry on her heart?

Ian shoved the questions away. Their answers didn't matter. She was Russell Bishop's daughter. Her mere presence in Bon Terre was unraveling twenty-five years worth of determination. Of iron will. Of survival instincts. When he looked at her, he saw the man who'd killed his father. That's who he needed to see. But increasingly he saw a woman. An amazingly resilient, brave, vulnerable woman.

He didn't know what it was about her, her courage or her defiance, her determination or her indomitable spirit, but with incredible precision, she'd slipped under his skin. Splintered. Drew blood. And in doing so, she threatened everything he'd ever believed in, right and wrong, black and white. His patience.

God, especially his patience.

It was the ultimate slap in the face—despite the danger she posed to him, he couldn't turn away from her. Her determination to dig into the past forced him to keep her close, when survival instinct demanded that he run her out of town. He—

A gunshot pierced the night and shattered the cricket chorus. Then another. Or maybe that was Ian's heart.

The beer bottle dropped to the porch, and Gaston whimpered.

Ian ran.

Chapter 10

"Tori!"

Ian tore across the damp grass and slammed headfirst into the past. The echoes of gunshots surrounded him. Memories chased from all directions.

"Tori," he yelled again. "Tori!"

He'd been a damn fool. He knew about the threats. The hatred. Knew someone wanted her gone. But he, Ian Montague, son of a murdered father, witness to the brutal aftermath of violence, a man sworn to protect those in his care, had let pride and anger cloud his judgment. *Just like with Meghan.*

Tori was in trouble.

He was all she had.

And he'd turned his back on her.

Now he ran. His bare feet slammed down on the damp grass, on leaves and twigs and the knobby roots of the oak trees, but he never broke his pace. He cut through the cloying Spanish moss, his heart hammering with every step he took.

Dear God, Tori.

The crickets were humming again. Louder. Faster. An escalating soundtrack to a drama he didn't want to relive.

Papa! Papa!

And then the house came into view, much as it had that cold night a quarter of a century before. Grand. Sheltering. Deceptively graceful. White in color, but bloodstained inside.

The memory exploded around him and through him, a well-placed land mine. He staggered from the impact but kept going. The wide steps he took two at a time, his feet barely touching the porch before he lunged for the front door.

Locked.

No lights shone inside, either. No sounds penetrated the relentless crickets.

Meghan's apartment had been dark and quiet, as well.

"Tori!" His voice carried through the night, reverberated in his mind. His heart. He should never have left her alone.

The back door granted no reprieve. Nor did the windows. Left with no choice, no time, he smashed a fist through a pane of glass, then reached down to finagle with the lock and let himself inside. His bare feet crunched down on broken glass, but he didn't give a damn. The pain was nothing compared to the possibilities.

The silence was deafening. No more gunshots, no cries, no whimpering. Only the old grandfather clock rhythmically marking the passing of time.

Training and instinct took over. Ian became a New Orleans beat cop again, responding to a 911 call, cautiously moving through unfamiliar territory. But he knew the Carondolet house. Knew every room, every secret. He wanted to yell out for Tori, demand that she answer him, but training told him to go slow. He didn't know who had fired those shots. A perp could still lurk in the shadows, primed and ready to attack.

His gun, damn it. In his haste to reach Tori, he hadn't grabbed his gun.

Keeping his back to the walls and his movements stealthy, Ian quickly discerned no one occupied the lower level of the house. He eased up the back staircase and down the long hall, checking each room as he went. The sewing room. Her grandmother's room. In the guest room, his heart stopped. The big poster bed held center stage, his rumpled sheets thrown back, a slight indentation in the pillow.

But no Tori.

And then he heard it, a slight whimpering. He turned and ran down the hall, realizing only one room remained. And that's when the coldness took over and vertigo slammed in. Everything slowed. Stretched. Elongated. He heard a roar rip from his throat, but it wobbled in the silence. His heart barely beat. He wasn't sure he breathed. He tried to run, but it felt more like a crawl.

A cold hand of horror grabbed his throat and wouldn't let go. He didn't want to go into that room again. Didn't want to see where his childhood ended. Didn't want to find Tori where her mother and his father had lain. He'd heard the rumors about crazy Estelle, knew she'd kept the room perfectly preserved, the last lingering remnant of the daughter she'd loved, but lost too early. Taking care of the room had turned into a surrogate for taking care of her child.

The locks she'd installed after the murders hung open. And he knew. God help him, he knew. Tori was in there. He could feel her. Knew he had to go to her.

Wasn't sure he was ready for what he would find.

Knew that didn't mater.

He opened the door and stepped into the past. Saw her. Almost went to his knees.

If he lived a hundred years, Ian knew he would never be able to erase this moment from his mind. Never forget the sight of Tori huddled in the corner of the room, her eyes wide and dark, the Colt Mustang in her hands and pointed at him.

Alive, damn it. Alive.

"Tori, honey? It's me. Ian." He knew enough about fear and trauma to recognize shock when he saw it. He wanted to tear across the room and pull her into his arms, but forced himself to move slowly. Cautiously. As non-threatening as possible. It was hard, though, so damn hard, when adrenaline invaded his reflexes and poisoned his thoughts. But she held a gun in her hands, and he wasn't sure she recognized him. Recognized anything.

"Everything's okay," he said in a strangled voice. He held his palms up, kept his gaze on hers. "I'm here now."

Those wide eyes of hers tracked his every step, but they didn't blink, and she didn't move. And it killed him. Just that afternoon she'd been all guts and resilience, blazing brighter than the sun, showing a zest for life unlike anyone Ian had ever known. At the time he'd labeled her attitude as defiance and vowed to squash it. He knew the danger of bravado, couldn't stand by and let her put her life in jeopardy like Meghan had.

But nothing prepared him for Tori Bishop stripped bare.

"It's me," he said, dropping to his knees.

At last, she blinked. "I t-tried...I w-wanted...c-call you..."

Her broken voice slayed him. "Sh-h-h," he said, curling his fingers around the barrel of the gun and turning it away from his gut. "It's okay now. I promise. I'm here."

Need crashed around inside him. Drove him. Punished him. He slid his hand down the gun toward hers, still curled around the butt, finger on the trigger. Her skin was alarmingly cold. But unlike the steadiness she'd exhibited when he first opened the door, she was shaking now.

The thaw, he knew. When frozen mountaintops turned into a raging river.

"Just give me the gun now, *chère*."

Surprisingly, she did. He took it from her hands and

quickly removed the clip. Three bullets remained. He secured the lock, then slid the gun out of reach and returned his attention to Tori. She was just looking at him. Looking through him. Like she was lost and didn't know which way to turn.

"What happened?" he asked, running his hands along her arms. "Are you okay?" Through the soft cotton of her pajamas, he felt her tremble. Felt the chill of her flesh. And all he could think about was warming her. Chasing away the coldness. Coaxing the resilience back into her amazing eyes.

And he couldn't take it. Couldn't fight it any longer. He could no more have not pulled her into his arms than he could have spun time backward and prevented the night that shattered their childhoods and erected a mile-high, impregnable wall between them. Nothing mattered at that moment but Tori.

He crushed her to him, ran his hands along her back, touching as much of her as he could. And there in his arms the thaw became a flash flood. A low mewling tore from her throat as she curled her hands around his neck and lifted her face to his.

Need burst through the shackles of constraint, and his mouth came down on hers. Hard. Desperate. He wanted to be tender. Wanted to go slow. Couldn't. The need was too great—the horrific thoughts that had driven him barefoot across their lawns. The possibility that he might never see her again. Never put his mouth to the hollow of her neck and feel her pulse point fluttering rapidly. Never test the limits and see if the past could be defeated.

One minute she lay sprawled in his lap; the next, they were on the floor, she beneath him. Her mouth was seeking, hungry, inviting him in. Against his chest, her breasts were dangerously soft, and all he could think about was tasting them, too. Her hands were everywhere, cool soft fingers running along his arms and his back, searing as she went. Her need destroyed him. It was so raw, so primal.

And in that moment nothing else mattered. Not who they were, not what lay ahead. All he knew was Tori, a fierce need to tear down the barriers between them and get as close to her as he could. To hold the world at bay.

He dragged his mouth from hers and skimmed along her face, needing to taste and touch every inch of her. And that's when he felt it. The moisture streaming down her face.

He pulled back abruptly and looked into her damp eyes, and like a splash of ice water, the haze of passion cleared, leaving only stark reality. Tori was in shock. He knew that, had known it the second he'd opened the door and found her huddled in the corner. But that hadn't stopped him from mauling her like a rutting animal, driven to take her, mistaking her need for comfort for that of desire.

She deserved better.

"Don't go," she whispered.

He wiped the moisture from beneath her eyes. "I'm not going anywhere, *chère*." He took a moment to bring himself under control. He had to think clearly, like a cop, not a man slashing through cobwebs. "What happened, Tori? I heard gunshots."

She pulled from his arms and looked around the room, fixating on the door. "I...I needed you. Needed to get your attention."

Nothing prepared him for what that revelation did to him, the violent collision of shock and prophecy. It's what he wanted, her letting him do his job, but the fact she'd actually turned to him made his gut clench.

"A phone call would have sufficed quite fine," he said softly, gently, trying to lighten the mood. "Ma Bell is a lot easier on the heart rate."

"The phone's not working."

He reached over to the nightstand and picked up the receiver, where a dial tone greeted him. "It is now."

She pulled the hair back from her face. "That's not possible," she said, but then took the receiver from his hands and brought it to her ear. "Oh, my God." She looked around frantically. "I fell asleep in here," she said in an oddly mechanical voice. "But then something woke me. A sound downstairs. The door was closed, but I didn't remember closing it. And when I tried to turn the knob, I found it locked."

Ian frowned. "It wasn't locked when I got here."

She stood and crossed the room, checking for herself. "I heard voices. Laughter and screams. That's what woke me."

Ian had been greeted by nothing but the relentless ticking of the grandfather clock.

"There was a light from the hallway. I could see it slipping in from under the door."

A bad feeling snaked through him as he stood. "What happened then, Tori?"

She looked at him. Looked lost. Confused. "I tried to call you, but the line was dead, and I realized there was only one way I could reach you."

He didn't know whether to be furious for the risk she took, or pull her back into his arms and kiss her senseless for taking it. "So you fired shots into the night," he muttered.

Her eyes met his. "And prayed."

Ian wasn't sure how he remained standing. Wasn't sure how he managed not to crush her in his arms. He was in about ten miles over his head and sinking fast.

"Stay here," he barked more gruffly than he'd intended, and strode from the room.

Tori wrapped her arms around her waist and watched Ian disappear down the hall. She wasn't crazy. She hadn't imagined things. Someone had been in the house, playing with her like a cat does a mouse, then scurrying away when he had her cornered.

Fury mingled with leftover fear. She hated both.

Long moments passed. Moments when she waited for

Ian to return. When she replayed the cold terror of sitting in her parents' room, wondering if Ian would hear the shots. If he would care enough to investigate. She'd never been more frightened in her life.

And then he'd been there, filling the doorway like an avenging warrior, all tall and broad and ready for battle, bare-chested and barefoot, his only weapon his hands, clenched into fists and ready to fight. His eyes had been fierce, but his touch held only gentleness.

Tori drew a hand to her mouth, still shaken by the unrestrained passion of his kiss, the need she'd tasted, the like need still crashing within her. Dear God, she'd never felt so…frenzied before, like a small boat tossed around in the choppy waters of the Atlantic, desperate for harbor but exhilarated by the ride.

And now, in the wake of the insanity, she wondered how they would ever go back to calm waters.

Frowning, she looked back toward the inside of her parents' room and saw blood. A trail of it led from the doorway to where she'd been crouched in the corner.

She swung toward the hall and noticed a trail there, as well. Leading to the stairs.

Ian. Instinct took over. She ran from the room and down the stairs. "Ian!" she called, but he didn't answer. Her heart started to pound all over again. He—

He stood at the parlor window, framed by the heavy brocade curtains and looking into the night. His bare shoulders were tense, his hands balled into tight fists.

The little boy who'd grown up too fast and turned into a fighter, now stood alone.

"Ian?" she whispered.

But he did not turn around.

She crossed the ominously quiet room and looked at the hardwood floor, where the flimsy light of the moon revealed a pool of dark red trickling from beneath his left foot.

"You're bleeding," she said, and deep inside, felt a like

response within her. "Ian," she whispered, lifting her gaze. "We have to—" But the words died when she caught sight of the back of his right hand. The cuts there. Fresh. Still bleeding.

"My, God," she whispered. "What happened to you?"

Now he did turn toward her, and for a moment, there, she almost swayed. His eyes. Dear God, his eyes. They were...decimated. If he'd looked like a warrior primed and ready for battle when he charged into her parents' room, now he looked like a warrior reeling from the aftermath.

His eyes met hers. "You, *chère.* You happened to me."

Emotion jammed in her throat. She didn't understand his abrupt withdrawal any more than she understood her need to pull him back. "Ian—"

"It's what you wanted, *c'est vrai?* Why you fired the gun? For me to come to you, even if that meant running over broken glass?"

A cruel little panic twisted through her. Because of his voice, she knew. The velvety undertone of accusation. "I didn't want you hurt," she whispered, staring at the shattered window.

"Life isn't about what we want, Tori, or you wouldn't be standing here right now."

"Ian—"

"Go back upstairs. The house is secure."

Like hell. She was darn tired of this man telling her what to do and what not to do. What to think. What to feel. Something had broken free upstairs. She was tired of pretending.

"I'm not going anywhere," she said, stepping closer.

"Damn it, Tori—"

She didn't let him finish. She pushed up on her toes and put her mouth to his.

Ian went completely still, but Tori didn't let his lack of response deter her. She wanted what she'd tasted upstairs, the unrestrained passion, the possibility. She wanted to feel like she had when he'd crushed her in his arms, like she mattered. Like he cared. She wanted to touch him on the same level, to affect the unaffected, to cut through the past and see what truths remained.

Dangerous, she knew, but still, she moved her lips against his in a gentle, coaxing rhythm, letting her hands settle against the hard muscle of his chest. The hair there was crisp and inviting, and beneath her palm she felt his heart beating rapidly, as though he ran hard, instead of standing absolutely still.

A need she didn't understand overrode the humiliation of his rejection. She spread her fingers wider, wanting to touch more of him but encountered cool metal instead. The silver chain she'd seen hanging around his neck. Curious, she slid her hand over a flat nipple until she found what lay nestled among chest hair.

Tori looked down at her palm, where twin images of St. Christopher awaited her. She knew many catholic men wore the medal to invoke the saint's protective powers, but she'd never known anyone to wear two.

Puzzled, she lifted her face and literally saw the veneer slide back into place. "Two?" she asked softly.

Ian the Unaffected met her gaze. "One's a gift from my father. The other was his, a gift from his father."

His answer was swift and brutal. "Oh," she whispered.

Ian tore away, and finally, finally the haze cleared and she realized what she'd done to him. He'd heard the shots fired into the night one time before. He'd run into the darkness. He'd found his father in that very same room.

And she'd forced him to relive every horrible second all over again. Regret was immediate.

"I don't know what to say." She reached for him, but he raised an arm to keep her away. "Somehow 'I'm sorry' doesn't seem like enough."

"Go back upstairs, Tori. It's late."

"No, damn it! I'm not walking away from this."

"Sure you are. I'm a cop, and this is technically a crime scene. You need to let me do my job."

A steely resolve marched through her. Ian and his veneers were wearing thin. "You're no more doing your job than I'm picking roses with my mother. You're shutting me out, damn it. You're trying to rewrite history, just like you accused me of doing. You're pretending we didn't almost make love."

And God, how it stung. She'd finally gone against her better judgment and reached out to him, and in return he was turning her away. She'd been right to be cautious of him. Men like Ian Montague only led to broken hearts and shattered dreams.

"You're tired and upset," he said in a horribly patronizing tone. "Someone tried to hurt you tonight—"

"No, they didn't!" she exploded. He had the cop veneer in place now, and she wanted to scratch it away with her bare hands. "If someone wanted to hurt me, they would have by now. They want to scare me. That's all."

"That's all? That's all!" He pushed the hair back from his face, exposing the bright gleam in his eyes. "Damn it, woman, you *terrify* me."

The words sent an odd little jolt through her. "Ian—"

"Tough Tori. You always have to be right, don't you? Always have to be brave." He made it sound like a crime. "When are you going to realize you're just inviting danger? Didn't tonight teach you anything?"

"Oh, yes. Tonight taught me a lot." The hollowness in her chest lengthened and deepened, turning more jagged by the second. "But everything is fine here now. I never should have bothered you in the first place. I was probably just dreaming."

That was true. Not just of her mother, but of the way Ian had looked at her on the way back from New Orleans, just before he kissed her. Of the way he'd looked that afternoon at the shooting range, when he'd slipped up and acted as if he cared.

But she was awake now. *Wide* awake. And she realized that her misguided attraction to this man could lead nowhere but heartache. "Just go," she said through gritted teeth.

"I can't do that."

"Why?" The question came out sharp, strained. "Why can't you just leave me alone—you've made it clear nothing would make you happier than to never see me again." And, God, how it burned.

He took a step toward her. "Is that what you think?"

"It's what I know." She held her ground, even though he stood so close she had to look up to see his face.

"If that's true, why am I here?"

That was easy. "Because you think you were put on the earth to rescue damsels in distress."

A faint light glittered in his eyes. "And why does that scare you so bad?"

Scared didn't even come close. Terrified was more like it. Not for her life, but her heart. "I'm not scared."

"Then maybe you should be," he rasped. Though he stood close enough to touch, he seemed to be slipping away, from her, from the world. "When I was a little boy," he said in an oddly distorted voice, "we had a magnolia tree in the front yard. Every year it grew bigger. Prouder. Mama loved that tree. One year I saw a perfect bloom, way up high. I wanted it for her. So I climbed the tree, even though my dad had forbidden me to do so, even though I knew if I was caught I'd get a whipping. He said the tree wasn't for climbing, that I'd only wind up hurt if I tried. But I didn't care. I wanted that flower."

Tori wanted to turn and walk away, but fascination wouldn't let her. She had no idea what point Ian was trying to make. She stared at him, but rather than seeing a tall, half-dressed man with haunted eyes, she saw a mischievous little boy with pecan-colored hair and an unruly cowlick, scraped knees, and daring eyes. She blinked against the image, tried to make it go away, but Ian just kept right on talking.

"I worked my way along the branches, toward this perfect flower. For Mama. I finally reached it, and sure enough, it was the prettiest magnolia you ever did see. Pure and perfect, big and bold and beautiful. Almost defiant, up high in this tree, where no one could ever harm it. But I was there, and I picked it. And in doing so, I lost my balance and fell to the ground.''

Words of commiseration surfaced, but Tori refused to speak them.

"I landed hard,'' he said. "Heard the bones crack. Mama was there in a flash, screaming, crying, yelling for my dad. I kept trying to tell her to hush, but she wouldn't listen. She was too worried about me. Almost hysterical.''

"And your dad?'' she couldn't stop herself from asking.

"He determined I'd broken my arm in two places, then turned me over his knee and paddled me good.''

"He spanked you? After you'd fallen out of a tree?''

"Some of my father's lessons were hard, but he meant well. I know that.'' He shoved the hair back from his face. "But this story isn't about me, *chère*. It's about the flower.''

She blinked at him. "The flower?''

"The big pretty magnolia I wanted to give Mama. I landed on it. Snapped all those perfect, bold petals, crushed them into the ground so hard that the damage could never be repaired. If I'd just left the damn thing alone—''

"Ian—''

"I never climbed that tree again. Never picked another flower for Mama. Never pulled the pinchers of a crawdad just to see what would happen. Never shot at minnows, just to see if I could hit them.''

She could seem him all too well, the little boy turned into a man by gunfire, but who'd never forgotten the flower he'd destroyed. Who'd never forgiven. Never learned how to live with the guilt he carried deep in his heart.

Your scars are not of the flesh, the palm reader had said. *Not all of them, anyway. Not the deepest.*

"What about my father?'' she asked quietly. "Would

you have shot *him* if you'd found him in the house, not me?"

His eyes flared. "I didn't find *him*, Victoria, though God knows I've wished for that too many times to count. I found you."

And too easily she remembered the way he'd looked at the top of the stairs, with the fading light of early evening casting him half in shadow, half in fading light.

"You remind me of that magnolia, *chère*." His voice was softer now, thicker, hinting at his Cajun ancestors. "Bold and defiant, strong, beautiful."

Deep inside Tori something shifted. Melted. Reached for something she couldn't quite grasp. Knew better than to trust. "And that's why you told me the writing was already on the wall," she murmured. The point of his story squeezed her heart, the reason he'd pulled away upstairs. "You think you're going to crush me, just like that magnolia."

"You think so, too. That's why you keep undermining me."

"Undermining you?"

"Someone put a bloody note on your door, and you attack rather than run. Kay reads you the riot act, and you just lift your chin. Hell, even the stupid palm reader—she talks to you of danger and loss, but you don't even bat an eyelash. But me..." he said, moving suddenly and crowding her up against the window. "The second I try to help you—*help* you, for God's sake—you tense up like I'm an alligator lying in wait."

Her heart hammered hard. "I'm not the one who pulled away just now," she pointed out in a strangely hoarse voice.

"No, but you should have."

Frustration burned through her. "I'm not some damn flower, Ian. You're not going to crush me."

"Don't be so sure of that." His voice was smoky, the words like ice. "Go to bed, Tori. Sleep tight. But realize that if you continue to muddy the waters, no matter how hard I try to prevent it, you're going to get hurt.''

The breath stalled in her throat. ''Are you threatening me?''

''Not even close. I'm merely acknowledging the writing on the wall. If you're as smart as I think you are, you will, too.''

Ian didn't sleep. Leftover adrenaline made sure of that. He stared out at the darkness for a long time before sprawling on the couch and listening to the clock tick off the seconds until morning. He refused to let himself think about Tori or what had happened upstairs. About how twisted up she had him, like the barbed wire at the back of his property. He knew better than to lose control like that. He knew better than to tempt fate. The grand dame always won, first with his father, then with Meghan.

Darkness gradually gave way to light, and with it Ian stood and stretched, ready to get on with the day. Thirty minutes later he'd showered but not shaved, pulled on a clean T-shirt and jeans, fed Gaston then returned to Tori's and started the coffee.

The call to his deputy caused something deep inside him to twist. *She'd lied to him.* He'd been so consumed by her story and her quest, so blinded by her liquid green eyes, that he hadn't even covered the basics like asking for identification. Making sure she was who she claimed to be.

But Lenny had. And he'd been downright gleeful about telling Deputy Fontenot all about Victoria's dirty little secret.

Ian wanted to pull her out of bed and demand answers, look into her eyes as she fumbled with the truth, but the survivor in him knew better than to let her see him like this. He needed to bring himself under control first. So he poured a mug of coffee, sat at the old table and tried to read the paper.

''What are you doing here?''

He looked up and found her in the doorway, soft and sleepy and rumpled. She hadn't dressed for the day yet, and her loose blond hair and makeupless state lent her an innocence he now knew to be a skillful facade.

"Well, good morning to you, too. Coffee?" he offered.

She wrapped her arms around her waist, drawing the soft cotton tighter around her breasts. "I asked you a question."

"Ah," he said, pushing the paper away from him. "You want answers. Funny, I'd like some of those, too." He stood. "Tell you what. I'll answer your question, if you answer mine."

"I haven't heard a question yet."

She looked tired, her face still a little pale. But her eyes, the green of her eyes sparked and sputtered magnificently, especially considering the early hour. "I'm here because of my job, sugar. An oath I take seriously. Someone broke into your house last night. I wanted to be here if they came back."

Her eyes flared. "You spent the night?"

He heard the shock in her voice, the fury. He ignored both. Of course he'd spent the night. Despite the fact they'd hit flash point and he needed to distance himself from her, he'd been unable to stay away, not after hearing those gunshots shatter the night. He'd waited on her porch for a long while, then quietly let himself inside, where he camped out in the parlor until the sun destroyed the darkness.

"Tsk, tsk. It's my turn to question, not yours."

She narrowed her eyes and breezed into the kitchen, heading for the drip pot on the stove. He watched her standing in a pool of sunlight, those soft cotton pajamas falling sensually over gentle curves, pouring coffee and ignoring him.

He moved behind her, not necessarily trapping her, but making it difficult for her to dart away. He ignored the subtle aroma of pralines and braced his hands on either side of the stove. Then he asked the question that felt more like a knife to the heart.

"When were you going to tell me about your husband?"

Chapter 11

Bracketed between Ian's body and the stove, Tori went very still. "My what?"

"You heard me."

She turned in the confines of his arms and looked up at him. Defiance sparked in her eyes. "I didn't see that my love life was any of your concern, Sheriff."

He couldn't stop himself. He'd spent a good part of the night recounting all the reasons he should never touch her again, but he found his hands settling on her shoulders. "After the way you came apart in my arms last night, you're damn straight it's my concern."

Color rose to her cheeks. "Damn you."

"Go right ahead, sugar. I knew you were trouble from the moment I saw you on the staircase, but I didn't take you for a cheater. Does he know you're here?" Ian growled. He didn't like how possessive he felt. How betrayed. "Does he know you're laying your life on the line and playing with fire?"

Ian wondered what he referred to—the past or the dangerous attraction he couldn't destroy.

Tori glanced toward the window he'd opened that morning, allowing a cool breeze to filter in and tinkle the wind chimes. Her chest rose and fell with jerky breaths.

"Well?"

She looked back at him. "I'm not married," she said through gritted teeth.

"Then why did the driver's license you gave Lenny say Victoria LaFleur, not Bishop?"

An unsettling light glinted in her eyes. "If you can have your demons, Ian, then I can have mine."

He didn't like how distant she sounded, how removed. "What else haven't you told me? What other secrets are you keeping?"

Again she averted her face to stare out the window.

Ian recognized a brick wall when he saw one, but never had one stopped him. If she wouldn't give him answers, he would find them on his own.

"Fair warning," he said, turning her face toward his. Big mistake. Her eyes were huge, wounded. Lost. And they pummeled him somewhere deep inside. "I will find out. If you're smart—" if he was lucky "—you'll be long gone before then."

"That's right. LaFleur. Victoria LaFleur. Driver's license is from Massachusetts." Ian listened for a moment, then added, "Everything you can find, got it? And I want it yesterday."

He hung up the phone and gulped the rest of his coffee.

"Can you really blame her, Ian?"

"You better believe I can blame her," he said, turning to face his mother. She'd stopped by the station on the way to the final planning meeting for the Spring Festival.

"You're being too hard on her," she lightly scolded. "Can you imagine how scared she must be? How alone she must feel? Coming to a town where everyone looks at her and sees a murderer? Where everyone makes it clear she's not welcome?''

Where she'd been terrorized and tormented, ridiculed.

Ian quickly rerouted the godforsaken protective instincts. ''Hank tells me he saw you out by Dad's grave.''

A sad smile touched his mother's lips. ''He always loved spring, said it was like God starting over. I thought he might like some flowers.''

The residual grief in her voice, the memories her words evoked, tightened around Ian's heart like a steel vise. He'd known this would happen. ''Mom, I don't think that's a good idea. You know what the doctors—''

''Ian Michael Montague. I'm not the fragile flower you think I am. I can visit my husband without falling apart.''

''I know you can, Mom. But I've also heard what's being said on the streets—having Tori here, digging up questions and stirring up rumors can't be easy on you.''

Laurel quirked a brow. ''Actually, *mon chou,* I'd have to say having little Vicky here is a lot harder on you.''

Something close to a growl tore from Ian's throat. ''That woman attracts trouble like Mardi Gras does Yankees.''

She glanced at the file he'd started on his desk, where he'd scrawled Tori's names in hard, dark letters. ''Why are you so angry with her?'' she asked, looking up to pierce him with the eyes he'd inherited from her. ''Because she dares to challenge big bad Ian Montague? Because she's kept secrets? Because of whose seed gave her life?'' His mother paused, letting the questions linger before continuing. ''Or is it, my dear son, because despite everything, she reminds you what it's like to live and feel, to hurt?''

Ian stiffened. Years of therapy had given his sweet mother an uncanny knack for going for the jugular. ''Shouldn't you be headed over to the coffee shop?''

She laughed. ''*Mais oui.* I should. And I will. Just as I know you will choose the right path, even if it's not the easy one.'' She leaned close and kissed him on the cheek. ''You're a good man, *mon chou.* I'm proud of you.''

That said, she turned to leave.

Ian stormed out behind her, knowing damn well he had to find some way to get Tori out of town. Not just for her own well-being, but for his own.

Because next time he put his mouth to hers, he might not be able to stop.

''I'll see what I can do, Victoria. The paper comes out day after next.''

She smiled at Autrey Roubilet and offered him her hand. ''Thank you.''

He closed his fingers around hers in a warm shake. ''It's my pleasure.''

They said their goodbyes and Tori headed down the street, toward the Java Café. She tried not to think about the scene in her kitchen that morning, the betrayal glittering in Ian's eyes. None of that mattered, she told herself. All that mattered was finding the truth about the night her mother died. She'd tried to call Carson Lemieux earlier, but had only reached his voice mail. She told herself not to be frustrated at his continued absence, but was. The lawyer had the answers she needed, answers that would allow her to pack up and leave this town before it consumed too much of her.

A breeze blew off the bayou, mingling with the warmth of the sun to create a picture-perfect spring day. Smiling despite the feeling that walls were closing in on her, Tori opened the door to the coffee shop and stepped into the muted lighting. A latte sounded like heaven.

She saw them too late. All the tables were occupied by various townsfolk, all of whom faced the back of the small shop, where Kay Roubilet stood next to an easel and pointed to a list on a large sheet of paper. The Spring Festival, Tori realized. It was only two days away. And Kay headed up the committee.

A sharp gasp cut through the murmurs, and the room went quiet. In full authoritarian glory, Kay glanced around. "What's the matter, folks? No one wants to—"

Tori knew the second the woman saw her. Her lips pinched and her eyes narrowed. "You're not welcome here, girl."

After everything else that had happened, the woman's hostility didn't faze her. "I didn't know buying coffee was against the law," she commented breezily.

Kay glanced toward the counter. "Penny, you tell this girl she's not welcome in your shop."

"Stop it." From the center of the room, a woman rose up from her chair. "Stop it right now," Laurel Montague said. "This girl has as much right to be here as any of us do."

Tori looked in shock at the striking woman, feeling a warmth and longing she didn't understand. Her son hid behind veneers, but Laurel stood tall and firm.

"Just because your son is as blind as his father was and thinks with the wrong part of his body—"

"That's enough, Kay." Autrey filled the doorway just behind Tori. "We don't air our laundry in public."

The vengeful woman glared at her husband. Her body went so rigid, so tense, Tori thought her on the verge of shattering.

Laurel made her way among the tables. "Come on in, *mon ange,* and join me for an espresso."

Kay's hatred Tori could take, but Laurel's kindness undid her. For an excruciating heartbeat, she remembered being a teenage girl, getting her period and having her heart broken, but having no mother to wipe the tears from her eyes and promise her it would be okay. She'd put on a sunny face and pushed forward, never realizing a bandage didn't heal a wound.

"Thanks," she said, "but I have somewhere else to be." Away from the cozy coffee shop, she amended silently. Away from Laurel Montague before she did something stupid like throw her arms around Ian's mother and never let go.

Laurel took her hands and squeezed. "Another time, then."

"Yes," Tori answered. "Another time." She glanced to the back of the coffee shop, where Autrey Roubilet had joined his wife. They stood talking in furious hushed tones. "Thank you," Tori added softly.

Laurel smiled. "Anytime."

Back outside, Tori breathed deeply of the warm spring air and gazed off toward the bayou. Her emotions ebbed precariously close to the surface, a sandbar lying in wait. She wanted to head over to the sheriff's office and look at the police records Ian had told her about, but first she needed to make one more stop. A stop she'd been putting off ever since her arrival.

Odd, she thought, ten minutes later. She'd never thought of a cemetery as a place of beauty, but here in south Louisiana, where the high water table necessitated above-the-ground interments, burial sites took on an otherworldly quality. Cities of the dead, she'd heard them called, and now knew why.

Beyond a rusty wrought iron gate, row upon row of weathered concrete and marble houses jutted up from a carpet of green grass and wildflowers. Haunting statues abounded, crumbling stone crosses and intricately carved angels. Elaborate urns contained withered floral arrangements, solitary remnants of undying love. No gaudy plastic flowers here, no cheap ornamentation, just graceful oaks and elegant magnolias.

Tori's throat tightened. She put a hand to the latch and let herself in. The breeze stirred her hair as she made her way among the monuments of lives gone by. She didn't know how long she walked before her heart stumbled and her breath caught, but there, finally, at last, she found who she'd come seeking.

"Corinne Victoria Carondolet Montague. Beloved wife and mother. April 4, 1948—November 16, 1977."

The wave of grief hit so hard Tori dropped to her knees and braced a hand against the tombstone. Someone had installed a statue of the Virgin Mary above her mother's grave, to watch over her for eternity. "Oh, Mama," she whispered. "I wish you were here. I wish you could tell me what happened." Wished she could put her arms around her and hold her…

The breeze picked up, becoming more of a wind and swirling around Tori like an embrace. She didn't even try to stop the silent tears. She'd felt a connection with the old house, but nothing had prepared her for the sense of peace she found here with her mother. Time passed. The vivid blue of the sky gave way to the gray of an afternoon thunderstorm, telling Tori it was time to leave.

"But I'll be back," she told her mother. "I promise you."

Another gust of wind, this one warmer than before. And the birds, they cawed a little louder, circling close.

Tori swiped the tears sliding down her cheeks and headed for her car. Composure, she reminded. She needed to pull herself together before she faced Ian and the investigation records.

The old gate creaked in protest when she let herself out. She made her way among the sprawling oaks and beautiful magnolias, across the gravel drive to where she'd left her car. She let herself in and turned on the engine, taking a deep breath before pulling onto the narrow highway.

The clouds swirled closer, thunder rumbling not so far away. When rain began splattering, she eased down on the brake, realizing oil spots could make the blacktop slick.

But the car didn't slow down.

Puzzled, Tori tried again, this time pumping her brakes the way her father had taught her. Nothing. In fact, the car seemed to be picking up speed on the rain-slicked highway.

A busy intersection lay dead ahead. She braced herself, seeing the stop sign but knowing her car wouldn't obey. She had no choice but to swerve.

She noticed the canal too late.

Ian pushed through the doors of the emergency clinic. Everything looked calm, orderly, the complete antithesis of the sharp edges inside of him. He strode to the admitting desk, where young Camille Boudreaux sat filing her purple fingernails.

"Where is she?" he demanded.

Camille looked up and smiled. "Well, Sheriff Montague, this is a nice surprise. Who is it you're looking for?"

"The car accident. I heard they brought a woman here."

"Ah, the Bishop girl," Camille said, and her expression darkened. "Such a shame, you know."

"Where is she?" he asked again. This time the fear twisting through him leaked into his voice.

Camille's eyes widened. "Second room on the right," she said, gesturing down the hall.

Ian took off.

"You can't go in there," he heard Camille saying, but kept right on walking. He'd been across the parish when the call came in, hadn't found out about the accident until well after the rescue operation. Details had been in short supply, sketchy at best. He knew only what the 911 operator had told him. That Tori had been in an accident, her car pulled from a canal. That she'd been taken by ambulance to the emergency clinic.

And that's all it had taken to trample his determination to put distance between them. Why *should* she tell him her secrets? he realized. He hadn't exactly gone out of his way to earn her trust and confidence.

The acrid smell of antiseptic grew stronger as he approached the closed door. By the water fountain two nurses stood laughing. Somewhere a baby cried.

An insidious fear overrode them all.

"Sheriff," old Dr. Pitre called from down the hall. "Something I can help you with?"

Ian didn't spare a glance for the man who'd delivered him thirty-three years before. He shoved open the second door and strode into the small room, drew up short.

She sat on a metal table, arms wrapped around her waist and bare legs dangling. Her pale hair was damp, tangled, shoved back from her face. Her eyes were huge.

Relief cut him sharply.

Then details came into focus. The large bandage on her forehead. The bruise on her otherwise colorless cheek. The pile of her muddied clothes huddled by the bed. The blanket draped around her shoulders, clutched by her bloodless hands.

The need to replace the wool with his body caught Ian by surprise. To hold her. Warm her. Keep her safe.

"Ian," she whispered, and the hitch to her normally strong voice kicked him hard.

He held himself very still, though inside he shook. Violently. "Good God," he practically growled, "you're determined to give me a heart attack, aren't you?"

A faint light crept into her shockingly green eyes. "Careful there, Sheriff. Keep looking at me like that, and a girl might get the wrong idea."

During the long drive to the clinic, hideous thoughts had hacked through his mind. That she could be hurt. That he might never see her again. That his final words to her had been spoken in anger and frustration, not the dangerous gentleness she stoked deep inside him.

"If you wanted to go swimming with the gators, you should have told me, sugar." He spoke the words as Ian the Unaffected would, ignoring the crazy desire to touch and assure himself she was real. Safe.

"Now why would I have done that?" she asked with an eerily somber smile. "If I recall correctly, the last thing you said to me this morning was something about wanting me gone before you found out what else I've been hiding.''

The reminder of the scene in the kitchen shattered his restraint and sent him striding to the exam table. The need was too great. Not even the widening of her eyes stopped him from bracing his hands on the outside of her legs and leaning close.

"Forget this morning," he muttered, then lowered his mouth to hers.

She tried to murmur something, probably in protest, but the movement of her lips just gave him better access. He lifted a hand to cradle the back of her head and slid his fingers into damp hair. He wanted to drink her in, soft and slow, leisurely, like a long sip of water after a brutally hot day. The taste and texture of her quenched his thirst, even as they ignited a fire it would take more than water to extinguish.

"What are you doing?" she asked against his seeking mouth.

Damn good question. Damn dangerous one, too. "Adrenaline does strange things to a man, sugar."

She put her hands against his chest and pushed him back. Her cheeks were flushed, her gaze defiant. "It turns you on?"

"Not it, *chère.* You." He slid his hand to the side of her face, running his thumb along her cheekbone. "Even sitting here like this, all banged up."

"Our girl is darned lucky," came a gentle masculine voice from the doorway. "Other than a mild concussion—"

Ian swung toward Dr. Pitre. "Concussion?"

The doctor whose long silver ponytail made him look more like a biker than a man of medicine nodded. "She got knocked around pretty good when the car went into the water. Think they said she hit a tree stump first. That's what broke the impact."

Ian looked back at Tori. She sat quietly on the table,

watching him with a strangely removed gaze. "What happened?"

"The brakes wouldn't work."

"Wouldn't work?"

"The rain had just started, and I was approaching an intersection. I tried to stop, but nothing happened. I had to swerve to avoid slamming into the other cars."

Ian frowned. He would have the car inspected, find out what went wrong with the brakes. But something else demanded his attention first.

He looked back at Dr. Pitre. "When can I have her?"

The doctor glanced down at the chart, then at Ian. "I'd like to keep her here a few more hours. Monitor her."

"Fine, I'll wait."

"Concussions are unpredictable," Dr. Pitre added. "I don't want her alone tonight."

Ian was beginning to realize he didn't want her alone, either. *Ever.* He looked back toward the exam table, where Tori sat watching him. The sight of her blond hair falling against the big bandage on her forehead, the knowledge of how much worse her injuries could have been, made his gut clench.

"Don't worry. She won't be."

The sun-dappled garden of roses stole her breath. Tori spun in a circle, enjoying the warmth of the breeze and taking in the dazzling shades of crimson and saffron and coral. Her laughter echoed on the breeze. Hope swirled.

Up above, an azure sky stretched on forever, dotted by a few amazingly fluffy white clouds. Smiling, she glanced across the yard toward a white picket fence. A man stood there, tall, silent, watching her with an unnerving intensity. She extended a hand toward him, but for a moment he just stood there. Then he walked toward her, bringing the spindles of the fence along with him. As he approached, the confines of the fence shrunk, drawing closer, closer, until they caged her off from the world.

She awoke abruptly. Her breaths came in choppy gasps. Her heart pounded. Darkness surrounded her. Tori sat up in bed, wincing when the room started to spin. The concussion, she knew. Dr. Pitre had warned against sudden movements.

Disoriented, she blinked, bringing the bedside clock into focus and discovering just how long she'd slept. She barely remembered Ian escorting her to the room, then pointing to the big bed.

Now she cautiously lowered her feet to the cool hardwood floor and gently stretched. A stillness permeated the house, as though no one else occupied the rooms. Silence screamed around her. Maybe he was downstairs reading, she decided. Or maybe he'd made sure she slept, considered his duty done, then returned to his house.

It would be better for them both.

Her memories of the accident were hazy, fuzzy. She remembered being at her mother's grave, but after that, everything blurred. The rain starting to fall. The slick highway. The brakes that wouldn't work.

The impact had jarred her. The air bag exploding in her face. And then the water, pouring in around her feet. She remembered the claustrophobia, the voices shouting from somewhere nearby. The stark awareness that she might never see Ian again. Might never feel his arms close around her again. Never know what it would be like to make love with him. To feel his body over and inside of hers. To—

She shoved aside the heated thoughts, just as she'd done in the car. They were ridiculous. Hardly the kind of thing a woman should think in her final moments.

But she had. Dear God, she had.

And that reality left her as frightened as the moment she'd discovered she had no brakes to stop her car.

Pray God she could find brakes to stop a desire that could only result in an equally destructive collision. She couldn't let him live her life for her, no matter how strong the draw between them. She couldn't let him put her up on a shelf like a doll.

She headed downstairs, escorted, as always, by the steady thrumming of the grandfather clock. She smiled, realizing she'd come to think of the stately clock as an animate object, almost a friend. It was as close to family as she had.

All the rooms turned up empty. He'd left her, she realized with a strange jolt. Relief, she told herself. Not disappointment. Frowning, she took the back staircase and headed down the hall. A bath sounded divine. Warm, sudsy, filled with the subtle aroma of warm vanilla. She could almost smell the scent already, she thought as she put her hand to the doorknob and strolled into the bathroom.

And forgot to breathe.

Never had a sight shocked her more. Thrilled her. Terrified. An army of candles flickered gently, sending off a soft aroma and drawing her attention to the sudsy water in the claw-foot tub. And the man sprawled inside. His long legs lay draped over the edge, his arms hung over the sides. His hair was damp and pushed back from a face that looked more relaxed than she'd ever seen it. His eyes were closed.

And for a moment all Tori could do was stare. And remind herself to breathe. Very few bubbles remained.

And dear Lord, he was beautiful.

Heat flashed through her, bringing with it a dizzying wave of discomfort. What kind of woman was she, staring at a man while he slept? Gloriously, unabashedly naked. In a bathtub.

"If you're thinking about joining me," came a deceptively lazy voice, "we'd better heat things up a little."

Chapter 12

The lazy words surged through Tori like a streak of raw lightning. She looked from Ian's damp feet hanging over the rim of the tub to his face, where slumberous eyes watched her.

Mortified, she turned toward the mirror, but he awaited her there, too. Her heart started to thrum. "Pardon?" she asked with strained indifference, suddenly fascinated by the wax dripping from a round, three-wick candle.

"The water," he said with equal disregard. "It's gone a little cold."

She chanced a glance back his way, couldn't resist a taunt. "I didn't think you believed in aromatherapy."

He pushed back against the edge of the tub, water dripping down his darkly tanned chest and sliding over the twin St. Christopher medals.

Pecs, Tori decided, shouldn't be that well-defined.

"You told me to make myself at home," Ian reminded.

She had, but this wasn't what she'd had in mind. "You're out of your mind, you know that?"

"Most cops are. It's the only way we can wake up in the morning." He reached for a bar of soap—vanilla scented—and slid it back and forth in his big hands, building a lather. "Did you want something?"

Her mouth went dry. The man had no shame. Another veneer? she wondered, or just another facet of Ian the Unaffected. He lay sprawled in a bathtub two sizes too small, yet he spoke to her as though they sat at the kitchen table fully dressed and sipping iced tea.

But what did she expect? Him to blush and pull a washcloth to his groin and cover up? Not hardly. Not Ian. Not when he had a body that made a woman's mouth water—not even the scars on his hands and heart detracted from the sheer beauty of him.

"I wanted to ask you about the auction house," she ad-libbed, keeping her eyes on his, "but it can wait."

"What do you want to know?"

Tori worked hard not to growl. She tore her gaze from Ian, concentrating instead on a ridiculous school of black, art deco fish swimming against the flamingo-pink wall. "I'm not having a conversation with you like this."

"Why not? I'd say you pretty much have me at your mercy."

The challenge in his voice enticed her to meet his eyes. "Somehow I doubt anyone ever has you at their mercy."

He didn't grin, didn't frown. "Don't be so sure about that."

But she was. Even naked, Ian Montague was a man who remained in complete command. "I'll be downstairs," she said, turning to leave.

"Tori."

She stopped in the doorway, but didn't turn toward him.

"Time takes its toll on everything, no matter how well constructed. No matter how strong. Some things can never be restored. Those that can, that survive...are priceless."

The breath stalled in her throat. Spoken in a hoarse voice, the words sounded ominously like an apology. Or at least an explanation. On the surface his comment applied to the massive furniture in antique shops around the world, but somehow, as she stood there working hard to breathe, she could only associate them with the man himself. As with the antiques, his veneers concealed the damage within.

"That's what the BTAA specialized in?" she asked, playing along.

"The auction house opened shortly after the Civil War," he explained, and his voice was as rough as the beat of her heart. "Too many families had too little left. They had no choice but to trade heirlooms for the cash they needed to live."

The thought saddened her. Too well she understood having no tangible icons of those who came before her.

"Word of the auction house spread like wildfire. Folks came from all directions for a chance at lost treasures of the South."

Tori heard water splash behind her but remained standing with her back to him. She didn't need to see more of him than she already had. "And?"

"The owners prospered—the town prospered. Hotels and restaurants sprung up. Shops. For a while, there, Bon Terre was like year-round Mardi Gras."

A wistful smile worked free from her heart. She loved the thought of the town alive and vibrant, shimmering like the diamonds her father allegedly stole. "If the auction house was the heart of the town, why was it never rebuilt?"

For a moment Ian said nothing. Even the water went silent. Only the grandfather clock continued. Tori was tempted to turn back toward him, but caution wouldn't let her.

"It's like I said," came his voice a heartbeat later. "Some things can be restored. Others can't."

"I see," she said, and did. No matter how strong the desire otherwise, sometimes the taint of scandal, like scars, could never be completely scrubbed away. And under its shadow the splendor, the potential, could never be attained. The haze would linger, keeping the sun from shining bright.

And no matter how hard you tried, no matter how badly you wanted, walking away with dreams intact always hurt less than seeing them shattered at your feet.

"I'll be downstairs," she said, and closed the door before his voice could touch her again.

He found her in the parlor. She sat at the ancient grand piano, her fingers poised on the ivory keys. With the grandfather clock presiding over her efforts, she tried to tap out the childhood classic, "Frère Jacques."

Ian leaned into the doorway, and watched. Listening wasn't that good an idea. But, God, was she beautiful. Her corn-silk hair fell loose around her face and shoulders, hiding the nasty bandage on her forehead. She again wore the soft cotton pajamas with roses and hearts cascading against an ivory background. And when he looked at her like that, all soft and serene, he no longer saw Russell Bishop. Just a woman. A woman who made him more than a little crazy. And that scared him.

The last woman who'd muddied the waters had wound up dead. And she hadn't even come close to stripping away his defenses like Tori did with the mere blink of an eye.

His body tightened at the memory of waking to find Tori in the bathroom. He'd been a fool to let himself drift off, but there in the warm water with the flickering candles and aroma of pralines, secure in the knowledge that Tori slept two doors down, he'd given himself permission to close his eyes. He'd never imagined he'd fall dead to the world. Nor had he imagined he'd awake to find Tori standing by the tub, an intoxicating mixture of shock and wonder swirling in her dark-green eyes. Desire had hit hard.

Thank God the bubbles had hidden just how hard.

Exposed wasn't a word Ian liked. Nor was *awkward.* But as he'd lain there sprawled in the bathtub, he'd realized just how cooked his goose was. He'd had two choices. Pretend her presence didn't affect him at all, or pull her in the tub with him and show her just how much it did.

A completely off-key note jolted him back to the moment.

The piano needed tuning in the worst kind of way, but that didn't stop Tori. Her attempt shifted to a cross between "Mary Had a Little Lamb" and "Twinkle, Twinkle, Little Star." Ian's response fell somewhere between cringing and grinning. He liked seeing her like this, though, bravado lowered, giving him a glimpse of the woman she worked so hard to protect. He wondered if she realized that she condemned him for wanting to do the very same thing she couldn't stop doing.

Protecting Tori.

He crossed the hardwood floor and joined her on the piano bench. "Care for some company?"

Her hands stilled on the keys. She glanced at him, her gaze traveling from his clean gray T-shirt down to faded denim pressed against her thigh, on to his bare feet. Then she lifted her eyes to his. And grinned. "You smell like vanilla."

"I prefer to think of it as pralines."

"You would," she said, lifting a hand to slide a few stray strands of hair behind her ear. "I don't think the boogeyman is coming tonight—why don't you go on home now?"

"I'm not leaving you."

Her eyes widened, darkened, as though he'd touched her intimately. "Did you ever stop to think it might be more dangerous for you to stay than to go?"

Every second since he'd brought her home. "Brakes don't just go out, Tori. And concussions aren't no big deal." Just that morning, he'd received the lab report on the knife stabbed into her door, and as he'd feared, no prints had been found. Worse, Carson Lemieux was still missing. Ian's gut warned the old lawyer wouldn't be found.

At least not alive.

And now someone had run Tori's car off the road. "You're hurt, and you're in trouble. I'm not walking out that door."

A bemused smile claimed her mouth. "What is it with you? Do you think the whole world is yours to protect?"

"Not the whole world." He couldn't help himself. Pale hair had slipped back into her face, prompting him to ease it away. He needed to see that bandage. To remember how high the stakes had climbed.

She looked down at her hands, still poised over the ivory keys. Her fingers were long and nimble, her unpolished nails gently rounded.

The image of them skimming along his body fired his blood.

"You didn't answer me last night," he said, and his voice sounded hoarse to his own ears. "Why does that bother you so much? Why won't you let me help?"

She resumed her attempts to tap out "Frère Jacques." "I don't need your help."

"*My* help?" he asked, moving her hands to the right section of the keyboard and pressing her thumb against Middle C. "Or anyone's help?"

She didn't depress the next note. "Damn it—"

"What happened to you, *chère?*" He asked the question as nonthreateningly as possible, running his fingers along the keyboard as he did so. "What made you so determined to take on the world single-handedly?"

She didn't answer. Not at first, anyway. So he kept playing, shifting from childhood songs to heavier melodies. Darker. Like Dvořák. The sounds of keys in minor merged with the grandfather clock and the wind in the trees to create an intimacy so heavy he felt it settling around them.

With his shoulder pressed to hers, he could also feel her breathing. Deeply.

"Do you have any idea," she said at last, and her voice was soft and low, like the music, "how it feels to have someone shadow your every step? Waiting for you to fall. Waiting to pick you up. Do you have any idea how degrading it is to be treated like an invalid? Someone who can't think on her own? Take care of herself?"

The tumble of words, the pain behind them, caught him by surprise. He'd asked, but hadn't really expected her to peel away one of the layers between them. "Whoa, there," he said, but didn't stop playing. He didn't let himself look at her, either. He knew she'd stop if he did.

"Of course you don't," she said, "because somewhere along the line, you decided to play hero to all us weak souls who can't take care of ourselves. It's how you define yourself. But I don't need rescuing, Ian. Not by you, not by my father."

"Your father?" The comparison hurt.

"I can think for myself," she said sharply. "Evaluate. Decide. I'm a grown woman."

And at last Ian understood. Russell Bishop hadn't had a choice but to keep his daughter under his thumb. If he hadn't, if she'd ever ventured out on her own and created a trail back to him, his house of cards would have crumbled.

And he would have lost the light in his life.

"Is that what all this is about?" he asked. "Your father?"

"He didn't want his little girl to suffer because of what happened in this house." The emotion in her voice hardened, sharpened, giving way to resentment. "So he took me, ran with me and totally erased that part of my life. Pretended my mother didn't exist. Even when I asked about Mama, he held quiet. My God, the day I told him I wanted to be a cop—"

"You wanted to be a cop?"

"He went a little wild. Now I know why. Not only do I look like Mama, but apparently my thirst for solving riddles is hers, too. He no doubt worried about what I'd find if I started looking."

Ian couldn't fight it any longer. He let himself look at her next to him on the piano bench, sitting there in her soft pajamas. "Tori—"

"Do you know what that feels like?" Her eyes were darker than normal, filled with a yearning he wanted to fill. "He engineered my entire life. In the name of love, he put me up on a shelf like a doll and hand-fed me what information he wanted me to have. He took care of everything! And in doing so he wiped out part of who I was. I can't go through that again!"

The heartbreaking pieces fell into place, and finally Ian realized just how much determination coursed through Victoria Bishop. And how much courage. He wanted to resent her father for doing this to her, but couldn't blame a man for taking drastic measures to keep those he loved safe.

"I know what you're thinking," she said. "I know what you believe my father did. But he wasn't evil, Ian. He's not the monster everyone here thinks he is. He was a good man. Gentle. Kind. His only crime was that of loving too much."

Now it was Ian's turn to look away. He stared at a large painting of an old plantation home, not wanting to see Russell Bishop through his daughter's dangerous green eyes. To think of the man as a father. To feel even an ounce of commiseration.

"Nothing adds up," she whispered. "The man I grew up with, the fisherman who coached soccer, doesn't match with the man who worked at the Bon Terre auction house. Yes, he loved antiques, but…I can't believe him to be a murderer. It's like I have two men as my father, and I can't mesh them into one."

Her quiet words stripped away the haze he'd been living

behind since the moment he found her standing on the staircase, wearing nothing but a robe. He'd been so focused on keeping the pain of the past buried, of making sure his mother didn't get hurt, he hadn't let himself stop to think about her. Victoria Bishop. The woman whose whole life was nothing but a lie.

He turned to straddle the bench and look at her, felt something shift deep inside him. Something sharp. Jagged. Lifting a hand to her face, he smoothed back her hair, giving himself an unencumbered view of those amazing green eyes. Not full of secrets or mystery now, not full of bravado or determination. Just longing.

"Maybe you shouldn't even try," he suggested.

"But—"

"Some riddles don't have answers, *chère*. It's all in the past. Just let it go."

She frowned. "I can't do that."

Seeing someone in pain and not trying to help went against every instinct Ian had. But he knew that if he touched her, if he put his mouth to hers the way he wanted, more hurt would ensue. Intimacy would not erase the past. It would only strengthen his desire to protect her from every evil the world had to offer, and for that, her resentment of him would grow.

He'd been right the night before. She really was like that magnolia—bold and defiant and beautiful—and he really would crush her.

She lifted a hand to his face. "Ian, don't be mad."

He winced, realizing she'd misinterpreted his struggle not to say to hell with the consequences and carry her upstairs, worry about tomorrow, tomorrow.

"I'm not mad, Tori. I'm worried."

Of all the reactions she could have given, laughter never even occurred to him. But that's what she gave him.

"You're a fascinating man, Ian Montague—big, bad soldier of fortune, yet you play the piano and worry like an old woman."

The escape path glimmered bright. "Want to learn?" he asked, realizing she'd come to his rescue and saved them both.

"Are you offering to teach me?"

"I'm not sure that's possible, but I'm willing to try."

Challenge sparked in her eyes. The hallmark bravado he'd come to admire. "I didn't think there was anything Ian Montague wasn't sure about."

"Trust me," he said, positioning her soft hands on the ivory keys. "There's plenty."

The night wore on. Tori lay on the old sofa, an afghan curled around her. Fatigue pulled at her, but she fought the draw, not ready for the eye of the storm to end. Ian sat at the grand piano, his brown hair having dried with a seductive little curl that made her wonder what it would feel like to touch. He'd long since given up teaching her how to play. He ran his hands along the keys now, producing dramatic, cascading sounds that stirred something deep within her. A yearning she didn't understand. The strains were dark and brooding, much like he'd been since she'd spoken of her father.

And Tori didn't understand. She sensed a struggle in Ian, a struggle that only made his music more passionate. She lay there fascinated by the rare glimpse of yet another veneer to this complicated man. And found herself wondering...

What if the past didn't stand between them? What if her father hadn't put her on a shelf built of love and secrets? What if Ian hadn't grown up too fast, taking on a man's responsibilities when he still occupied a boy's body?

The music stopped abruptly, and Ian turned toward her. Lamplight cast his face in shadow, making the whiskers on his jaw look darker, the line of mouth more harsh. His eyes were narrow and guarded.

And with his left thumb he rubbed the inside of his right palm.

His gaze met hers. "Her name was Meghan."

Four simple words, but the hoarseness to his voice sent Tori's heart into a low, staccato rhythm, much like the somber tune he'd been playing. She pushed upright, keeping the afghan securely around her. "*Whose* name was Meghan?"

He stood and crossed to the window, drew back the curtains and stared into the night.

"Ian?"

"Madame Rousseau was right," he said, turning to face her. "About the woman I lost. Her name was Meghan."

Tori's throat tightened. While she'd been lying there marveling at Ian's music, letting it weave around her and through her, he'd been thinking about another woman.

You've loved before, the palm reader had said. *Briefly. Intensely. And then you lost. And you blame yourself.*

"I'm sorry," Tori whispered, meaning the words on too many levels to count.

Ian showed no reaction. "She was a witness on a murder case I was working," he said in a voice devoid of emotion. "An attack on a prominent businessman. She was his protégée. And she saw his partner shoot him in cold blood."

Tori drew a hand to her heart. "Oh, my God."

"There were ties to organized crime. She risked her life by coming forward, admitting what she'd seen. I wanted her in protective custody but she refused."

And died because of it, Tori realized before he finished his story. Ian had tried to protect the woman he loved, but she'd ignored him and, as a consequence, wound up dead.

The pieces clanked into place with brutal clarity, and at last Tori understood. No wonder Ian couldn't leave her alone, when he'd made it clear he wanted her gone. No wonder her refusal to cower earned his contempt. No wonder he shadowed her with his body, while keeping her at an emotional distance through all those veneers.

She was a flesh-and-blood reminder of the man he believed responsible for killing his father, and the woman he'd loved but lost. She didn't know how he could stand to even look at her.

"I found her in her apartment," Ian said. "Dead where she'd slept. I don't think she ever felt the gunshot."

Horror clogged Tori's throat. She rolled to her feet and crossed the hardwood floor, but Ian held up his hand. "No, Tori, don't. It was a long time ago—I don't need your comfort. I just thought you should know what happened."

"Why?" she rasped.

"I think you know why."

She did. "Tell me, anyway."

His gaze turned smoky. "I don't give a damn who your father was, not anymore, but I can't forget who you are, Victoria Bishop. A beautiful, warm, determined woman. Seductive without even trying."

She watched him standing there framed by the heavy curtains, the glitter in his pewter eyes, the mouth that could condemn as easily as it could seduce, and felt everything inside of her go hot and liquid.

"I want you so bad I can hardly see straight," he ground out, "much less think straight. I want you upstairs and in bed. I want to love you until we're both too weak to move. But what you shared tonight…whether you knew it or not, you told me why that can never be. You confirmed what I told you last night, that, given the chance, I'll crush you. I only thought it fair I tell you why I'm not tempting fate any more than I already am. Why I'm standing across the room, even though I want to be inside you so bad it's shredding me."

Words failed her. So did breath. She just stood there staring at him, fingers curled around the back of an old wing chair, her whole being on fire from his words. He was right, God help her. God help them both.

"Go to bed, *chère*. I'll keep the boogeyman away."

Her defenses melted into a river of need. She knew what would happen if she touched him right now, they'd go up like a bonfire on Christmas Eve.

He was doing it again, she realized. Trying to protect her. Making decisions for her. But this time he was right.

She turned toward the stairs, paused before taking them. Her heart pounded so hard she could barely hear the grandfather clock. "I'm sorry," she said.

The light in Ian's eyes dimmed. "So am I."

The call came with the first rays of the sun. A break-in down at the paper. Two of Ian's deputies were out on another call, a third home with a sick wife and child. Ian didn't want to leave Tori but had to.

Twenty minutes later, with Tori tucked safely in *his* bed, in *his* house, protected by *his* security system and *his* dog, Ian pulled onto the near-deserted streets of downtown Bon Terre. He hated leaving her alone, but she'd promised to call if she heard so much as a peep. And she'd promised to stay put.

Autrey Roubilet met him outside. During the night someone had broken into the renovated warehouse that served as the production facility for the local paper, and smashed up one of the printing presses. Autrey was beside himself. The paper only came out once a week, but with a delivery scheduled for tomorrow, he couldn't afford to be down a machine.

Forty-five minutes passed before Deputy Fontenot appeared and took over as primary. A window had been broken, but chances of lifting incriminating prints were slim— too many employees in and out of the building on too regular a basis.

Ian called his house, but after four rings voice mail answered. Telling himself Tori was still sleeping, he ignored the irrational pounding of his heart and picked up coffee and beignets on the way home.

But when he walked into his bedroom, he found the sheets empty. Same with the bathroom, the kitchen, the whole damn house. Gun in hand, he ran across the adjoining yards, ready to read her the riot act for going against

his orders and scaring him half out of his mind. He'd actually thought they'd reached a common understanding the
night before.

But when he reached the house next door, he found no
trace of her there, either. Just walls pushing in on him. The
past tangling with the present and turning his blood to ice.
It was happening again. All over. And just like before, he
couldn't do a damn thing to stop, to protect. When would
he learn, damn it? How many times did he have to fail the
same lesson?

"Tori!" He ran onto her front porch and yelled for her
over and over. The birds answered, singing gaily. And the
breeze, it lazily swayed the branches of the oaks that kept
too many secrets. "Tori!"

He heard it then, a subtle rustling of grass. He pivoted
toward the back of their houses, where Gaston came bolt-
ing out from the woods. Barking. Frantically.

His world slowed to a crawl. "What the hell—" he
started, but then froze. She came staggering out behind his
dog, hair loose and tangled. No longer did she wear her
pajamas, but rather, one of his khaki work shirts hung from
her shoulders, extending all the way down to her knees.

"Come back here, you worthless mutt!" she called
laughing, but Gaston ran straight for his master.

That's when Tori saw him. She released the leash and
presented him with a Tori-gorgeous smile. "Hate to break
it to you, Sheriff, but your dog can't retrieve worth a
darn."

The breath tore in and out of Ian. Blood roared through
his ears. The sight of her loping toward him with his dog,
beautiful and laughing and alive, stripped him bare. Here
she was grinning, and he couldn't even breathe. All those
veneers he kept tacked into place, the veneers that kept
him unaffected, fell away like someone had peeled him
alive.

"Your dog is a mess," she said, reaching the steps, but
Ian turned and walked inside. He didn't trust himself right

now. Didn't trust himself to see the wild green of her eyes without crushing her in his arms. Didn't trust the need tearing through him like a tornado in the swamp, uprooting even the strongest foundations.

"Ian?"

Standing at the window, he tried to concentrate on Gaston running in circles around one of the oak trees, but couldn't ignore the aroma of pralines drifting up from behind him. He didn't know how far away she stood, knew it wasn't far enough.

"You don't want to talk to me right now," he warned. His voice sounded harsh even to his own ears.

"What's wrong? Has something happened?"

The alarmed questions ripped away the last of his veneers. Emotion broke free. "What's wrong?" he exploded, spinning toward her. "What's wrong? I told you to stay put, damn it. I told you not to go anywhere."

"I just took Gaston for a walk—"

"But I didn't know that! Do you have any idea what I thought when I came home to find you gone? When I heard the silence? Do you have any idea what went through my mind?"

A strand of blond hair scraggled against her lips. "No."

"Then let me tell you." He walked across the room slowly, deliberately, like an animal stalking its prey. He kept waiting for her to back away. Better yet, for her to run. But tough Tori did neither. With her hair all loose and tangled, she just stood there watching him, looking disarmingly sexy with his shirt hanging from her shoulders. Her eyes were dark and wide, her cheeks flushed and her mouth slightly ajar. He saw the glimmer of confusion in her gaze, but couldn't do a damn thing to protect her from it. From him. Not anymore. He was just a man. And she was everything he'd ever wanted.

"Better yet," he said, closing in on her. "Let me show you."

Chapter 13

Instinct warned Tori to back away, but fascination held her in place. Her heart pounded a relentless staccato rhythm. Only a few feet of dusty hardwood flooring stood between her and Ian, but the deliberation with which he approached her transformed the old-fashioned parlor into an endless eternity.

Over the past few days she'd seen Ian Montague ominously belligerent, exasperatingly charming and frustratingly nonchalant, but she'd never see him like this. So alive and...exposed. Coldly furious and yet heartbreakingly vulnerable. The masculine precision of his movements made him appear taller, broader but somehow battered. Like a man walking out of a forest fire, charred and exhausted, but still standing.

And that's when she realized it. The veneers...they were gone. Burned away. Stripped clean. All of them, the Southern good ol' boy, the hardened, unaffected cop, the soldier of fortune, even the passionate pianist. And at last Tori had the answer to a question that had niggled since the night she met Ian—what he hid beneath all those layers.

Need. Pure, raw, unadulterated need.

The kind of need that could reduce even the strongest of defenses to smoldering ashes.

"I couldn't stop thinking," he said in a darkly quiet voice, "that I was too late." He stepped into her personal space and stopped a heartbeat away, so close the heat and tension of his big body sloshed against hers.

And somewhere along the line, her heart forgot the necessity of a steady rhythm. It stuttered and stalled, ached. Her throat burned.

Ian lifted his hands to her face, then scorched a path down her neck to the vee of the khaki shirt she'd found in his closet only an hour before. Where his fingers touched, her skin burned.

"I couldn't stop thinking that I might never have the chance to touch you like this," he murmured as his fingers nimbly slipped the buttons through their holes. "That I might never know how your eyes darken when I do this," he added as his fingers slid over the lace of her bra and the flesh of her stomach. "I might never hear that sexy little catch in your breath."

Tori couldn't stop it. The little mewl ripped free when he skimmed a finger beneath her breast. The yearning came next. Intense. Fierce. She wasn't sure how she stayed standing. Still winded from her foray with Gaston, she struggled to breathe, but her lungs shut down on her. Every nerve ending crackled like live, exposed wire, ready to maim with the slightest touch.

Shock, she knew. Desire. They crashed and swirled, reducing the core of who she was into something hot and molten, like a blacksmith melting down the strongest of alloys so he could create something new and unrecognizable but infinitely more beautiful.

Ian slipped his shirt from her shoulders and let the fabric pool at her feet. His hands settled against her arms. "I couldn't stop thinking that I might never know how it feels to touch you like this," he murmured, then leaned closer and ran his mouth along her collarbone. "To taste you."

A shiver ran through Tori, a ribbon of heat stretching from her breasts to the core of her femininity. Delicious. Drugging. Leave, she commanded herself, but could no more move than she could give him back the innocence and hope he'd lost that long-ago night. The night both their lives had been shattered. The night that had propelled them onto this very collision course.

There, in the musty parlor with the stately grandfather clock watching, she now stood before him in nothing but her bra and panties, and a dangerous sense of inevitability. "Ian—"

"Sh-h-h." He skimmed a finger along the arch of her collarbone, then pulled back and framed her face with his big hands. His eyes lit, revealing a fire that burned from the inside out. "Do you know the worst thought of all?"

She tried to look away from those hypnotic eyes of his, but couldn't. Couldn't breathe, either. Couldn't think. "No," she whispered, but wasn't sure sound came forth.

He slid his hands to the back of her head, tangling his fingers in her hair and tilting her face to look up at him. His thumbs remained to stroke her lower lip. She felt her eyes widen, her heart stall out.

"I couldn't stop thinking," he ground out, "that I might never feel you beneath me. Over me. Around me."

Something hard and immovable gave way, like a boulder rolling from the front of a cave to reveal the world waiting beyond. The light and the beauty, the endless possibility. She struggled against the sensory overload, but couldn't stop herself from lifting her hands to the wrinkled cotton of his shirt and easing free button after button. She saw her fingers trembling, knew that he saw, as well. She could feel his gaze on her, burning hot like the sun, but she refused to glance up. Wasn't sure she could stay standing if she did. His eyes were too all-knowing, too penetrating, and she wasn't ready for him to see what she could no longer hide.

The truth. The way he made her feel. Want. Forget.

When the shirt finally hung open, she pressed her palms to the warmth of his hard stomach and slid them up over his chest to his shoulders, where she eased the fabric down his arms. He didn't try to stop her. Nor did he help. He just stood there and let her go at her own pace.

She didn't know what her own pace was—had never before undressed a man. Never stood trembling, staring at such a beautiful masculine chest, at the tanned strength of it, the well-defined pecs and flat mauve nipples, the tempting mat of dark curly hair. And the medallions. The silver chain hung around his neck, the twin medals dipping low. The urge to touch was strong. She scooped them up in her hand and tried not to weep. But the sight of them, the memory of what they represented, clogged her throat with an emotion she didn't understand. Moisture flooded her eyes. Like everything else, Ian Montague kept the core of who and what he was hidden from the world. Buried. Protected.

But now she held the well-guarded secret in the palm of her hand. The fact he let her humbled. But it also terrified.

The last of her defenses melted away, swirling into a dangerous, eddying pool of need. Nothing mattered, she realized, nothing but the sensations cascading through her. Driving her. Demanding. Emotional as well as physical, both trampling the mental, the caution. She stepped closer and brought her mouth to her palm, where she kissed each medal.

Ian's hand came down on her shoulder. To stop her, she wondered. Or steady himself. He swore softly, the words torn out of him and seared into her. His eyes, she realized. She needed to see his eyes, to see if they damned or—

They didn't damn.

They stole her breath. He looked down at her with such

aching tenderness and longing, such naked vulnerability, Tori almost cried out. When he lowered his mouth to hers, all the reasons to stay away from him jumbled and blurred, flitted away.

Her knees went weak. She'd never been a coward. She'd never shied away from risks. Life was for living, bumps, bruises and all. The need that scorched through her right now, the desire that charred a path between reason and emotion, survival and revival, embodied life at its most pure and elemental.

Ian Montague kept himself hidden from the world, but he was letting her see him now, the truth of who and what he was burning in his eyes. And the reality of that seared through Tori, heightening every nerve ending. The feel of his big hand on her shoulder, of his mouth making love to hers, arced all the way down to her toes. Her blood felt like fire, her bones like melting ice caps.

Dear heaven, she'd never felt more alive in her life.

Standing there bathed in the midmorning sun, nothing else mattered. Not the past nor the future nor the fight she'd been putting up to stay away from him and stand on her own two feet. Nothing. Just Ian. Being as close to him as possible. Chasing the shadows from his eyes and taking the raw edge off his heart.

And finally, finally, Tori realized what she'd been fighting all along. Not Ian, but herself. Herself and the way Ian made her feel. Made her forget. The way her blood heated whenever she was around him. The way he could melt her defenses with just a look. What the man could do with a smile. But there weren't enough of those smoky smiles, and that broke Tori's heart.

Needing to see him, she eased back but felt his hands tighten against her body the second she moved.

"It's okay," she whispered. "I'm not going anywhere."

His eyes met hers. "Oh, yes you are." He slid his hands to the small of her back and had her off her feet before she realized his intent. The feel of his hard body seeped into hers like a drug, prompting her to wrap her legs around his waist. Through the cotton of her panties, she felt the warmth of his skin and wondered if he felt the moist heat of hers.

Again his mouth found hers. Gently at first. Little kisses. Almost teasing. Nipping. Playful. But building with each one. A little longer. A little harder. A whole lot hungrier. Hotter. Each time he tore his mouth away, her heart stuttered and her body cried out. She wanted his lips against hers. She wanted them to stay. She wanted him to ease the ache turning more excruciating, more demanding, with every second.

And finally he did. He put his mouth to hers and slid a hand up through her tangled hair to cup the back of her head, and walked toward the stairs. With her legs around his waist and pressing her intimately to his body, the deep, openmouthed kiss became shockingly erotic. They moved as one. She could feel his body against hers and craved even more intimate movement.

At the top of the stairs he turned toward the room where she'd been staying, pushed open the door and strode through a shaft of sunlight toward the big beautiful four-poster bed. The bed with his sheets. The bed where she'd lain night after night, seduced by the aroma of sandalwood and soap, daring to imagine what it would feel like to have the man himself there with her, not just his essence.

His mouth slowed its movement against hers, until he just stood there with her body curled around his, their lips together, but not moving. She felt the steady thudding of his heart, felt the deep breaths tearing in and out of him. It was all she could do not to rock against him. To press. To demand he brace her back up against the wall and take her like that, fast and frantic.

"If this isn't what you want," he said in a strangled voice, "you'd better tell me right now."

The words, the restraint behind them, would have shattered her remaining defenses, but none remained. Her need for this man extended beyond anything she'd ever known. Ever known possible. The draw defied logic. Caution fell to the wayside.

"Put me down," she said.

The hands cruising along the heated flesh of her back stilled. The mouth nibbling at her jawline stopped. And for a minute, there, she wasn't sure he breathed. But he did as she asked. He eased her down the rigid length of his body and returned her to her feet. And then he stepped away from her, like a soldier stepping back into formation.

Tori's breath caught. She looked at him standing all rigid in the muted light filtering through the curtains and saw, literally saw, the struggle to slide a veneer into place. The swirling pewter of his eyes hardened. And his mouth, the mouth that had seduced seconds before, became an unyielding line.

The poignancy of his gesture almost launched her back into his arms. She'd told him to put her down. And though clearly he didn't want to, he'd done as she asked, letting her go, despite the excruciating candor of what he'd just revealed.

"Instead of telling you what I *don't* want," she whispered, putting her hands to the fly of his jeans and pulling the tab down, "I'd rather show you what I *do* want."

A sound she barely recognized tore from his throat. But he said nothing, just stood there and watched her slide his jeans over his hips, leaving him in nothing but his medallions and his underwear. Somewhere along the line he'd kicked off his shoes. So had she.

The tingle of her body became an unbearable ache. The gray cotton had the shape of boxers, but hugged his hips and thighs like briefs. The combination stole Tori's breath. She'd known from the size and shape of his hands that he would be impressive, but nothing prepared her for the reality of the man himself. The fabric clinging to the thick ridge left nothing to the imagination and told her—*showed* her in bold detail—just how badly he wanted her.

Ian saw her eyes go dark and felt his control slip another notch. Standing there in her lacy white bra with matching panties, she was killing him. It had taken great restraint not to take her, downstairs, there on the hardwood floor of the parlor to the steady tick of the grandfather clock.

But she deserved better than that.

She deserved better than being taken on the floor or the stairs, having her back pressed to a wall so that he could drive into her and put an end to the irrational need that blotted out sanity. She deserved tenderness and respect. The subtle sexuality she exuded, the raw trust in her gaze, triggered protective urges unlike anything he'd ever experienced. He wanted to crush her in his arms and never let go. Lock her away from the world and keep her safe. Prevent the past from crashing in on them and stealing this moment. Keep her here, like this. Keep her his.

Nothing else mattered. He realized that now.

She smiled, bringing light to the darkest corners of his heart. "You're beautiful," he told her, drinking in the sight of her standing there more naked than not, awash in the filtered light of the morning sun. She'd come to him like this in his dreams since the very first night. Before, actually. He'd just never had a face to go with the desire.

Something deep inside reacted to the fact he could find no darkness anywhere. He should have realized there'd be no hiding in the shadows for Victoria Bishop.

"You're not so bad yourself," she said. The mystery in her eyes deepened, darkened, as she let her heavy-lidded gaze dip down over his rigid body.

In turn, he drank in the sight of her, letting his own gaze skim over the lace of her bra and down her flat stomach, to where the sunlight glinted—

"What the hell?" he barked, blinking hard.

She tensed. "What?" she asked, then must have seen where he stared, because she drew a hand protectively close. "Oh."

The diamond stud winked at him from her belly button.

He'd always thought of body piercing as mutilation, not erotic, but with Tori his body tightened even more. He tore his gaze away and met hers, where a mischievous but defiant gleam warned that her little surprise carried more significance than just a whim. And again he realized just how deep her need to be free ran.

"Don't tell me you did this in New Orleans," he muttered, giving her the reaction she needed.

Her smile turned daring. "Then don't be mad at me."

He wanted to be mad at her. Furious, actually. Now he knew why it had taken so long to find her in Jackson Square. While he'd been frantically tearing through the plaza, she'd been having her belly button pierced.

But instead of anger, he could only grin. "You're determined to do me in, aren't you?"

She stepped closer and ran a whisper-fine kiss across his mouth. "It's been the most effective way of cutting through your veneers."

In another time, another place, the point-blank statement would have pierced the haze of desire and resurrected his defenses—those very veneers to which she referred. But along with the wash of morning sunlight came a wash of truth, and he could only return his mouth to hers.

She really was going to do him in.

Hanging on by a thread, he went down on a knee and pressed his mouth to the diamond stud. He heard her sharp intake of breath, felt her shudder. With his hands holding her hips, he skimmed his tongue around the symbol, to show that he accepted her just the way she was. He wanted to slide lower, put his mouth somewhere far deeper, but didn't want to scare her. Didn't want to go too fast.

Kissing his way up her stomach to her chest, he ignored the desire to pull a nipple into his mouth and made his way up her neck. When he again stood, it was only for a heartbeat. He braced a knee against the mattress and eased her down beneath him. She went willingly, one arm curled around his neck and pulling him down with her. He didn't know how much longer he could hold out. He wanted to be inside her. To feel her welcome him deep, to feel her arms and legs close around him and hear the cries of pleasure tear from deep in her throat and know that they were for him and him alone.

But this was Tori, a woman whose resilience and courage hid a stabbing vulnerability, a gentleness and innocence he wanted to protect and cherish, not crush.

You remind me of that magnolia, chère. Bold and defiant, strong, beautiful.

And you think you're going to crush me.

You think so, too.

But, God, he didn't want to. The thought of crushing her, of hurting her in any way, shape or form ripped at him. She didn't deserve any more pain. She didn't deserve any more disillusionment. She deserved happiness.

"Ian?"

He looked at her lying beneath him, pale hair fanned out against the pillow, green eyes slumberous and mouth swollen, and felt a surge of something so fierce, so primal, he could find no name for it.

"What's wrong?" she asked.

Like a blind man running through the swamp, tripping and stumbling, he tore at the tangled vines of his heart. "Nothing."

"You look angry."

"Not angry," he ground out, skimming a finger along her cheekbone. "In awe."

A slow smile curved her lips. "I'd rather you in something else."

That did it. The point-blank words stripped away the last of his control. Only need remained, sharp, demanding, hacking away at him. He kissed her hard, deep, all the while his hands fumbled with the front closure of her bra. When the clasp finally opened, he felt something break free in him.

First he explored with his hands, letting his fingertips

learn the shape and texture of her breasts, the feel of her silky smooth skin and her nipples. Her breasts were full and round, soft, and when he let himself look at them, the sight of the pebbled pink areolas almost made him groan out loud. The need to taste, to learn and memorize and imprint, to close his mouth around her nipple and suckle almost slayed him.

He made his way down her neck to her collarbone, sharing little kisses as he did so. He loved the way she arched and twisted beneath him, the little sounds of satisfaction slipping from her throat. She had her hands on his lower back, and her legs fell open, letting him settle between them. He wanted to rock against her, to ease the pressure building between them.

But even more, he wanted to draw out every second.

When his mouth found her nipple again, she arched. "Ian," she rasped, and he began to suckle. She lifted a hand to the back of his head as though to hold him in place. The simple, endearing gesture made him want to stop and just hold her, promise her everything would be okay, but he couldn't stop now, and the feel of her fingernails grinding into his lower back told him she didn't want him to, either.

He reached for her panties, which he quickly discarded. He'd felt the moist heat through the soft cotton fabric, but not even that prepared him for how slick he found her. How ready. He eased one finger inside, tried not to groan.

"Ian," she whispered, tugging against his boxer-briefs. He helped her shove them down his legs, and soon he lay there between her thighs, nothing but flesh and desire between them.

His mouth went slack against her breast. How could he have been so stupid?

"What?" Her question was urgent, breathless.

He met her eyes. It was the cruelest of ironies—Ian the protector had come unprepared.

But how could he have been prepared for this flash fire?

He hadn't run from his house to hers with the intent of making love to her. He'd just needed to make sure she was okay. Alive. How could he have known the sight of her tripping along behind Gaston would destroy the fortress between them as if it were nothing more than a flimsy matchstick village?

"I don't have anything," he hoarsely admitted, and his body protested by hardening even more.

The soft light in Tori's eyes surprised him. "I do."

He pushed up on one arm. "What?"

The light turned into a smile. "How many times do I have to tell you I can take care of myself?" she asked softly, then slipped from his arms and leaned toward the nightstand. From the drawer she withdrew a box. From the box she withdrew several foil packages.

"Will these help?" she asked with a wicked smile.

Ian looked from the challenge in her eyes to the object in her hands. The urge to be inside her battled with something sharp and jagged he didn't understand. He didn't want Tori to have condoms on hand, *just in case*. He didn't want Tori to be prepared for a moment like this. The thought of Tori and another man—

"Ian."

The breath ripped in and out of him. He never thought—

He swallowed the surprising surge of possessiveness and looked into her eyes but couldn't say anything.

"I bought them for you," she whispered. "For us. After the other night..." She closed her eyes and looked down.

He tilted her face toward his. "After the other night what?"

Her gaze searched his face. "When I thought someone was in the house, when I thought I was in trouble, all I could think of was you. Your smile and your touch, how much I wanted you there with me. Not just because I was scared at that moment, but because I'd been scared since I saw the way you looked at me at the shooting range. The coldness in your eyes. I couldn't stand for that to be my last image of you.''

Ian went very still. He'd hurt her, he realized. In trying to protect her, he'd done just the opposite.

''And then you were there,'' she said, and touched a hand to his face, ''filling the doorway and my heart and I knew…I realized no matter how strong someone is, you can only fight inevitability so long. I knew it was only a matter of time before we found ourselves just like this, or died trying to prevent it.''

The admission wound through him, settling dangerously close to his heart. ''No one's going to die,'' he said, pushing the hair back from her face. Her eyes were wide and dark and shockingly moist. Vulnerability hid in her gaze, but trust glistened there, as well. And that trust reached down and touched what remained of his soul.

She took his hand and placed a foil package into his palm. ''Love me, Ian. Make everything else go away.''

His heart exploded in his chest. He tore open the packet and protected them, then she extended an arm and pulled him down to her. Their mouths met first, a hungry battle of small and deep kisses. He slid a hand down her torso to between her legs, where he found her wet and ready.

''Now,'' Tori whispered, lifting her hips for him. She cried out when he slipped a finger inside, arched up against him. Sensation cascaded through her, but rather than satisfying, the hunger grew. She knew Ian went slowly for her, but if she didn't have more than his finger inside her soon, she knew she'd go out of her mind. ''Please. Hurry.''

His eyes were glazed, almost fevered. ''Ah, *chère*. I tried to warn you about this.''

She tried to look away from him, couldn't. The way he lay atop her let his hair fall around his cowlick, prompting her to lift a hand and ease the brown strands back from his forehead. ''Warn me about what?''

He moved a finger inside her, joined it with another. ''When I prefer to linger.''

The breath stalled in her throat. She felt herself convulse around his fingers, but tried to hold the dam in place. She didn't want to let go without him. "I'm all for lingering," she whispered, reaching down and finding the length of him. She closed her hand around him, squeezed. "But let's do it together."

A groan tore from deep in his throat. He withdrew his fingers, for a shattering heartbeat leaving her empty and craving. She arched up against him, and felt the tip of him pressing against her. "Now," she said, guiding him. "Please."

He pushed inside, filling her with the most profound sense of awe she'd ever known. She opened for him, tilting her hips to give him a better angle, wanting all of him. But he held back.

"I won't break," she murmured against his mouth, then pressed a hand to his hips and tilted up to greet his thrusts.

When he tore his mouth from hers, she cried out his name, but he put a finger to her lips. "You asked me to love you. I'm asking you to look at me."

The words touched her heart. She wanted to look at him, wanted to look up and see the fever in his eyes, the hair falling against his forehead, but for a moment couldn't bring her eyes to meet his. Somehow that seemed even more intimate than the way she lay beneath him in the broad daylight with their bodies joined, their hearts beating as one.

"Tori," he whispered, tucking a finger beneath her chin. "Trust me."

That got her. She did trust him, otherwise she could never be making love with him. She glanced up at him, almost gasped at the naked vulnerability in his gaze. She knew her heart bled into her eyes, because he gave her back just the same. He found her hand, then brought it alongside her face on the pillow and twined their fingers together.

There, holding her like that, he picked up the rhythm of

his thrusts. The deeper he went, the more fevered his eyes became, but she never looked away. The sight, the reality, thrilled her. Wrapping her legs around him, she tilted her hips and gave him an even deeper angle, sending them both straight over the edge.

It was another free fall, but, unlike all those times before, this time they fell together. No slapping branches or stinging accusations. Just a flood of sensation, crashing and swirling, tangling just like their arms and their legs. Soft sounds of feminine pleasure mixed with primal masculine exertion as they barreled through time and space. And when they landed in a glorious heap, sated and breathing hard, Tori knew that the risk of injury extended far beyond a broken arm.

But for that transient moment she didn't care.

Rain fell from a gunmetal-gray sky in steady sheets. Every now and then, lightning rolled across the horizon, not splintering streaks, just flashes of illumination. The ensuing thunder rumbled with equal finesse.

Tori stood on the back porch with her hands curled around the old railing. Her face tilted toward the sky, she welcomed the rain flitting against her throat. The early-evening breeze, no longer heavy and hot from the day, but cooled by approaching darkness, lifted the strands of her hair and caressed her exposed flesh.

She could breathe out here. Finally. For the first time in countless hours. She could breathe. And she could think.

And she could cry.

The tears slid silently down her face. She let them, welcomed them. They were too pure and real to swipe away.

Upstairs Ian lay sleeping in the big bed. While the sun rode high in the afternoon sky, they'd made love over and over, lost in a tide of inevitability that had been building since the moment she saw him standing at the top of the stairs. A simmer could only build for so long without boiling over.

That's why she'd bought the condoms. And she'd thought that would be all it took to prepare herself for making love with Ian.

She'd never been more wrong in her life.

The man… A shudder ran through her. Again. Still. The man made her feel more alive than anyone ever had. Than she'd ever imagined possible. The man brought her body and soul singing to life. Being with him was like being in a brilliantly lit meadow at springtime, turning in circles, faster and faster, breathing in the heady scent of nectar and feeling the warmth of the sun, glorying in the beauty, but not knowing where to turn or explore first.

Tori lowered her head. If that *was* true, why was she crying?

Because it *was* true. And the reality of it, the power, frightened her. When she was with Ian, she forgot all those hard life lessons she'd learned. She forgot about her own two feet and the shelf. She forgot everything, except the way those simmering pewter eyes scorched clear through to her soul.

She wore his shirt and nothing else, and when the breeze picked up, the scent of sandalwood and soap became so strong she almost thought he stood behind her.

"There you are."

Tori stiffened. A thick blanket settled around her shoulders, but she didn't turn around. Couldn't.

"Tori, *chère,* you okay?"

The timbre of his voice, the puzzlement and concern, washed around her and through her, brought her body thrumming back to life. She wanted to turn and see him, but found herself unable to move. Breathe. He wasn't the first man she'd slept with, but he was the first with whom she'd shared such raw, no-holds-barred intimacy, an intimacy that left her feeling naked from the inside out. And now, after the heat of the moment, she didn't know how to look him in the eye. She felt so…exposed. Vulnerable. This man had explored every inch of her body. He'd made

love to her for hours, shown her pleasures she'd never even
dared imagine.

And she'd done the same with him.

"Sweetheart?"

She braced herself for the feel of his hands settling down
on her shoulders, or maybe him turning around, but nothing happened. He didn't touch her, didn't so much as
move.

Gratitude welled through her. Because for the first time
in her life, Tori realized she stood on the verge of shattering. She gazed out across the lawn, toward the oaks
shielding her yard from his. Spanish moss swayed in the
breeze, making her realize that just like those tangled
strands would lose their allure if separated, she and Ian
could never pretend passion hadn't exploded between
them. There was no going back to before. Their relationship would never be the same.

And that's what frightened her.

She'd been working hard to stand on her own two feet,
but she'd let Ian sweep her right off them, literally and
figuratively. She hadn't held anything back. She'd responded to him wholly, instinctively. She'd given him everything. When she'd been in his arms, he in her body,
nothing else had mattered, not the past, certainly not the
future. She'd let go of everything and found nirvana.

And she knew that when she looked at him, she would
see the awareness in his eyes. The memory of the uninhibited way in which they'd explored and satisfied each
other's bodies.

How could she pretend to be immune to this man when
he'd heard the sounds tearing from her throat? Felt her
body tense, then shudder in release. And if she couldn't
feign immunity, how would she ever keep the lines of her
life separate? How could she give her body to a man who
believed a murderer's blood flowed through her veins? A
man who threatened her need to—

"Look at me, *chère*. Please. I need to see you."

The endearment undid her. Against better judgment, she did as he asked, and crumbled as she'd expected. The sight of him standing in the fading light of early evening stole her breath. He stood there all tall and compelling, wearing nothing but the twin St. Christopher medals and a pair of unfastened faded jeans. His messy hair reflected the countless times she'd run her hands through it, finally discovering how it felt to play with his cowlick. His jaw badly needed a razor. His mouth was swollen from the intimacies they'd shared. And his eyes…

His eyes were on fire.

Her body went liquid. He touched her with only his gaze, but she felt as though his hand once again stroked intimately. No one had ever affected her so deeply, rattled the foundation of who she was, what she thought to be true.

"My God," she said, drawing a hand to her steadily thrumming heart. "What have we done?"

Chapter 14

Ian brought her hand to his mouth and kissed the backs of her fingers. "If the past eight hours are any indication, I'd say we did what we both wanted from the very first."

She searched his eyes, those amazing eyes of his that could condemn with coldness and seduce with heat. And there she saw the truth. "We forgot."

"Forgot what?" he asked with a wicked grin. "I can't think of anything we didn't remember."

The words sent awareness tripping through her. And along with it came a cold, hard certainty. "We forgot who we are," she told him, pulling the blanket tighter around her. "Just like that day on the levee."

A moment of silence passed. A long, deep moment when he just looked at her. The pewter of his eyes revealed the struggle, the search. The stance of his body showed his displeasure. But when he lifted a hand to her face and wiped the moisture beneath her eyes, he gave her only gentleness.

"No, *chère*," he said in an achingly tender voice. "We

didn't forget. We found something more important, and we let go.''

Emotion clogged her throat. He made it sound so easy. But it wasn't, and she knew that. Magic in bed, sex, didn't erase the wall between them. Not just the past, but how the events of that one night shaped the man and woman they became.

"I'm scared.'' The admission cost her, but he deserved honesty.

"I didn't think tough Tori was scared of anything.''

"I'm scared of you.'' Curiosity motivated the admission, but he didn't give her the swagger or cockiness she expected.

"Me?'' His expression hardened. "Did I hurt you? I thought you wanted—''

Too late Tori remembered Meghan, and the festering guilt Ian still battled. "I did want,'' she said, cutting him off before his thoughts ran down a destructive path. "That's what scares me. The way you make me feel. Forget.''

He shoved a hand through his hair, leaving it to fall wherever. Then he swore. Softly. "This is about what I told you the other night, isn't it? About crushing you.''

"Ian—''

"I was just trying to scare you off, *chère*. Just trying to prevent everything that's happened since then. Forget about the magnolia. We're beyond that now.''

The note of certainty in his voice scraped as much as it seduced. "I'm not sure I *can* forget.'' Not sure she should.

"Let me help you then,'' he said, drawing her into the circle of his arms.

She wanted to lift her hands to his chest, to push him away before she lost all sense and reason. But even more, she wanted to feel the warmth of his flesh beneath her fingertips. To kiss his medallions again. "Ian—''

"You're a gutsy woman,'' he said, cutting off her protest. "Don't turn away from me now. Not when we finally realize what we've been fighting all along."

Her defenses lay in ruins. She tried to resurrect them, but her heart took a pickax to her efforts.

"I don't want to fight anymore," she whispered. Because she didn't. Dear God in Heaven, she didn't. She was tired of taking on the world single-handedly.

"Then don't." Ian took the blanket from around her shoulders and laid it on the porch, then drew her down beside him. When his mouth found hers, she opened willingly, just as she'd done all day.

And there, to the sound of soft rain and rolling thunder, Ian quickly discovered what she wore beneath his shirt.

Her heart.

Early-morning sunlight streamed through the kitchen window. Ian set a cup of coffee and glass of orange juice on a tray, tucked the local weekly paper under his arm and headed upstairs. He hoped she still slept. He wanted to be there when she awoke, to stroke the pale-blond hair from her face and see what heat and memories lingered. There was something naked and unguarded about the first look of the day.

He wanted to share hers.

They hadn't found sleep until the wee hours of the morning, and even then, Ian had barely let himself drop off. Instead, he'd just held her, savoring the feel of her body draped over his. With the sunrise he'd slipped from bed, gone home to feed Gaston and grab supplies, then returned to fix Tori breakfast.

Now he stepped into the bedroom and for a moment just stared. He'd always loved the antique four-poster bed, but with Tori tangled in the sheets, he found the sight even more spellbinding. He could watch her forever, he knew, watch her chest rise and fall with her deep, rhythmic breathing.

But even more, he wanted to touch. Still. Again.

Setting the tray on the nightstand, he sat on the mattress and feathered a hand along the side of her face. She murmured something sleepily and turned into his hand.

The innocent, trusting gesture wound around his heart with staggering force. "Wake up, sleepyhead. Time for breakfast."

A little sigh escaped, then a languorous stretch as her eyes slowly opened. Blinked. Blinked again. Fixated on him. *"Ian."*

"Who else were you expecting?" he teased.

Recognition came fast and hot. Awareness flared. The sudden rush of color to her face surprised him, given the uninhibited manner with which they'd explored each other's bodies the night before. She pushed up in bed, grabbing at the sheet when she realized she wore nothing at all.

"Thought you might be hungry," he said with a lazy smile. "For food, that is."

She glanced toward the nightstand. "You made me breakfast?"

He found her discomfort oddly endearing, deeply satisfying. Obviously, she didn't have much experience with morning-afters. To ease the tension he ignored the rumpled sheets and smell of lingering sex, the damningly ready state of his own body, and climbed in bed next to her, bracing his back against the carved headboard. He then handed her a cup of coffee as if he'd done so dozens of times before, kept the orange juice for himself and opened the paper between them.

She leaned over his arm. "Did the world change overnight?" she asked in a sleepy voice.

The simple question ground into him. God, if only she knew. "I can't imagine it didn't," he answered easily, skimming the headlines. "It says right here—" His words died the second he saw the big black letters.

"It says what?" she asked, leaning closer.

Blood roaring through him, he folded the paper shut.

"Ian?"

"There was an explosion," he told her, shoving the paper to the floor. He fumbled through his veneers, but they all slipped away, forcing him to look at her while the shock of the article still rocked through him. He knew what she would do if she saw it. He knew the conclusions she would jump to. The risks she would take. And he simply could not let her put her life on the line like that.

"An explosion," he said again, and if she saw the wild glint he couldn't keep from his eyes, if she saw the savagery he couldn't quell, he had only passion to blame. "For those at the epicenter, the world definitely changed," he added. "The aftershocks are expected to linger for days."

Her eyes glazed over. "It must have been pretty powerful."

"You have no idea." He spoke the truth, but that didn't stop shards of guilt from slicing him up inside. Nor did it stop him from leaning over and easing her down to the mattress. Keep her safe. Keep her alive. That's all that mattered.

"What should we do?" she asked a little breathlessly.

It was a damn good question. "Hang on for the ride," he suggested, and lowered his mouth to hers.

Contentment spread through her like an early-morning mist. Groggy and sated and surprisingly sore, Tori pushed up on one arm and looked at Ian sleeping next to her, sheets tangled at his hips. His breathing was deep, rhythmic, the features of his face relaxed and unguarded. Except for the medallions, his broad chest was bare.

Absently she reached out and brushed the brown hair at his forehead, loving the way it curled around his cowlick. And her heart caught. She'd been so frightened of this, she remembered. Of him. Of herself. But she felt no fear now. Only a bone-deep sense of rightness. Of trust.

Memories washed over her and through her, of the way

he'd held her, stroked her, brought her body humming to life and demanding more. She'd never known it possible to make love for hours on end. No wonder he slept. The man had to be exhausted.

With a soft smile she eased from bed, careful not to wake him. She would bathe and clean up, then see about lunch. On the other side of the bed, she stooped to find her discarded bra and panties, but found the weekly paper instead. She started to tuck it under her arm, but a headline froze her in place.

Prominent New Orleans Lawyer Carson Lemieux Missing.

"Oh, dear God," she whispered. Her heart beat erratically and her vision blurred. She skimmed the article, found that the lawyer's town house had been ransacked the day she and Ian went to New Orleans. No one had seen or heard from him since. His family feared the worst.

No wonder he'd stood her up. No wonder she'd reached no one at his office since then, just voice mail.

Dizzy, Tori sank to the rug alongside the bed. Missing. Bloodstains in his Garden District home. Robbery suspected.

Tori suspected something far worse.

"*Chère?* Is something wrong?"

She looked up to find Ian sitting on the side of the bed, shoving the hair from his face. "The lawyer," she said, picking up the paper. "The lawyer who said he knew about my father. They think he might have been murdered."

Ian swore hotly and stood. "Let me see that."

She barely heard him, couldn't stop staring at the words. "I can't believe he could be dead."

Ian's hands curled around the edges of the paper. "Tori, I mean it, let me—what the hell?"

The barked-out question shattered the haze. She looked up at him towering over her, found him glaring at the back page. "Ian?"

He grabbed the paper and pulled it toward him. The string of expletives shocked her. The rigid stance of his body unnerved.

"What?" she asked, pushing to her feet. "Is there more?"

He wadded the paper into a tight ball and threw it across the room. Then cold, furious eyes met hers. "God, Tori, how could you? Are you out of your mind?"

Her heart stalled out. After the long hours of murmured endearments and encouragement, the accusation in his voice hurt.

"Didn't you hear me, Ian?" she asked a little desperately. "Carson Lemieux is missing. They found his blood—"

"What were you thinking?" he went on. "What were you trying to prove in having this little dare published for the whole town to see?"

She stared at him for a long moment, while his questions and his actions found their way together. Her throat tightened. With great deliberation she reached for the crumpled paper and smoothed it open, saw the letter to the editor she'd dropped off a few days before, the letter in which she challenged the town to let go of the past. "Oh."

"Oh?" he roared. "That's it? Oh?"

She searched his face, looking for a trace of the passionate lover with whom she'd shared the night, but found only the hardened veneer of the cop. And the way he looked at her, the fury in his eyes, cut straight through to her heart. She'd known he would be angry—that's why she hadn't told him. But she hadn't expected a reaction this severe, and she hadn't expected a confrontation while they both stood naked.

She grabbed a blanket from the bed and drew it to her body, unable to stand there exposed while he looked at her like that. Of course, Ian didn't bother covering up in turn. But why should he? He wasn't the one being interrogated. He wasn't rattled. He—

It hit her then, hard and brutal, and her heart flat-out stopped. Then came the chill, from the inside out. No wonder the news about the lawyer didn't faze him. No wonder he was focusing only on her letter to the editor, when the fact that a man with a connection to her might have been murdered held far greater significance.

"You knew," she whispered. "Dear God, you knew."

It wasn't a question, but a statement of cold hard fact.

He stepped toward her. "Tori—"

She backed away. "That's what this was all about," she rasped, gesturing to the rumpled sheets. Thoughts blurred, merged. Reality shifted. "You made love to me so I wouldn't see the article!" She almost gagged on the words.

His pewter eyes took on a dangerous glitter. "I made love to you because I wanted to. You wanted it, too."

She clenched the blanket tighter. "Are you telling me you didn't see this article before you kissed me?"

The breath sawed in and out of him. He squeezed his eyes shut, then opened them to the truth. "No," he said with astonishing blasé. "I knew you would find out eventually. I just didn't see any reason for it to be that very moment."

Everything inside her felt jagged and broken. Violated. She'd given this man her trust and her body, and he'd used both against her. "You think the fact that we're lovers makes it okay for you to use my body as another way of dictating what I do and don't do? See? Think?"

"That's the hurt talking, Tori."

"It's the truth," she flung back.

"Maybe I didn't go about it in the best way, but I didn't want you hurt by this. I didn't want—"

"You didn't want. *You* didn't want! Well, what about *me,* Ian?" The hurt hollowed her out. "What about what I want? What I need? Did you ever stop to consider that?"

He stood there tall and naked, unyielding. But his eyes

turned smoky. "Every hour, of every day, since the moment I found you in this house."

The melting words sent her reeling. She fought the dangerous temptation to fall back into the spell and focused on the facts. The day in New Orleans, the dark change in his mood after he'd made a phone call. The withdrawal on the way home. She felt so naive. She'd attributed both to Madame Rousseau's words, when all along he'd been manipulating her, withholding information she had a right to know.

"When were you going to tell me?" she demanded with remarkable calm. Later she would fall apart. But now, in front of Ian the Unaffected, she would give him nothing but the same.

"I could ask you the same question about your little letter to the editor," he said implacably, as though they spoke of the weather. "I want you to recant it. Submit a follow-up letter to Autrey stating that you were upset, that you didn't mean to condemn the whole town. Tell them—"

She just stared at him. "Nothing's changed, has it?" she realized sickly. Not with him. She was the one who'd made the mistake, who'd let dreams and desire override what she'd known all along. "Despite what we shared last night, when morning came, you're right back to making decisions for me."

"I don't want to see you hurt."

"Go," she said, picking up his jeans and shoving them at him. God, he was still naked. "Send a deputy over if it makes you feel better, but leave. I can't see you right now."

"I'm not going anywhere." His stance loomed as unyielding as his words.

"This isn't your choice, Ian. It's not your decision. It's mine, and I've made it."

He stalked toward her. "Don't do this," he warned.

She shoved against his chest, but when her fingers

touched the cool surface of the St. Christopher medals, she pulled her hands back. "Don't do what? Live my own life? Make my own decisions? Don't be upset that when I thought we were making love, you were employing a tactic to keep me in the dark?"

"Don't pretend last night didn't mean anything."

"Oh, it meant something," she said. Her gaze darted to the sheets, rumpled from their loving, and she felt her stomach clench. Her heart lay in shreds, but from deep inside she found the strength to say what needed to be said. "It means I don't have to wonder anymore. I don't have to wonder if making love would change anything between us. Because now I know it won't."

His nostrils flared. "You're upset right now, Tori, I know that. But when you calm down, you'll realize—"

"Calm down? Don't you get it, Ian? I'm not some doll you can just put up on a shelf. I'm not a child who needs decisions made for her, but that's exactly what you keep doing." Her vision blurred. "You were right about the magnolia," she said. "You can't help it. You don't have a choice. Crushing is the only way you know."

Those simmering eyes of his went cold. Ice cold. Cold as death. And as though on cue, something inside her died. The veneer was back, hammered into place with brutal precision. And she knew. The passionate man with whom she'd shared her body and heart would never be let out of his cage for long.

"You're doing it right now," she told him, praying her voice didn't crack on the truth. "You're doing it to yourself. You're slamming a veneer in place as fast and hard as you can. Ian the Unaffected," she mocked. "It's the only way you know, but I can't live with that. I can't be with a man who can't be with himself."

He looked at her for a long moment, his eyes like shrapnel. Something hot flashed in their depths. Something sharp and volatile. Then he shut it away. "I don't recall asking you to live with anything."

He spoke with freezing precision, and the words landed like a slap to the face. "No, you didn't, did you?"

She'd just assumed. She'd responded to his jagged need, erroneously labeling mind-numbing sex as intimacy. Lovemaking.

He jerked on his jeans. "Blame me if it makes you feel better. If it's easier. But sooner or later, maybe when you lie alone in this bed tonight, you need to realize that when you muddy the waters, when you ignore warnings, you get hurt."

His voice was hard, the words blunt. "But tough Tori doesn't want help, and I can't make you accept it. I'm not going to beg. And I'm not going to apologize for wanting to keep you alive. But I'm not going to hang around like a lap dog, either." He yanked up the zipper. "I can't stop you from hurting yourself, but you won't get the weapon from me. If you lock the door tonight, know that you're not doing it to keep me out. I don't make the same mistake twice."

That said, he turned and walked away.

Tori moved mechanically through the rest of the morning. Everything inside her felt numb, sick. She'd let passion blind her to caution. She'd let desire override all those life lessons she'd learned. Her own body had betrayed her, coming to life beneath the clever mouth and talented hands of a man who let himself feel nothing. He'd shattered her defenses and had her begging for more, every kiss, every sigh leading her blindly and passionately into quicksand.

Now every time she heard a creak, she turned, thinking he'd come back. Praying he hadn't. Hoping he had. Just the sight of the big antique bed, the memory of what happened there, broke her heart.

A loud knock at the back door sent her pulse hammering. *Ian.* She stood there breathing deeply, not wanting to see him, but knowing she had to pull on an impassive mask the way he did, stroll downstairs and blandly tell him to go to hell.

A quick glance in the mirror confirmed her features were blank. In the kitchen she tried not to shake as she put her hand to the knob. She pulled open the door and stared.

"Victoria?" asked an older man with the most shockingly white hair she'd ever seen.

She blinked. The man in the tattered tan overcoat looked vaguely familiar, but she couldn't place him. "May I help you?"

His gaze darted toward Ian's house, then back to her. "Actually, I'm here to help you."

"Oh?" Tori glanced down by his feet, half expecting to see a case of household cleaners or insurance brochures. But found nothing. "I'm sorry, sir, now's not a good time."

He took a step closer. "The name is Carson," he said in a low, urgent voice. "Carson Lemieux."

Chapter 15

Tori went very still. All but her heart—it started to pound. Disbelief fought with relief. Hope pushed against both. Just a few hours ago she'd thought her journey to Louisiana had slammed into a brick wall. But now a glimmer of light shone from cracks she hadn't imagined possible. "Mr. Lemieux. Oh, thank God! I thought—"

"That I was dead?" he asked quietly.

"The newspaper said—"

"Exactly what I wanted it to say."

The ominous statement chilled her. She looked at the tall, thin man standing in the shade of her back porch, shock giving way to a barrage of questions. He looked…tired. Haggard. His shoulders were slumped, his white hair badly in need of a comb. "I don't understand— are you all right?"

His gaze cut toward Ian's house, then back at her. "It's not safe to talk in the open like this. May I come in?"

Unease tightened its grip. The lawyer seemed agitated, uncomfortable. But then, his house had been ransacked.

His blood had been found. "Yes. Yes, of course," she said, stepping back and letting him into the large kitchen. "What happened—"

"I didn't think the sheriff would ever leave you alone."

Tori stiffened, but refused to yield to the flood of emotion. "He won't be back," she said, and shut the door.

"I'm glad to hear it," her father's attorney said when she turned to face him. He was frowning. "Saul Montague's son is the last person you should be listening to. There's something broken inside him. I was worried he'd break you, too."

The words, spoken in utter kindness and sincerity, cut with uncanny precision. She kept the flash of pain from her face, but deep inside, she felt the bleeding start once again. Instinctively her gaze traveled out the kitchen window and beyond the grand old oaks, where the outline of Ian's house could be seen.

"What's going on?" she asked. She turned from the memories, refusing to think of the terrible mistake she'd made with Ian. She'd told him all along she didn't need him. And she didn't. Carson Lemieux was standing in her kitchen.

"You said everyone thinks exactly what you want them to. But why? Why do you want everyone to think you're dead?"

"Same reason your father did, I suspect. To protect you."

"Protect me?" The words grated. "From what?"

"They don't want us talking, Victoria. They don't want you to know the truth. That's why they broke into my house. As a warning."

"*They?* Who's they?"

He gestured toward the kitchen table, where the remains of the breakfast tray Ian had prepared sat. "Perhaps you should sit down first."

"No." The word came out more adamant than she'd intended.

A faint smile lit the lawyer's eyes. "I should have known Russ Bishop's girl wouldn't take anything sitting down."

Tori's heart took a peculiar little stutter step. Lemieux knew her father, had called him friend. "Tell me," she said. "Please. Who is 'they'?"

Deep lines of tension replaced the whimsy in his eyes. "The FBI."

"What?"

"They've been looking for you and your father for twenty-five years. You're a wild card. They can't risk you learning the truth about your father."

"He didn't kill anyone."

"In my heart I know that, Victoria. But the evidence says otherwise."

Tori just stared. Emotion clogged her throat. Since the day she'd arrived in Bon Terre, she'd heard her father's name and reputation maligned. He'd been called a thief and a murderer. Now, for the first time, someone spoke of him without hatred and contempt. "But if you believe—"

"The diamonds," Lemieux said. "No matter what I believe about Russ, the diamonds remain unexplained. And it wouldn't look very good if word got out that an FBI agent vanished along with more than a million dollars in uncut diamonds. Hardly the kind of reliable, steadfast image the bureau wants to perpetuate."

Her breath caught. "An FBI agent? What are you talking about?"

"Your father, sweetheart. He was one of the best."

The walls of the quaint kitchen closed in on her. She swayed, groped for one of the old spindle-back chairs. Curling her fingers around the top, she barely felt the splinters digging into her palm. "That's not possible—there must be some mistake."

"There were lots of mistakes—your father's occupation wasn't one of them. That's how he met your mother. They worked on a case out of New Orleans together. He was burned out, decided to walk away from undercover work and create a simpler life. A life with your mother. And you."

The words came at Tori distorted, through a tunnel of disbelief. The idea of her gentle father as a covert FBI agent was as foreign as him being a cold-blooded killer. But then she thought back on her childhood, the way he'd changed their identities and vanished without a trace. The skill and precision with which he'd taught his little girl to shoot a gun. The way he always seemed to be looking over his shoulder, bracing himself, waiting for something Tori never understood.

The very facts that lent credibility to Ian's story, lent even more to Lemieux's. An FBI agent. A man of law, not crime. A man of honor, not malice.

"I'm sorry," Lemieux said. "I know this must be a shock."

Shock didn't even come close. Her heart was hammering so hard she could hardly catch her breath, but for the first time since she'd come to Bon Terre, the events of that long ago night were starting to make sense.

"He was undercover at the auction house, wasn't he? He wasn't behind the smuggling, but the one trying to bring it down."

"The bureau lured him back for one last assignment. He knew Corinne would object, so he didn't tell her. And he almost pulled it all off. He had the bust arranged, everything. But he underestimated Guy Melancon, didn't count on him catching on at the eleventh hour."

Tori drew a hand to her chest, but the sickness spread. The pain her father must have suffered. The sacrifices he'd made.

"What happened?" she asked, though she already knew.

"Your father also underestimated your mother. He never realized that in leaving her in the dark about his activities, he'd prompt her to begin an investigation of her own. Guy caught her snooping around the warehouse, taking evidence. He had her followed.''

The memory hit swift and brutal. Ian had told her about the phone call his father had received the night of the murders.

"The diamonds," Tori murmured.

"She was desperate, scared that something terrible would happen to her husband, the father of her child. She wanted to help him.''

"And that's why she died," Tori realized with a sharp twist to her heart. "She was trying to protect him.''

"No," Lemieux countered, "she died because she took chances she had no business taking and stumbled across the truth. She interfered with the investigation, that's what got her and the sheriff killed. Guy knew of the deceit by then, the impending bust, and took out a hit.''

Tori struggled to take it all in, the facts and implications. If her father had been honest and told her mother about his return to the bureau, she'd be alive to this day.

"You were with him that day," Lemieux added. "He'd taken you to a carnival. No one ever saw him after that. My guess is he heard about the shootings and realized he'd be implicated. He had no choice but to run. He was grief-stricken and scared.''

But he was also innocent. "Why didn't the FBI help him? If he was one of their own—"

"He vanished, Victoria. He ran.'' Dismay laced the lawyer's voice, twisted his face. "And the diamonds, key evidence, disappeared along with him. That's not the MO of an innocent man. There was nothing anyone could do for him, not even me.''

"But why would he do that? Why would he run, rather than fight to clear his name?''

"You.''

Her heart kicked, hard. "Me?''

"He had a child to think of and a price on his head, not

just from the bureau, but as retribution for the smuggling operation he brought down. If he showed his face, he would have more likely ended up in the plot next to your sweet mama, than with a cleared name. Your father wasn't a man to trust others with his life. Or with yours.''

Tori's throat tightened. She thought back on her childhood, the devotion her father had given her. Her girlfriends had thought her dad was the coolest. None of their fathers had spent a fraction of the time with their children. But instead of realizing the burden he carried in his heart, she'd grown to silently resent his overprotective tendencies. Now the truth behind his actions awed her. He'd traded his life, his good name and his freedom, to protect her.

Lemieux crossed toward her. ''It was safer for him to take you and the diamonds and make a clean start.''

The subtle accusation bumped up against the shock of discovery. Tori looked at the man her father had called friend, and realized that not even he fully believed his innocence.

''He didn't take the diamonds,'' she said. ''We lived a simple life. He was a fisherman, for God's sakes.''

''They never turned up.''

''Then someone else took them.'' Of that, she had no doubt. ''Ian,'' she whispered. Just saying his name hurt. ''He needs to know.''

Lemieux's expression closed up. He glanced out the window, his gaze lingering in the direction of Ian's house before returning to her. ''Be careful, Victoria. You're a living, breathing link to a busted operation the government tried to bury. If you go to the press, the FBI will have a lot of explaining to do. Secrets, scandal, a runaway agent...it's hardly the image they want. You could create quite a problem for them.''

''But so could you,'' she pointed out.

A harsh laugh broke from the lawyer's throat. ''I value my life and my freedom. They know that. But you...you have a personal stake.'' His expression was grim. ''Think carefully before you make your next move. Your father worked long and hard to give you a life untainted by the past. Before you shine a spotlight on it, think about what's to be gained. What's to be lost. The bureau isn't going to rush to the defense of a man everyone thinks killed his wife and stole a fortune in diamonds. You won't clear your father's name, but you will destroy the anonymity he sacrificed everything to give you."

The chill deepened. Lemieux's warning sounded loud and clear.

"If you're not willing to help, why did you ask me to come down here?"

"Because you deserved to know the full truth, and I might be the only one still living who can give it to you."

Gratitude warred with frustration. Carson Lemieux had risked his life to tell her the truth, but now there was little she could do with the coveted information. He'd shared his story with her out of a debt to her father, but he wasn't willing to go public with the allegations.

"It's not fair," she whispered.

Lemieux frowned. "Life rarely is. But I wanted you to know your father wasn't a murderer. He was a hero."

A tear slipped over her lashes. "Yes," she agreed. "He was."

And because of that he'd lost everything.

He stood across the town square, his tall form easily distinguishable despite the booths and rides set up for the Spring Festival. On duty, he leaned against one of the columns lining the porch of Lafitte's Landing Bed and Breakfast and scanned the swelling crowd. The late-morning breeze played with his hair, longer now than when she'd first arrived and curling at his nape. A few rebellious strands fought with his cowlick to fall against his forehead. He looked casual and relaxed, completely at ease. Not even the shady porch dimmed the wattage of his smile.

Tori braced a hand against the side of the library and

tried to look away. Couldn't. She stood not twenty feet from Ian, and though she'd gone to great effort to ensure he didn't see her, the fact he seemed oblivious to her presence stung. The fact he laughed, stung worse.

A young woman with soft red hair laid a hand on his forearm and gazed up at him, speaking in quiet tones. Ian watched her intently with those laser eyes of his, a slow smile curving his lips. Then he leaned down and whispered something in her ear, and the woman playfully swatted him and laughed.

With detached fascination, Tori wondered how it was possible to breathe, while her heart quietly shattered.

Around her, sights and scents whirred and blurred. Couples of all ages laughed and danced to the knee-slapping sounds of zydeco music. The aroma of Cajun cooking abounded. Alcohol flowed like water.

But the cacophony barely registered. She didn't belong here at the Spring Festival. Didn't belong here in Bon Terre.

Go to him, some little voice inside countered. Tell him what she'd learned. Tell him she'd been right all along. Her father was an innocent man, his only crime that of trying to protect those he loved.

The parallel gave her pause. When it applied to her father, she referred to the crime as minimal, something forgivable. Yet when it came to Ian, she found the very same trait unpardonable.

It was different, she told herself. Her father had a blanket of love to motivate his actions. Ian had only the past.

With a sad smile she glanced around the town square, easily locating his mother, the librarian, even Kay and Autrey. Everyone looked happy. At peace. Even Ian, she thought, her gaze once again drawn to him. He stood among a circle of friends, people he'd probably known his whole life. This was where he belonged. Here he could be Sheriff Montague, Ian the Unaffected, and no one expected anything different of him. No one dreamed of the man he kept hidden beneath all those veneers. No one mourned for the little boy who'd grown up entirely too fast.

But Tori didn't belong here. Because she did dream, and she did mourn. The man leaning against the column had been shaped and hardened by an act of violence completely out of his control. And though Tori understood, she couldn't live with the consequences.

Nor could she trust herself. Now that she and Ian had been lovers, now that she knew what it felt like to have him around her and inside her, she didn't trust herself to think clearly. To think at all. His touch melted her defenses like the sun turned ice caps into puddles. Despite her best intentions, she'd fallen into the very well she'd tried to avoid.

He looked up and caught her gaze, as though she'd broadcast her thoughts directly into his heart. The amusement drained from his eyes, the smile fell from his mouth, and again the stern face of Ian the Unaffected took over. He didn't wave, didn't incline his head, didn't wink, didn't do anything to indicate that yesterday at this time they'd been making love.

Having sex.

Tori lifted her chin and stared right back, refusing to let him see any evidence that his shrapnel eyes were ripping her to shreds. Tough Tori, he called her, and for once, she wanted him to be right.

And then he did it, hammered the last nail in her heart. He extended a bottle of water toward her in a mock toast, then drew it to his lips for a long swallow. The woman standing next to him glanced toward the library, glared when she saw Tori, moved closer to Ian. He neither encouraged nor discouraged her, just stood there as if he didn't flat give a damn.

If you lock the door tonight, know that you're not doing it to keep me out. I don't make the same mistake twice.

Neither did Tori. Giving him nothing in return for nothing, she lifted her chin and turned her back to him, casually walked away. She wanted to go slowly, so that he might catch up with her. She wanted to run, so that he didn't.

But she did neither, and neither did he.

Fifteen minutes later she stood on the vacant lot where her father had worked undercover at the renowned Bon Terre Antique and Auction House. Now, twenty-five years later, nothing remained but a tangle of weeds, a faded sign and the taint of scandal. At last the cloud of mystery surrounding her mother's death had cleared, but in the glare of the truth, Tori didn't find the closure she'd come seeking. Only a profound sense of sadness for all that had been lost.

In the car her suitcases sat waiting. At the airport a seat on a plane to Boston had her name on it. This time tomorrow, she would be home, and this whole nightmare would be over. There was nothing for her in Bon Terre, never had been.

Her father had been right all along.

''Ian, honey, you listening to me?''

Ian looked away from the library and into a pair of simpering brown eyes. ''Of course I am, Charla. I'm always game for a crawfish boil.''

She gazed up at him, her pretty lower lip jutting out just as she'd done when Ian asked for his class ring back in what seemed like another lifetime. ''I asked if you wanted to dance.''

''Oh.'' He lifted a bottle of water to his lips, but he'd long since polished it off.

''She's not here anymore,'' Charla said with a frown. ''She left half an hour ago.''

Ian glanced at his watch. Actually, it had been thirty-three minutes since Tori walked away, but the tightness in his chest had yet to diminish. Nothing had prepared him for the sight of her standing across the street, the shell-shocked look in her normally flashing eyes. The mechanical stance to that sinuous body of hers. The need to go to her, to put his mouth to hers and breathe some life back into her had been like a punch to the gut.

"How about a rain check, Char? I need to talk to Deputy Harrison."

Charla eyed him dubiously. "You know where to find me."

And he had for a long time, he'd just never found the motivation to do so. Forcing a smile, he worked his way through the crowd, looking for the young deputy he'd posted outside Tori's house that morning. No matter what had gone down between them on a personal level, his job remained to keep her safe. And he couldn't quite let go of the nasty feeling that something hovered just out of sight. Out of reach.

"There you are, son," he said, locating his newest deputy. He still remembered the kid in diapers; it was hard to get used to him in a badge. "Everything okay at the Carondolet place?"

The rookie polished off a funnel cake before answering. "Real quiet, Sheriff. Ms. Bishop stayed inside most of the day. Only came out when Ms. Roubilet came around."

Ian stilled. "Ms. Roubilet? You mean Kay?"

"Yeah, I think it was her anyway. She was wearing some kind of long coat, but it sure looked like her. Drove a big white Cadillac like her."

The well-honed instincts of a cop took over. "That's odd," he said, trying to put the pieces together.

"I thought so, too. I mean, I heard about Kay not wanting Ms. Bishop here, and all. I was about to head up to the house, just in case, but then the two of them strolled out onto the porch and said goodbye. For a minute, there, I thought Ms. Bishop was crying, but then she smiled and Ms. Roubilet left."

The words, the image they invoked, stabbed hard. "Son of a bitch," Ian growled. "Thanks, son. Good work." He pushed through the crowd, blood going from simmer to slow boil. It was time to let go of the past and quit holding a grudge. Tori had not only lost her childhood and her innocence, but the events of that long-ago night held her locked in a cage she might spend the rest of her life fighting to escape.

"Kay!" The older woman sat with Autrey, Ian's mother, and several other committee members at one of the back tables. "A word with you please."

Laurel stood. "Ian, I was wondering—" Her words broke off and she stepped closer. "Has something happened?"

His mother was too perceptive. Always had been. "I just need to speak with Kay, Mom."

"Where's Tori?" Laurel asked, frowning.

Ian caught the look that passed between Kay and her husband. "I'll explain later, Mom, but for now, I need to talk with Kay."

Autrey stood. "What's this about, boy?"

"That's what I'd like to know." Not giving a damn about their audience, Ian moved to stand beside the older woman's chair and glared down at her. "What were you doing at Tori's house this morning? What did you say to her?" *How did you make her cry?*

Kay set a plastic cup on the table. "I don't know what you're talking about, Sheriff. I haven't seen that woman since she barged into my meeting at the coffee shop."

"Deputy Harrison saw you, Kay. Saw your Caddy. The overcoat was a nice touch, but not good enough."

The blood drained from Kay's face. "Oh, no," she whispered.

"Honey?" Autrey moved behind her chair and put his hands on her shoulders. "You forget to tell me something?"

She shook her head from side to side. "No."

Fury almost blinded Ian. "That *woman,* as you call her, has been terrorized since the day she arrived in this town. Bloody notes stabbed to her door—" The second the words left his mouth, realization hit. The note. On a sheet of newspaper from the day after the murders.

Autrey ran the newspaper.

"Son of a bitch," he growled again, closing in on Autrey. "It's been the two of you all along." He reached to the clip on his belt, where his cuffs dangled. "We need to have a little talk down at the station."

Kay bolted out of her chair. "No!" she shrieked. "It's not what you think. I didn't want her hurt—I just wanted her gone!"

"She's an innocent woman," Ian said, sickened. "Now, you can come on down to the station with me, or we can do this right here in the middle of everyone."

Autrey sent Kay a defeated glance. "You shouldn't have gone there today, dove. I told you to leave her alone."

"I didn't go there! I was getting ready for the festival!"

"If not you," Ian said acidly, "then who? Who else looks like you and drives a white Cadillac?"

Kay's expression crumpled. "No," she whimpered.

"Dear God," Autrey whispered, crossing himself.

Ian lost it. He grabbed the older man's shirtfront and twisted. His mother screamed. "Who, damn it?"

Autrey didn't fight back. He looked like a man facing his own mortality, and not liking what he saw.

Kay gazed at him with pleading eyes. "Autrey, don't."

"I have to," he told his wife.

Ian was ready to haul them both down to the station. "Mom, go find Deputies Harrison and Fontenot. Tell them to meet me—"

"Guy," Autrey said.

Over the jangly zydeco music, the older man's voice barely registered. "What?" Ian asked.

Autrey looked him dead in the eye. And this time when he spoke, he did so with punishing clarity. "You asked who else looks like Kay and drives a white Cadillac. I'm telling you. Her daddy. Guy Melancon."

The gaiety of the festival whirred around Ian like a kaleidoscope out of control. "He's dead."

"To you, yes, he is. But not to me, and not to Kay. And apparently not to Russell Bishop's daughter. He never quit looking for her daddy. Never quit hating. Blaming. Never quit looking for the diamonds, even now, twenty-five years after he faked his own death."

Ian strode through a near-deserted Logan International Airport, cell phone to his ear. It was almost two o'clock in the morning. "What do you mean it's a vacant building?"

"Just that. The address you gave me is for an old tenement on the south side of town. No one has lived there for years."

Ian swore hotly. He'd been so hopeful. It had taken hours to track Tori's movements and discover she'd boarded a plane to Boston, and that's when he'd remembered the driver's license she used to buy her handgun. The Boston address. He'd alerted the local authorities and boarded the next plane.

"She's got to be somewhere, damn it. People don't just disappear into thin air." But Ian knew that wasn't true. Russell Bishop had vanished without a trace all those years before—apparently he'd taught his daughter well.

"She could have gone anywhere from here," the skeptical Boston detective pointed out. "Without more to go on—"

"Search the surrounding communities."

"Already tried that. There's no record of a Victoria Bishop or LaFleur anywhere in Massachusetts."

"What about her father? Russell Bishop? Maybe LaFleur?"

"Nothing."

"Damn it!" He'd been such a fool. Panic, he knew. By the time he'd realized how deeply "tough" Tori had slipped under his skin, the thought of losing her had twisted him up inside. Consequently he'd done the worst thing possible in her eyes. He'd held on too tight. And in doing so he'd sent the woman he loved straight into the arms of danger. "Way to go, Montague," he muttered under his breath.

"What's that?" the detective asked.

"Nothing. Keep looking. I'll see what else I can come up with." Ian flipped the phone closed and kept walking. He didn't know where he was going. Where there was to go. He'd traveled for hours, adrenaline surging so hard he could hardly sit buckled in his plane seat, only to run into a brick wall.

He'd lost her.

A cold fist closed around his throat. Just last night they'd been making love. He'd finally accepted what he'd been fighting, that with her fire and tenacity she'd brought light to his life. He could still see her standing on the staircase that very first night, that day in New Orleans when their relationship had taken a dangerous turn. With her pale hair blowing in the breeze, her eyes had sparkled when he talked of the lobsters following the Acadians from Nova Scotia—

His heart kicked hard.

Nova Scotia.

The sun climbed high in the azure sky by the time Tori pushed open the back door and stepped into the small house. After a four-hour flight from New Orleans to Boston, she'd reclaimed her car and caught the overnight ferry across the Bay of Fundy to the country where she'd spent the better part of her life. Now, almost twenty hours after she'd turned away from Ian, she set down her suitcases in her Nova Scotia home. And smiled.

Her whole world had changed, and yet here in the small house she'd shared with her father since she was four years old, everything looked the same. Warmth washed through her, and for a moment she half expected to smell her father's pipe, to see him sitting in his old recliner or hear him booming out a welcome.

But that life was over and done with now, just like the one she'd left behind in Bon Terre.

Emotion scratched at her throat, but she refused to let it surface. She was home now, the familiar surroundings as sustaining as she'd always found her father's embrace. She could crawl into her own bed with her own sheets, go to sleep surrounded by her own belongings and without the punishing smell of sandalwood and soap. With any luck she wouldn't dream.

Bone tired from traveling, she did just that.

The pounding woke her. She opened her grainy eyes and blinked against the morning sun. The bedside clock read 10:03, less than thirty minutes after she'd closed her eyes. She lay still for a moment, thinking she must have imagined the noise, until she heard it again. Louder. Urgent.

Ian.

Her heart revved and stalled. Adrenaline rushed. He'd followed her. Maybe he wasn't so unaffected, after all. Maybe—

That was ridiculous. Ian Montague had no idea where she lived. She'd made sure of that. Not even her driver's license had her real address—her father had insisted upon maintaining their U.S. residence. She hadn't known why at the time. Now she did. It was his way of hiding even deeper, protecting them both.

Another knock reverberated through the house. One of the neighbors, she decided. Miss Rosemary, no doubt. She'd seen Tori's car in the driveway and come to welcome her home.

Not ready to get up, but eager to see a familiar face, Tori rolled from bed and slipped on the robe she'd worn that first night with Ian, and hurried for the front door. She pulled it open without thought.

"Thank God," he said. "I'm not too late."

Chapter 16

He stood on her welcome mat, looking very much like a world-weary traveler. Beneath his tattered trench coat, he wore gray slacks and a black dress shirt. His eyes looked slightly bloodshot, his complexion pasty.

"Mr. Lemieux. What are you doing here?"

His eyes flashed urgency. "Are you all right?"

Her heart started to pound. Hard. Because of yesterday, she knew. Because of this man's connection to her father. "Why wouldn't I be?"

"We need to talk," he said. "I didn't tell you everything before. There's more. And I'm afraid your life is in danger."

A warm breeze blew through the front door, but Tori fought a chill. "Danger? What kind of danger? What are you doing here?"

His expression turned guarded. "It's not a good idea to talk about it in the open like this." He glanced back at the quiet street behind him. "If I followed you so easily, there's no telling who's right behind me."

The implications of his words drove home her mistake. She'd packed her bags and walked away from Bon Terre, just like everyone had wanted her to do from day one. But in doing so, she'd never considered that she might be followed. Her blood ran cold when she thought of the long hours of the night she'd spent dozing on the ferry, the fact that someone else aboard might have been following. Watching. Waiting.

Ian, she thought a little frantically. *Dear God, Ian. What had she done?*

"I think it's time to call the police," she said.

Carson Lemieux eased back the flap of his trench coat to reveal a pistol tucked into his waistband. "I think it's time to let me inside."

Her heart kicked, hard. She moved to slam the door, but he was surprisingly strong for a man of his years. He shoved his way into the front room. "Mr. Lemieux—"

"Where is he?" he asked.

She backed away, deeper into the house. "Where is who?"

"Your father."

Everything inside Tori went very still. "My father?"

"And don't tell me he's dead. We both know that's the oldest trick in the book."

The breath stalled in Tori's throat. She stared at Mr. Lemieux, trying to find the concerned lawyer from the day before, but seeing only a wild glint that reminded her of the glassy gaze in her father's eyes as his thoughts had dwindled into nothingness. "He's dead," she said, heart pounding hard. "He had Alzheimer's. He passed on right after Christmas."

But Mr. Lemieux wouldn't back down. "I need to see him, Victoria. And I need to see him *now.*"

Confusion gave way to a nasty blade of fear. "He's *dead.*"

"He's a liar and a cheat, is what he is. A thief."

Her heart staggered. "What are you talking about?"

"I've waited twenty-five years to find him. To catch up with him and make him pay." He eased the gun from his slacks and turned it over in his hand. "I'll be damned if I'm going to get this close and come away with nothing."

Tori's gaze riveted on the semiautomatic. "Make him pay? For what?"

A little smirk twisted Lemieux's lips. "Destroying me."

Vertigo whirred closer. She stared at the white-haired man who held a gun on her, the man who'd told her a placid story that satisfied her curiosity and prompted her to return home. The man who'd cleverly gotten her away from Ian. The man who'd followed her to Nova Scotia and led her straight into a trap.

And she knew. God help her, she knew. "You weren't his friend, were you?"

A laugh tore from his throat, not one of joy, but laced with bitterness and contempt. "Now, that depends upon how you define friend. I thought we were. I treated him like the brother I never had. Brought him into my business, cut him in on everything. And look how he repaid me."

It hit her then, the vague familiarity that had nagged at her, a truth too chilling to believe. *"Guy Melancon."*

He executed a mock bow. "At your service, ma'am."

All the jagged pieces rained down around her, skittering close but refusing to fall completely into place. She'd been set up, she knew. Just like her father had.

"But the fire," she said, "…the body they found."

He looked quite proud of himself. "Just that, a body with a bullet through the skull, the right height and build, but too badly destroyed to identify. Back then, forensics weren't what they are today."

The enormity of his deception staggered her. "You faked your own death."

"It was the only way to get out alive."

"My God—the lawyer, you killed him, didn't you?"

"Lemieux knew too much. He was your father's friend. His confidant. If he'd gotten to you first, he would have sent you back into hiding, deeper than before. And then we wouldn't be standing here right now.'' He stepped closer, tracing the tip of the gun down her face. ''I lost everything, little Vicky. Everything. Because of your dear papa. And I want it back. Now.''

He *had* lost everything, she realized. Including his mind. Hers raced, searching for an out. This man had stolen her past; no way would she let him touch her future.

And she knew that's what he wanted—he couldn't let her live now that she knew his secret. ''I don't have anything to give you.''

''Yes, you do,'' he said. ''The diamonds.''

She swallowed hard. ''You think my father took them?''

''I know he did. Your misguided mama found them in the warehouse and ran off with them, for God only knows what reason. She probably thought she was saving Russell from himself. She had to be taken out. She knew too much. She had to be destroyed before she destroyed me. But the diamonds vanished.''

''My father didn't take them,'' she said adamantly. Her gaze skimmed the small room in which she'd spent countless hours with her father. She wondered if he saw what was happening now, and she vowed silently to exact the justice denied him in life.

''I searched that old house from one end to the other,'' Melancon roared. ''But they're not there. Because your sainted daddy took them. I've spent twenty-five years learning everything there is to know about Russell Bishop, his maverick career with the FBI, his refusal to depend on others. It's amazing what a dead man can learn. Your dad's superiors felt real bad about not being able to protect your mama, figured that's why Russell took the diamonds and ran. Because they'd let him down, and he didn't trust them with your life. Or his own.''

Tori wasn't about to point out that even if her father had taken the diamonds, now, twenty-five years later, they would have been liquidated. Guy's quest had consumed him, trapped him in a place where time had no meaning. Only vengeance.

She drew a hand to her heart, feigning shock. It wasn't that much of a stretch. "Oh, my God."

"What? What is it, girl?"

"The safety deposit box."

"What about it?"

Her throat tightened. Her heart hammered. *Dear God, Ian.* She'd vilified him for trying to protect her, trying to keep her safe, and look what had happened.

"There was a locked box," she murmured, knowing she had only one chance of coming out of this alive. And seeing Ian again. Telling him what she now knew to be true.

Anticipation lit the dull glaze in Guy's eyes. "Show me."

Adrenaline shot through her, but Tori kept her movements steady as she led the man who'd single-handedly destroyed her and Ian's childhoods down the hall. She felt him half a step behind her, felt the gun against her back. It chilled her to lead the vile man into the sun-dappled room of her youth, where she'd once kept dolls scattered from end to end, refusing to put them on the shelf her father built for her.

But in walking away from Ian and the way he made her feel, want, she'd put herself on a shelf. And now she had only one chance to jump down.

"I-it's here," she said, letting emotion quake through her voice. Since the time she was a little girl, the men in her life had underestimated her strength. Her determination. Now she prayed Melancon would do the same. She went down on a knee beside her bed and put trembling hands to the door of her nightstand.

"Don't dally, girl."

She felt him hovering over her shoulder, but knew what she had to do. Her heart hammered hard. She had no choice. She pulled open the small door and reached inside, slid her hands along the clutter of books and candles. And found the object of her desire.

Then she swung around. "You're not the only one whose life was destroyed, Mr. Melancon."

His gaze fixated on the Lady Derringer her father had given her for her fifteenth birthday. "You little bitch," he growled.

"Survivor," she corrected. "There's a big difference."

Quickly confidence returned to his gaze. "You won't shoot."

Slowly Tori stood. A cool strength streamed through her. "My mother was a cop, and my father was an FBI agent. You murdered her in cold blood and framed him to take the fall. You took away my childhood and my family." She swallowed against the tightening of her throat and felt the glitter move into her eyes. "Now why is it you don't think I'll shoot you?"

A little smirk played with Melancon's lips. "Because if you pull that trigger, you know I'll do the same."

"It's a risk I'll gladly take," she said, and knew that it was. For her mother. And Papa. They were with her now, she knew. She felt them on either side of her. "I'll say it one more time, Mr. Melancon. Put down your gun."

He lunged for her instead. They went down in a tangle of arms and legs, the sound of a gunshot the last thing Tori heard before her world went black.

"Looks like you were right, Sheriff. Several units are there now."

In the back seat of a taxi, Ian clenched his cell phone tighter. He'd never felt so helpless in his life. His fault, he knew. If he hadn't held on so tight. If he hadn't worked against her instead of with her. "Melancon? Has he shown up?"

"I don't have details," the dispatch officer told him. "The call came in from a neighbor about twenty minutes ago."

Ian went very still. "Call?" he asked in a quiet voice that belied the frenzy inside him. "What call?" He himself had notified the authorities hours ago. There should have been no reason, no opportunity, for a call from someone else.

"I'm afraid there was a shooting," the officer said. "I don't know more than that yet."

The news hit Ian like a bullet to the heart. He reeled on impact, fought for breath. "A shooting?"

"The units haven't reported in yet. I'll let you know as soon as we know more."

Ian almost crushed the phone in his hand. "How far are we?" he demanded of the taxi driver.

"Just a few more minutes," the elderly man answered.

"Make it fewer." Ian leaned back against the seat, trying to breathe. Not succeeding. He'd come as close as humanly possible to moving Heaven and Earth to reach Tori in time, but he'd failed. He'd pushed her away when he should have held on tight with his heart, but not so tight with his actions. In trying to keep her, he might have lost her forever.

The sights of the small fishing community blurred. Everything looked quaint and simple, the antithesis of the cold terror twisting through him.

The second the taxi turned onto the street, horror exploded anew, and his world slowed to a crawl. It was a sunny spring day, but Ian saw only a cold November night. Squad cars were everywhere, their lights flashing garishly. An ambulance waited with its back doors thrown open. Clusters of neighbors stood watching, wringing their hands and crying.

Ian's heart flat-out stopped. He threw open the door and was on his feet running before the cab even parked. He heard shouts and questions, saw a young officer try to block his path.

"Let me through!" he roared. "Let me inside."

"This is a crime scene," the scrub-faced kid protested, but Ian pushed past him and ran inside.

After the bright sunshine, the darkness matched his memories. He blinked against the momentary blindness, trying to make out shape and form and substance. An army of cops filled the small house, uniformed officers and detectives. An older man rapidly snapped pictures.

And then Ian saw the gurney.

"Oh, God, Tori." He barely got the words out. The past whipped up and slapped him hard, sending him running down the hall. *Not again,* was all he could think. *Not again.* "Tori!"

An older officer reached for his arm. "Sir, you can't—"

"The hell I can't," he roared, then stopped dead in his tracks.

She looked small and vulnerable, fragile. All but her green eyes, they glittered with a strength and courage Ian had come to crave. She sat on the edge of the bed, hands clasped in her lap. A paramedic tended a nasty gash at her temple—there was blood in her hair.

The sight almost felled him.

But then she smiled. "Ian," she said simply, and took the breath from his lungs. "What took you so long?"

Relief burst through him, like sunshine after a long cold night. He was across the room before anyone could stop him, dropping to his knees and taking her hand, drawing it to his lips. "Tori." He wanted to crush her in his arms and hold her tight, feel her heart beating against him, but she was injured, and he didn't want to hurt her.

Her smile wobbled. "You look like hell."

He couldn't help it. He laughed. Here she sat in a blood-stained robe and surrounded by cops, her eyes huge and shocky, but somehow everything seemed right.

"Do you have any idea—" His heart had yet to recover. He wasn't sure it ever would. "Any idea—"

"Yes." She drew their joined hands to her face, pressing his fingers to her cheek. "Yes," she said, moving her mouth against his palm. "Yes."

"Tori—"

"I'm sorry," she shocked him by saying, and suddenly tears washed through the courage in her eyes. "So sorry."

"What in God's name for?"

She gestured toward the gurney in the hall. "If I had just trusted you, instead of turning on you. If I'd listened, instead of resenting—"

"No," he said emphatically. "This is not your fault."

"But it is," she said. "I walked away from you, when I wanted nothing more than to stay. Because I was scared. Instead of living life, like I claimed I wanted to, I ran. I jumped right back up on the shelf, came back to my cage, and in the process I almost lost everything."

Her words humbled him. His tough, brave Tori was taking responsibility for his own stupidity. He moved his fingers against the soft skin of her cheek, knowing that if he touched her for the rest of his life, it would never be enough. "This isn't your fault."

"I didn't listen—"

"And neither did I. I should have told you that Carson Lemieux was missing. I should have realized you were strong enough to handle the truth, that together—"

"Sir, we need to get her to the hospital."

Ian swung toward the paramedic. There was so much more to be said, but unlike their parents, they had the gift of time on their side. "I'm going with her."

"He killed Lemieux," Tori said, staring at Melancon's inert form on the gurney. A team of paramedics tended to a gunshot wound in the right side of his chest. "He killed them all."

Rage tore through Ian. He'd lived with a thirst for vengeance for twenty-five years, and now the child's loss joined forces with the man's need to protect. Avenge. Guy Melancon had threatened or destroyed everything Ian loved. The need to punish made him a little crazy. Critical condition or not, if he'd laid one hand on Tori— "Did he hurt you?"

"Not today," she said quietly. "And not ever again."

"What the hell did he want?" Ian growled. "Revenge?"

"The diamonds. My dad was an FBI agent, Ian. Not crooked, but undercover, trying to bring Guy down. Guy thought Papa was still alive. Guy thought Papa had the diamonds."

Disbelief stabbed through Ian. Kay and Autrey had not told him that. But finally the lies and deception made sense.

"Ms. LaFleur is one lucky young lady," the paramedic said.

"Not lucky," Ian corrected, "but smart and capable." He drank in the calm serenity in her gaze and felt his heart twist. "Look at me now, Tori." Cops and paramedics surrounded them, but Ian didn't give a damn. He could only think of Tori, and how close he'd come to losing her.

"I'm not unaffected," he said in a voice hoarse even to his own ears. "I'm on my knees, and so in love with you I don't have a clue what to do about it."

A tremulous smile lit her eyes. "I think I can help you out there," she said softly. "If you're willing to wait a few days."

He'd wait a lifetime. "Tell me."

She smiled. Just a simple point-blank smile, that reached clear down to his heart. "Take me back to Bon Terre, Ian. Take me home."

Secrets. Echoes of long ago. Remnants of lives gone by. Every house concealed them, but as Tori stared at the old Greek Revival, she saw the future, not the past. Azaleas bloomed with abandon, while wisteria tangled up the intricate ironwork. Bushy ferns lined the wraparound porch and swayed in the breeze.

And deep inside Tori, something stirred.

She'd spent more of her life in Nova Scotia than Bon Terre, but the moment she'd returned to the sleepy bayou town, she'd known this was where she belonged, here among the sprawling oaks and towering cypress trees, with the man she loved more deeply than she'd ever imagined possible.

For as long as she lived, she'd never forget the sight of Ian charging down the hall of her house in Nova Scotia. The wildness in his eyes. The ferocity.

She'd faced Guy Melancon with an uncanny calm, never once letting emotion get the better of her. But the second she'd seen Ian, her heart had stopped, and she'd almost wept.

Everything else was a blur. The trip to the emergency room, the doctor stitching her forehead. The session with the detectives when she'd recounted what had happened with Guy. The meeting with the FBI, who'd confirmed Guy's story about her father being an agent. And at long last, with Guy's confession, Russell Bishop's name had been cleared. Once he recovered, Guy would spend the rest of his life in prison.

Ian had been by her side every minute, holding her hand and lending her his strength. She didn't know why that had scared her so badly before. After the doctors had cleared her, Ian had taken her to a hotel and made love to her all night long. She didn't know why that had scared her before, either. In his arms, his body, she found strength and freedom and an intoxicating sense of feminine power. He didn't want her on a shelf. He'd done a wonderfully thorough job of proving that.

Now she walked up the path to the old house. After driving in from New Orleans, Ian had received a call from the station and, reluctantly, had left her with his mother while he went on an emergency call. An hour later he'd called to say he'd be detained awhile and asked his mother to take Tori home.

Which she had. But Laurel had declined Tori's offer to

come inside for coffee, so now Tori opened the door, alone.

The muted smell of vanilla washed through her. She stood there in the foyer and breathed deeply, giving her eyes a moment to adjust to the shift from sunlight to early-evening shadows.

That's when she saw the rose petals.

They lay scattered across the frayed throw rug and over the hardwood floor, a trail of red and pink leading up the stairs.

She followed them.

The path stopped at the door to the bathroom, where the aroma of vanilla grew stronger. Heart thrumming, she put her hand to the knob and pushed inside, tried not to gasp.

Candles greeted her. They were everywhere, on the counter and on the floor, even on a small shelf, all shapes and sizes, flickering valiantly. And in the old claw-foot tub, bubbles awaited.

Emotion came hard and fast, clogging her throat and squeezing her heart.

"Hold it right there, *chère*."

The steely command froze her in place. She absorbed the sound and texture of the masculine voice, the rough-hewn tenderness and welcome strength. Then, on a moment of pure inspiration, she picked up a taper candle and spun around.

There was no one there.

Not right behind her, anyway.

He stood down the hall at the top of the stairs, half in shadow, half in light. A dark T-shirt covered his chest, black jeans his legs. His jaw desperately needed a razor. And just like that first night, a light gleamed in his pewter eyes. But this time, instead of a gun, he held a gold silk robe.

Tori looked at him standing there, all tall and strong and completely without veneers, and wondered how she'd ever walked away from this man. Life didn't offer guarantees, but it did offer love and trust, faith and hope. And loyalty. Commitment.

Ian Montague embodied all that and more.

"You did all this," she whispered, awed. "For me."

"For us." He started toward her. "I thought maybe we could start over," he suggested, his voice as smoky as his smile.

"Yes," she said, meeting him halfway. Happiness and promise swelled through her. "Let's."

Epilogue

"You're sure about this?"

"Absolutely."

"It's pretty big. This could take a while."

"The day is young."

"My point exactly." Ian gestured toward the center of the room, his smile as naughty as his voice. "When I see a big bed like this, and hear you use words like stripping and rubbing, chemicals aren't exactly what come to mind."

Tori laughed. "You're a bad, bad boy, Sheriff Ian Montague."

"And that's why you like me," he drawled, brushing a kiss across her lips. "Shimmy on out of those grubby clothes and I'll show you just how bad I can be."

Heat swirled through her. She looked at him standing there in the filtered light of early morning and felt her heart swell. His sleep-rumpled hair fell around his cowlick; three-day-old whiskers covered his jaw. His eyes were smoldering; his smile smoky. And though he wore work clothes—torn, faded jeans and an old white T-shirt—he looked more magnificent than he had two months before, when he'd stood waiting for her at the altar, a black tuxedo covering his big body. Four weeks had passed since they returned from their honeymoon on the lush island of Kauai, but the olive skin Ian inherited from his Cajun ancestors remained deeply tanned.

Looking at him, Tori was tempted to abandon her weekend project and take her husband up on his offer. But now that she was pursuing a degree in Criminal Justice at Tulane, Saturday and Sunday were the only time they had to restore the beauty of the old Carondolet place. The refinishing work was hard, but she loved watching the old house come to life. Just like Ian. No longer did he default to veneers, relying instead upon the power of truth and trust.

He skimmed a finger down the side of her face. "Well?"

She swatted his hand away. "We've got work to do, Montague." Then, to give him a taste of his own medicine, she put her mouth to his. "The sooner we start, the sooner we finish."

"You enjoy torturing me, don't you?"

"Isn't that why *you* like *me?*" she asked, grinning.

He growled. "Fine. But don't say I didn't warn you, *chère.*"

Her grin turned into a laugh. "No problem there."

Tori crossed the room and opened the window, inviting the crisp air inside. It was one of those brilliant storm-washed mornings, the sky all the more blue for the intense hours of thunder and lightning the night before. Birds chirped gaily. The geese had yet to arrive, but the cool temperature told her the graceful birds would soon make their annual journey south.

They went to work disassembling the big four-poster bed she'd slept in upon her arrival in Bon Terre. They would strip it today, smooth and sand it tomorrow. Only then would they know whether the original beauty of the wood could carry the piece, or if a new coat of stain was needed.

The first finial came off with ease, but the one atop the massive post on the left of the headboard wouldn't budge. "Can you come help me with this?" she asked Ian.

He crossed the mattress and came up behind her, wrapping his arms around her waist. "There was a time I thought I'd never hear those words from your mouth."

"What words?" she asked, turning to face him.

"Come help me." He pulled her closer. "We've come a long way since then."

Standing on the big bed in the circle of her husband's arms, Tori smiled. "Funny, I was going to say we've only just begun."

He kissed her thoroughly before pulling back. "What do you need help with?"

It took a moment to remember what planet she was on, much less what she needed help with. "This finial. It's stuck."

He worked at it a few minutes before deciding he needed his rubber mallet. A few taps later, the finial was free.

"Here you go," he said, lifting it. "Whoever put this here didn't want— What the hell?"

Surprised by the sharp edge to his voice, Tori stepped closer. "What?"

He squinted down inside the pillar. "Can you get my pliers?"

Tori hurriedly found and handed them over. She pushed up on her toes to watch Ian work, but the post was a good foot taller than she. So was Ian, for that matter.

"Sweet Mary," he drawled a heartbeat later. With the pliers, he pulled out a plastic bag.

Shock drilled through Tori, held her motionless. "Oh, my God." Morning sun filtered through the gauzy curtains, shimmering off the contents of the bag. "The diamonds."

Ian turned toward her. "In an evidence bag. Your mother must have put them here for safekeeping."

And there they'd stayed, for over twenty-five years, the one puzzle piece no one could account for, the missing link that would fully and completely exonerate her father.

Emotion streamed through her. "I knew he didn't take them."

"They were here all along," Ian said, shoving the hair back from his face. "Right under Guy's nose. Talk about poetic justice."

Tori smiled. "Mama outsmarted him."

"Like mother, like daughter," Ian said, drawing her into his arms. "My blood still runs cold when I think of the way you tricked Melancon that day in Nova Scotia. When I think about the risk you took, what could have happened—"

She pulled back. "Don't. It's over now." Guy Melancon would spend the rest of his life in prison. Kay and Autrey were there, too, guilty of aiding, abetting and harboring a criminal.

"I could have lost you."

"But you didn't." She pushed up on her toes and kissed him. "And you won't."

"You're damn straight I won't, Victoria Bishop LaFleur Montague."

They would have to call the authorities and turn over the diamonds, but Tori wanted to savor the discovery a little longer. The past could finally be laid to rest. The future was theirs. No shadows. No veneers. The days and months and years ahead beckoned, as dazzling and priceless as the rediscovered diamonds.

Pouring the love in her heart into a smile, she splayed her palms against her husband's chest. "I'm thinking I might like a demonstration in other methods of stripping, after all."

His smile turned languorous. "Would you now?"

"*Mais oui,* I believe so."

"This could take a while," he warned. A wicked light glinted in the pewter of his eyes.

Thoughts of refinishing the bed dissipated. "I've got all day," she murmured, and went on to prove just that.

* * * * *

If you enjoyed what you just read,
then we've got an offer you can't resist!

Take 2 bestselling love stories FREE!

Plus get a FREE surprise gift!

Clip this page and mail it to Silhouette Reader Service™

IN U.S.A.
3010 Walden Ave.
P.O. Box 1867
Buffalo, N.Y. 14240-1867

IN CANADA
P.O. Box 609
Fort Erie, Ontario
L2A 5X3

YES! Please send me 2 free Silhouette Intimate Moments® novels and my free surprise gift. After receiving them, if I don't wish to receive anymore, I can return the shipping statement marked cancel. If I don't cancel, I will receive 6 brand-new novels every month, before they're available in stores! In the U.S.A., bill me at the bargain price of $3.99 plus 25¢ shipping and handling per book and applicable sales tax, if any*. In Canada, bill me at the bargain price of $4.74 plus 25¢ shipping and handling per book and applicable taxes**. That's the complete price and a savings of at least 10% off the cover prices—what a great deal! I understand that accepting the 2 free books and gift places me under no obligation ever to buy any books. I can always return a shipment and cancel at any time. Even if I never buy another book from Silhouette, the 2 free books and gift are mine to keep forever.

245 SDN DNUV
345 SDN DNUW

Name	(PLEASE PRINT)	
Address		Apt.#
City	State/Prov.	Zip/Postal Code

* Terms and prices subject to change without notice. Sales tax applicable in N.Y.
** Canadian residents will be charged applicable provincial taxes and GST.
 All orders subject to approval. Offer limited to one per household and not valid to
 current Silhouette Intimate Moments® subscribers.
 ® are registered trademarks of Harlequin Books S.A., used under license.

INMOM02   ©1998 Harlequin Enterprises Limited

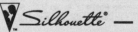

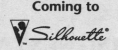

Silhouette®

COMING NEXT MONTH

INTIMATE MOMENTS

#1183 LOVERS AND OTHER STRANGERS—Dallas Schulze
A Family Circle

Rebellious Reece Morgan was back in town, but not for long. Shannon Devereux knew his reputation and feared getting too attached, but keeping things casual wasn't easy. Reece was falling for Shannon, but when she ran off after announcing she was pregnant, could Reece convince her that this former bad boy was now marriage material?

#1184 UNDER THE KING'S COMMAND—Ingrid Weaver
Romancing the Crown

Navy SEAL Sam Coburn had his mission: help the king of Montebello catch a kidnapper. But he hadn't counted on being partnered with naval officer Kate Mulvaney. Sam and Kate had shared a passionate affair years ago, and she was the one woman he'd never forgotten. But Kate had kept secrets from Sam, and now, in order to fight the enemy, they had to face their own true feelings first.

#1185 PROTECTING HIS OWN—Lindsay McKenna
Morgan's Mercenaries: Ultimate Rescue

After a devastating earthquake, Navy Lieutenant Samantha Andrews and Captain Roc Gunnisson were sent to the L.A. Basin to establish a medical relief center. Sparks flew as the two strong-willed soldiers battled for control and denied their desire. But when a survivalist group kidnapped Sam, Roc realized she was the only thing truly worth fighting for.

#1186 A CRY IN THE NIGHT—Linda Castillo

Search-and-rescue leader Buzz Malone had to find his missing son—a son his ex-wife, Kelly, had kept secret—before a raging forest fire did. But the Rocky Mountain wilderness wasn't the only thing on fire. Working together, Buzz and Kelly realized that their passion burned hotter than ever and decided to try again—if they made it out alive.

#1187 TAKING COVER—Catherine Mann
Wingmen Warriors

When Dr. Kathleen O'Connell, U.S. Air Force flight surgeon, forbade Captain Tanner Bennett from flying, she never thought they would be teamed up to investigate a suspicious plane crash. Working with Tanner wasn't easy, but denying her attraction to him was impossible. And when their lives were suddenly on the line, the only place for Kathleen to take cover was in Tanner's strong arms.

#1188 ON THIN ICE—Debra Lee Brown

Posing as a roughneck on an Alaskan oil rig to nail a corporate thief was Seth Adams' one shot at winning back his FBI job. Falling for his lead suspect, Lauren Fotheringay, wasn't part of his plan. As for innocent Lauren, she didn't realize what she had stumbled into. As the danger grew, she trusted Seth to protect her life, but she was less certain he could save her heart.

SIMCNM1002